The Pot Thief
Who Studied
Edward Abbey

The Pot Thief
Who Studied
Edward Abbey

A Pot Thief Mystery

J. MICHAEL ORENDUFF

OPEN ROAD
INTEGRATED MEDIA
NEW YORK

Copyright © 2018 by J. Michael Orenduff

978-1-5040-4993-1

Published in 2018 by Open Road Integrated Media, Inc.
180 Maiden Lane
New York, NY 10038
www.openroadmedia.com

To my grandchildren, Bram and Saskia

*Thanks in part to Edward Abbey, they will grow up on a planet
that still has wild and free places.*

The Pot Thief Who Studied Edward Abbey

Prologue

Life imitates art—but badly.
—Edward Abbey

According to the brochure, the process began with the model totally naked.

She smeared herself from head to toe with alginate, a slimy material made—as the name suggests—from algae. The alginate served three purposes. First, it retained the finest details of the surface once it dried. Second, it allowed the cast to be removed from the model without pulling away skin and hair. And finally, it insulated the model from the heat given off by drying plaster.

An assistant to the art professor covered the alginate with several layers of overlapping gauze swatches. Those initial layers of gauze were DayGlo green so that when the body cast was later being cut away, the green gauze would alert the artist that he should cut no deeper.

After reaching this minimally modest state in which she looked like the wife of the Jolly Green Giant, the artist and the assistant covered the green gauze with plaster. Then another layer of gauze, this time white. Then additional alternating layers of white gauze and plaster until the future cast was thick enough to contain the approximately four hundred pounds of liquid clay it would be filled with once it was off the model.

My students were doing 3-D work, so I'd brought them to the unveiling. Or, in this case, the unplastering.

The model looked like a standing mummy. The only spots not plastered over were her nostrils, into which straws had been inserted so she could breathe while the plaster hardened.

In order for her to remain motionless, a wooden framework was wedged around her. Even though it appeared secure and tight, it must have been difficult for her to stay in one position. The guards at Buckingham Palace do it, but they aren't covered in plaster. Just red coats and those silly furry hats.

Using a drywall knife with the blade adjusted to a mere eighth of an inch, the artist scored the dry plaster starting at the arch of the model's left foot and continuing up her leg, over her hip, along her rib cage, up to her armpit and then along the underside of her arm down to her fingertips. A similar incision was made on her right.

Reason told me otherwise, but I couldn't suppress the fear that blood would flow from the razor's path.

The third slit started at her fingertips and ran along the top of her arm, across her collarbone, up her neck, across the top of her head and then down the other side to the end of her other hand. The final incision ran up the inside of her legs, stopping just at the top of them.

She may have been willing to be covered with plaster for several hours, but she wasn't crazy enough to allow someone to run a razor between her legs.

The artist increased the razor's depth by another eighth of an inch and ran it through the grooves he'd made on the first pass. Each time he repeated this process, I held my breath. But of course he never cut the model. He stopped when he saw the DayGlo green gauze.

If you were paying attention to the geometry, you realize the plaster cast now had almost a complete front half and back half, a clamshell in effect. The small remaining connection between her legs would give way when the two halves were removed.

The wooden framework was moved away.

The artist inserted a thin putty spatula into the slots in the plaster and twisted it. He pushed here a little and tugged there a bit. When he was satisfied that the full body cast was loose enough, he and his assistant worked their hands into the now widened cracks and tugged at the cast.

The front and back sections came off almost intact. A few small pieces remained on the model, but it would be easy enough to connect the two sides of the cast, fill in any gaps and use it as a mold. The front mold had the two straws sticking out of its nose.

After the two halves were rejoined securely, liquid clay would be poured in. After it hardened, the plaster mold would be removed to reveal a life-size clay statue of the model.

The model had not fared as well as her cast. Much of the alginate had pulled away with the gauze and plaster, so she was almost completely naked. This had been anticipated, of course. The assistant was standing ready with a hospital gown. He held it in front of her, but she made no move to stick her arms into the sleeves. Probably too stove up to move.

Rather than just leave her exposed, the assistant took the initiative and pushed the gown toward her. When his hand bumped her arm, she toppled backward. There was neither a yell nor a scream, merely a thud when she hit the floor.

The assistant hurriedly removed the plastic discs taped on to protect her eyes.

"Are you all right?"

When she didn't respond, he grabbed her wrist and felt for a pulse.

Then he yelled, "Call 911!"

1

One month earlier—the start of the fall semester

On my first day as a college student, I'd walked from Dartmouth to the University of New Mexico.

It took me less than five minutes, because my family lived on Dartmouth Drive, about a hundred yards east of the UNM campus.

At the real Dartmouth back in New Hampshire, I assumed the nip of fall was in the air and colorful leaves were on the ground. In Albuquerque it was over a hundred degrees and the ground was hard-baked caliche.

Three decades later, I'm scheduled to teach a course. The air is still hot and dry, but the caliche is now covered with xeriscape, a fancy word for landscaping with gravel.

I can't believe they want me to teach a course. Neither will you when you learn how it all came down. A guy walked into my pottery shop last spring, stuck out his hand and said, "I'm Milton Shorter, head of the University of New Mexico Art Department. Are you the owner?"

I shook his hand and said, "Yes, I'm Hubie Schuze."

I was relieved he didn't know me and didn't recognize my name. I was responsible for his predecessor going to prison.

"You make pots?" he asked.

I told him I did, and he asked if I was interested in teaching a noncredit course in pottery making.

"Does the noncredit part apply to the students or to me?" I asked.

He chuckled and said, "The students get zero college credit. But to balance that out, your pay won't be much more than their credit."

I liked his sense of humor. "How low is the pay?"

"Fifty bucks for each student, plus tips."

"Teachers get tips these days?"

"Remember, these are noncredit courses. I'm told you may get cookies, fresh produce from their gardens or handmade birdhouses."

It was only two nights a week for six weeks. It was scheduled in the Botanical Garden Building, a ten-minute walk from my shop in Old Town. I thought it might be fun.

I was right. Olga Perez gave me tamales after the second session. The scents of limestone, corn masa, slow-cooked pork and ground dried pasillas told me Olga would get an A.

Except I wouldn't be giving grades. The course was offered through the Division of Continuing Education. I suspected it was scheduled at the Botanical Garden to ensure it didn't adulterate the intellectual climate on the main campus.

The students were mostly retirees looking for a hobby. They weren't even matriculated.

Which at their advanced age was probably a good thing.

I had six students. I appreciated the extra three hundred bucks but not nearly as much as the tamales.

A few weeks after the course ended, Shorter asked me if I'd be willing to teach a second course for the fall semester. For credit. And on the main campus, no less. I figured maybe Olga put in a good word about me.

My new course was ART 2330, Anasazi Pottery Methods. My job was to teach students how New Mexico's ancient potters made the works I illegally dig up and sell at my shop in Albuquerque's Old Town.

If you're wondering why the University of New Mexico would hire a pot thief to teach a course about Anasazi pottery, you've skipped over two even more vexing questions.

First, why would they hire someone they'd previously expelled?

Second, why would the art department hire the person responsible for sending their former department head to prison?

I guess I have some explaining to do.

My name is Hubert Schuze and—as I just admitted—I'm a pot thief. I was previously a treasure hunter. Then Congress passed the Archaeological Resources Protection Act (ARPA), redefining treasure hunting as theft. As I like to point out, who knows more about theft than Congress?

Because I had been an undergraduate thirty years ago, I figured reading something by another former UNM student might put me in a collegiate mood. The alumnus who came to mind was Edward Abbey. But John Hoffsis at Treasure House Books on the square in Old Town told me Abbey didn't write about colleges. John recommended I read *Desert Solitaire*, a memoir about Abbey's service as a park ranger combined with a diatribe against the National Park Service for selling out to what he called "industrial tourism," despoiling the wilderness in order to serve the interests of road pavers, motel builders and fast-food joints.

In this regard, he is a kindred spirit. As you might imagine, I frequently dig on public land. Despite my attempt to scour the remotest areas, I often encounter cigarette butts and Styrofoam cups.

People who smoke don't have the lungs for long uphill hikes. People don't buy coffee in Styrofoam cups if they plan to drink it six hours later. Cigarette butts and Styrofoam cups are not carried in by hikers. They are driven in by people in air-conditioned gas guzzlers using loop roads that allow everyone to get within a five-minute stroll of what was once unspoiled wilderness. Abbey wrote that loop roads are "extremely popular with the petroleum industry—they bring the motorist right back to the same gas station from which he started."

I understand the desire to make every square inch of the planet accessible. If I live long enough, I will eventually be too frail to hike out to the petroglyphs west of Albuquerque, much less climb up to cliff dwellings and dig for pots. I'll probably long for a level paved road to take me back to the remote places so fond in my memory. But making wilderness accessible is a contradiction. Once it's accessible, it's no longer wilderness.

You dream of seeing one of the hidden waterfalls in the slot canyons of the Four Corners area, where New Mexico, Colorado, Utah and Arizona meet. But when you get there, you also see the Visitor Center, with Coke machines and a sandwich shop. A paved parking lot full of Winnebagos. A pet "restroom" area and concrete picnic tables. Utility poles and wires spoiling the clear blue sky. People asking the rangers, "How long will it take me to get to the waterfall?" as if this were an episode of that deranged television series *The Amazing Race*.

My morning paper a week earlier had a teaser for the upcoming episode that read "Tensions rise in Thailand as one team forgets their fanny pack."

How can you forget a fanny pack when an entire team of videographers, lighting specialists and sound-boom operators are watching your every move?

Better question: Why do we watch people doing things instead of doing them ourselves? Get off your couch, turn off your television and get out in the wilderness.

While there is still some of it left.

If you happen to run across me with my hands in the dirt, do me a favor—don't tell the rangers.

As editor of the UNM student newspaper, *The Daily Lobo*, Abbey adorned the front page with the quote, "Man will never be free until the last king is strangled with the entrails of the last priest."

In what I can only assume was a tongue-in-cheek joke, he attributed the quote to Louisa May Alcott.

The university president was not amused. He had all copies of the issue destroyed and removed Abbey from the editorship.

That was in the '50s. Had he tried to remove the editor of the student newspaper in the '60s, the students would have burned down the presidential residence along with the ROTC Building. And maybe the football facilities for good measure.

Given the Lobos' ineptitude at football, no one would have cared about the latter.

According to Abbey, "Anarchism is democracy taken seriously." I'm not an anarchist. My five-six frame carries a one hundred and forty pounds of flesh and bone and only an ounce or two of nerve, so I like having police to protect me from bad guys. But when it comes to the Archaeological Resources Protection Act, I'm as lawless as it gets.

ARPA does not protect ancient pots. It protects them only from people like me. Professional archaeologists can dig them up and study them in a basement lab. But people who love those pots enough to want to share them with the world are not allowed to do so. God forbid that an average citizen should own one and display it proudly.

Okay, the expelled-from-university part . . . As a potter myself, I know the women who created the pots I dig up are happy to have me rescue their handiwork and make it available for all the world to see. And it doesn't hurt that I usually turn a healthy profit doing so.

I don't feel any guilt about that. It's not as if I can give the money to their heirs.

It was the first such profit that got me expelled from the UNM graduate program in anthropology. While the faculty were directing the other students where to dig, I took a walk away from the official site and did my own excavation.

I thought showing the three Anasazi pots I found would bring praise from Professor Gerstner. What it brought instead was a lecture about digging only where directed to do so and a demand that I turn the pots over to him.

That was prior to the passage of ARPA. I hadn't found the pots on the official dig site inside Gran Quivira, so the pots were legally mine. But that didn't keep Gerstner from kicking me out of the program when I sold them.

I used the money for a down payment on my building in Old Town and went into the pottery-selling business.

Now the department-head-going-to-prison part.

Walter Masoir, a retired UNM anthropology professor, enlisted my help four years ago to recover some pots that are sacred to the people of the San Roque pueblo. The pots had been looted over a century ago and passed through any number of hands before finally being donated to the UNM Department of Anthropology and Archaeology. Shortly before he retired, Gerstner convinced the faculty to repatriate all the department's Native American artifacts to the tribes from which they had originally come.

Masoir argued that it makes no more sense to operate an archaeology department without artifacts than it would to operate a chemistry department without test tubes, but most of the faculty went along with Gerstner's plan. The artifacts were repatriated.

Except for the San Roque pots.

But nobody knew that, because San Roque is closed to outsiders. Masoir was the only white man ever to learn their language. So when one of the Ma (as the residents of San Roque call themselves) told Masoir they didn't have the pots, he came to me and said he believed Gerstner had kept them as a retirement nest egg.

Which I managed to find out was true. I also discovered the head of the art department, Frederick Blass, was acting as Gerstner's fence. And proved he killed Gerstner when they quarreled about splitting the loot.

You may be wondering how the task of returning the pots to the Ma people required solving a murder.

It didn't.

What required me to solve the murder was that I was accused of it.

Life is full of ironies. That's how we know God has a sense of humor. Edward Abbey put an outrageous quote on the front page of the *Daily Lobo*, but he was allowed to stay in school. I dig up and sell pots legally and I'm kicked out.

Here's another irony. My best friend, Susannah Inchaustigui, is a fan of murder mysteries. She almost enjoyed it when I was accused of Gertsner's murder, because it gave her a chance to deal with a real case rather than a fictional one.

How many murders can an innocent man be charged with? That's another irony. I've violated ARPA a thousand times and never been caught. But I've been wrongly charged with murder three times. I sometimes wonder if one is intended to offset the other on the cosmic scales of life.

2

Susannah swallowed a sip of her margarita and asked me if I was required to attend the orientation session for new faculty prior to teaching a credit course in the fall term.

"I had to do that in the spring."

"Seems strange they would require that even for a noncredit course," she said. "Why didn't you ever mention it to me?"

"I was embarrassed. They kicked me out of the session."

The five o'clock cocktail hour is a tradition with us. The margarita is usually the cocktail, and Dos Hermanas is always the place, two blocks from Spirits in Clay and just down the lane from La Placita, where Susannah works the lunch shift as what used to be called a waitress but is now called a server.

We used to meet every weekday. But since I moved in with Sharice, we meet only twice a week. Before she was my girlfriend, Sharice was my dental hygienist. She works for Dr. Batres, who provides free basic dental care for indigents two days a week from five until seven in the evening. It is on those days that Susannah and I still meet at Dos Hermanas.

I sometimes poke fun at the doc because his name never appears on anything without "Dr." in front of it. He probably has it monogrammed on his underwear.

But I admire Dr. Batres for donating his services and Sharice for staying after work to assist. Since he is not charging, neither is she, but he does give her comp time.

"How did you manage to get kicked out of new-faculty orientation?" Susannah asked.

"It was a session on language and inclusion. The first presentation was fascinating, a Navajo guy who'd been a code-talker in the Second World War. He was over ninety but looked a lot younger, and he told us some great stories. Then the trouble started. The second speaker was a woman who signed her ten-minute presentation."

"She handed out signed copies of it?"

"No. She signed it rather than speaking it." I mimicked sign language by holding my hands out and moving my fingers into different configurations.

Susannah laughed. "You look like that guy at Nelson Mandela's memorial service who was pretending to be the sign-language interpreter but was really just faking it."

"At least the hearing portion of the audience at the Mandela service could listen to the speeches. In my case we just sat there staring at the signer."

"She didn't speak as she signed?"

"She did not."

"She didn't have someone else speaking as she signed?"

I shook my head.

"She had the presentation displayed on PowerPoint slides?"

"Nope."

Susannah plopped her margarita down on the mosaic tile-topped table where it landed, appropriately, on an image of an agave. "So she just stood there and signed for ten minutes to an audience that probably didn't have one person who could understand the signs?"

"Exactly."

She retrieved her margarita and took a sip while thinking it over. "Maybe she can't speak."

"You might be right. After she finished signing, she just stood there. It was like when Sharice takes me to the symphony. The orchestra stops playing, and there's an awkward pause before the applause begins because most of us don't know if the piece is over or if it's just a pause between movements. I didn't know if she had finished signing or was just pausing to catch her breath."

"You don't have to catch your breath when you're signing, Hubie."

"That was a joke, Suze. I guess the equivalent phrase in signing might be 'give her fingers a break'? Anyway, the pause lasted long enough that someone started clapping, and of course the rest of us joined in. When the applause stopped, she held up a placard that read 'Now you know what it's like when a deaf person attends a spoken event.'"

She frowned. "Like hearing people don't know that deaf people can't hear? After all, that's what deaf means."

"Not according to the speaker . . . er, signer. She distributed a leaflet explaining that deaf is a culture and signing is their native language."

"That's ridiculous. Signing is not a language any more than Twitter is a language. It's just a means of conveying a language."

"That's what I said. Except my example was typing. And that sent the deaf lady into a tirade."

"A tirade?"

"It seemed like a tirade. She was moving her fingers really fast and had a hell-bent-for-leather look on her face. When I tried to question her use of the word *culture*, the moderator said I was being hostile and asked me to leave."

"Was the deaf woman short with bobbed hair and a nose so big it deserves its own zip code?"

"You know her?"

"No, but I saw her in a class last semester. There was a deaf guy in the class. Ms. Nose was his signer."

I said, "I've heard some theory about when you lack one sense, the others become more acute to compensate for it."

"Yeah, like blind people can hear better than we can."

"Right. So maybe her nose is so big in order for her sense of smell to make up for her being deaf."

"That's funny. And not very nice. But that woman doesn't deserve nice. We had a guest lecturer on Raymond Jonson. She stood to the side and a bit behind him. I think she was reading his notes and signing from those."

"So she was probably deaf and couldn't hear the lecture?"

"That would be my guess. But she didn't stick to his notes. She made snide remarks about him. Like he didn't know what he was talking about and he was a spoiled brat."

"How could you know she was signing that?"

She loaded a tortilla chip with salsa. While she chewed it, she signed to me.

When she finished, I said, "So now it's your turn to imitate the guy at the Mandela memorial service?"

"No, I just signed that I knew she signed snide remarks because I watched what she signed."

"You know sign language?"

She smiled. "My whole family knows it."

Susannah has a variety of smiles. This was the closed-lips one that seems to say *My mouth is full of happiness, and I don't want to open it for fear that it will dribble down my chin.*

"Someone in your family is deaf?"

She opened her mouth and let the happiness out. "Can you guess which one of us?"

I knew it wasn't her. I let my mind drift among random memories of my conversations with her mother, Hillary; her father, Gus; and her two brothers, Matthew and Mark.

"Is it Mark?"

The smile returned. "How did you figure it out?"

"He sometimes sounds like he has a slightly stuffy nose."

"I am so proud of him, Hubie. We knew he was deaf almost immediately because he didn't turn toward sounds. Mom spent the year after he was born learning oral training techniques. I remember her holding him when he was still a toddler. She would put her face close to him and move her lips in some way until he began to copy her. She would stick out her tongue and he would do that too. Matt was enough older to think it was hilarious. Eventually, Mom would hold an object like a ball and coax Mark into saying 'ball.' Or something that sort of sounded like 'ball.' When he was about three, they hired a professional oral trainer. She lived with us until Mark started high school. Eleven years, Hubie. Four hours a day, seven days a week. That's how long Matt had oral training. And now he speaks so clearly that you didn't even know he's deaf."

"Do you two still sign?"

"Once Mark reached a certain level of oral competency, we were all forbidden to use signs. They wanted him to take off the training wheels, so to speak. But signing is so cool because it enables us to communicate when we don't want anyone to know what we're saying. Like when Mom served you that leg of lamb, I signed to Mark, 'Look at Hubie's face when he tastes the lamb.'"

"There's a sign for Hubie?"

"No. Proper names usually don't have a sign. You spell them out." She spoke the letters H-U-B-I-E as she simultaneously demonstrated the sign for each one with her left hand.

"A lot of ordinary words also don't have signs. For example, here's the sign for 'love.'" She crossed her hands in front of her chest with all the fingers and thumb curled in like a fist. "But there is no sign for 'affection.' You have to finger spell it. So you normally just use 'love' because it's easier to make one sign than to sign the nine letters of 'affection.' But if the context requires 'affection'—say you're reciting a poem that uses that word—then you have to spell it out. And that's one of the reasons why sign language is not a language. Signing is a wonderful invention, but the signs are merely another way of referring to a word in a spoken language."

"But suppose your parents hadn't made the effort to train Mark to speak. Couldn't he have grown up just using sign language?"

"How would he learn it? Mom might have been able to teach Mark what the sign for 'love' means by making that sign when she hugged him or when he saw two people kissing in a movie. But she could never get him to understand the difference between 'love' and 'affection' unless he could read."

"I don't get it. If he could learn the distinction between 'love' and 'affection' by reading, why couldn't he learn it by someone signing to him?"

"The next time you see a sign language interpreter doing her job, watch her hands and notice how often she spells out words.

American Sign Language has about ten thousand signs for whole words or concepts."

"You can make that many signs with just two hands?"

"I can't. Almost no one can. Most signers use only a few hundred of the most common signs. *The Gallaudet Survival Guide to Signing* has five hundred signs. But when an interpreter has to sign what a hearing person is saying—like the speakers at Mandela's memorial—they have to finger spell most of it."

"Because there are so many words that don't have signs?"

"Exactly. English has a million of them."

"Sure. But no one knows them all."

"You probably come close. You're the only person I know who reads the dictionary."

"That's because I'm probably the only person you know who owns one. Everyone else looks up words on their phone. But even if there were a sign for every word, that wouldn't make it a language. It would just make it a different way of *communicating* a language."

"Exactly," she agreed. "You can also communicate with Twitter, but that doesn't make it a language."

"Okay, so you learned to sign because Mark is deaf. Why did you learn Basque?"

"Good question. It would've made more sense to learn Spanish. And it would have been easier because we hear it all the time here. But learning Euskara was the best gift I ever gave my grandfather. He was so happy I wanted to learn it. And it gave him something to do after he got too old to help with the ranching chores."

"He was a good teacher?"

"He was horrible. He was forgetful. He would explain how to conjugate a verb we had already gone over a week ago. He nagged me about my accent. He skipped around randomly from verbs to nouns to adjectives to pronouns. He taught me idioms without telling me what all the words meant. And he was only semiliterate, so I'm a terrible speller in Euskara."

"So I guess you didn't enjoy the lessons."

"On the contrary. They are my fondest memories of him." She ate another chip. "So you only had presentations from the Navajo guy and Ms. Nose? Usually, someone covers sexual harassment."

"Oh, they had that too. It was before the language session. A woman from Student Affairs lectured us about it. What I remember about it was all the acronyms. There's SMART, which stand for Sexual Misconduct and Assault Response Team. There's CAR, which is Counseling Assistance Resource, which provides free transportation for victims wanting to see the Sexual Assault Nurse Examiner, which of course is called SANE."

Susannah rolled her eyes. "Maybe they should spend less time thinking up acronyms and more time actually preventing sex crimes."

"Evidently, they're doing a good job. There were only twenty-four reported sex crimes at UNM last year. Since they have about twenty-seven thousand students, that works out to less than one for every thousand students."

"That's little solace to the victims. Each of them experienced a personal rate of a hundred percent."

"Hmm. I hadn't thought of it that way."

"I think of it that way, because I'm the student representative for Student Programs Against Sexual Misconduct."

I resisted pointing out that the acronym of her group would be "SPASM."

The staffer from Student Affairs had urged us to be vigilant. Probably a good idea. It had never occurred to me that someone in my class might be a victim of sexual harassment. So I was alert when it happened.

It also never occurred to me that someone in my class would be murdered. Unfortunately, I *wasn't* alert when that happened.

3

The door to the pottery studio could be opened only by a university ID with a magnetic strip on it like a credit card. I didn't have one.

A university ID, that is. I did have a credit card.

It was maxed out.

The students all had IDs and had let themselves in. They were looking down at their desks.

The scene sent me back to my undergraduate days, the students arriving early for Professor Hillerman's class in journalism in order to get a good seat. We had no idea he would later become famous for his books featuring tribal police officers Joe Leaphorn and Jim Chee. To us, he was simply a learned and engaging teacher.

Even if Leaphorn and Chee were real, they would never catch me digging up pots. Not because they aren't crafty enough to do so, but because I never dig on reservations. Bureau of Land Management acreage belongs to you and me. So we should be free to dig on it, right?

But the reservations belong to the people who inhabit them.

Actually, that's not technically true. The lands are held in trust for them by the federal government. So the good ol' US of A has two categories of land—the 98 percent we stole from the Indians and the 2 percent we hold in trust for them.

Students actually read books back when I was an undergraduate. Between classes (and sometimes during if you were bored and sat in the back) we'd pull out dog-eared paperbacks of the popular titles of the day—*The Color Purple* by Alice Walker, *Love in the Time of Cholera* by Gabriel García Márquez or *The Joy Luck Club* by Amy Tan.

A black woman, a Venezuelan man and a Chinese American woman. But we didn't choose them for their diversity. We read them for their insight into the human condition. Those were heady days, filled with arguments about the meaning of life. We never reached a conclusion, of course.

And that sent us to Sartre.

He didn't reach a conclusion either, but he made not reaching a conclusion sound deeply meaningful.

One popular book I did not read was *The Silence of the Lambs* by Thomas Harris. Remember I mentioned how little nerve I have?

I pulled myself out of my reverie and tapped on the window.

A young black woman wearing turquoise earrings was the one who finally came to the door. She opened it slightly and raised her chin.

"You need something?" she asked assertively through the narrow crack.

"Yes. I need to get in."

She continued to hold the door semi-closed. "You a student?"

"No, I'm the teacher."

She shrugged and returned to her potting station.

I placed a box on the table at the front of the room and cleared my throat to get their attention. Not very original, and even less effective.

They were all looking down intently. But not at books. At phones.

Amy Tan and Gabriel García Márquez have been replaced by Facebook and Twitter.

"Hello," I said cheerfully.

A blubbery kid with red hair and blue-framed glasses was the only one who looked up.

"Hi," he said, and looked back down.

"Okay," I said in what I hoped was a collegial tone, "turn off your cell phones."

"That sucks," said the young lady with the turquoise earrings.

No one ever said anything like that when I was an undergraduate, but I'd discussed my teaching assignment with both Susannah, who's a part-time student in art history, and with my nephew, Tristan, who's studying computer science. I was steeled for the new realities of acceptable behavior and language.

"Sorry," I said, "but I'm old-fashioned. We're going to have class discussions. So no cell phones."

"There's something else that sucks," said a gawky young man with a snake slithering around his arm. "The lab fee for this course is a hundred dollars."

The snake wasn't actually slithering. It was only a tattoo. But it was so well done that it appeared to move when he did.

"What's the lab fee for?" I asked.

"Clay."

"The university doesn't supply clay?"

"They don't supply any consumables for free. They make us pay for them."

The turquoise-earring girl said to the gawky kid, "You're lucky you aren't in the jewelry-making class. They're charging us two hundred because we use silver." I guess that explained why the turquoise pieces were set in silver. Must have been a studio assignment.

Another student brought up the parking fee. They kicked that around for a few minutes, then switched to the athletics fee, which they quite reasonably objected to. When they left the topic of fees and started arguing about whether the vegan selections in the La Posada Dining Hall were really vegan (after all, the tomato plants were pollinated by insects), I realized their free-ranging conversation would consume the entire two hours of our initial session if I didn't take control.

I clapped my hands and said, rather loudly, "Quiet!"

They looked at me as if I'd struck them.

After a few moments of blissful silence, I said, "Don't pay the lab fee."

They stared at me some more.

The redheaded kid said, "They won't give us any clay."

"What's your name?"

"Alfred."

"You won't need the university's clay, Alfred. We're going to dig our own."

A big, goofy smile appeared on his face. "Really?"

"Sweeeet," said the gawky kid.

"They won't let us do that," said Earring Girl.

"What's your name?" I asked her.

"Aleesha. What's yours?"

"Hubert Schuze."

"Do we have to call you Dr. Schuze?"

"I'm not a doctor. I'm not even a professor. I'm an adjunct."

"What's an adjunct?"

"Adjuncts are local people with unique skills that qualify them to teach a course even though they aren't normally teachers."

"What's your skill?" asked Alfred.

Aleesha said, "He makes pots, dummy."

Alfred slapped himself on the forehead and said, "Duh."

I winced, but the other kids laughed along with Alfred. I figured if "sucks" is now an everyday word, maybe "dummy" is now a term of endearment.

Aleesha's phone moved across her table seemingly of its own accord. She picked it up. Her thumbs tap-danced on its surface.

"Aleesha. Your phone is supposed to be off."

"It is off. I'm just answering a text."

"When I say off, that means off for talking and off for texting."

"I can text and still listen to you."

"I'm sure you can. But I can't talk while you text."

"Well, that's a *you* problem, isn't it?"

I laughed. "I consider it an asset rather than a problem."

I removed two bubble-wrapped objects from the box and placed them on the table. I took the empty box and walked to each potting station and had the students put their cell phones in the box.

"You can have them back when the class is over."

"This really sucks," said Aleesha.

"You're right."

She smiled for the first time. It looked good on her.

"I am?" she said.

"Yes. You said my skill is making pots, and you were right. But I also have another skill—forging pots."

That got their attention.

A muscular guy wearing a T-shirt with an iguana image narrowed his eyes and asked what I meant by *forging*.

"What's your name?" I asked him.

"Bruce."

"I assume you're an art major."

"Yeah."

"What does forging mean to you?"

"Like copying someone else's work."

"Exactly. That's what I do."

"That's illegal."

"You all know Manet's painting *Olympia*?"

They nodded.

"Then you probably know it's a redo of Titian's *The Venus of Urbino*."

"No," said the bearded Hispanic guy, "it's not a redo. It's an appropriation. And Manet's version was later appropriated by Yasumasa Morimura, who inserted himself as Olympia."

"And your name is?"

"Raúl Zamoria."

"Morimura's *Olympia* is my favorite painting," Alfred gushed.

"Of course it is," said Aleesha.

Alfred reddened and lowered his head.

Raúl said, "Art history is simply the evolution of appropriation. Appropriation is creativity in context. Forgery is neither."

I made a mental note not to get into an art-history discussion with Raúl.

I unwrapped the first object I'd brought in the box, a black-on-white *olla* with a swirl-patterned exterior and a rare bulbous neck. The students gathered around the table in admiration, asking if it was real, how old it was, where it was from, and what it was worth.

I told them it was genuine, from Tularosa, probably from the eleventh century, and worth about four thousand dollars.

"Can I hold it?" asked Albert.

"Only if you can afford to pay me four thousand if you drop it."

The class laughed.

"I'll take a chance." He turned to Aleesha, who was looking at the pot over his shoulder. "Would you give me some room, please?"

"What? You think I'm going to push you?"

Bruce said, "Give the guy some room."

Aleesha shrugged and moved aside.

Alfred cradled the pot softly in his hands then held it to his cheek before gently returning it to the table.

"You'll make a good mommy," said Aleesha. I winced, but everyone else laughed.

I unwrapped the second pot.

"Wow," said the gawky kid. "You have two of them."

"I didn't get your name yet."

"Nathan."

"Examine the two pots carefully, Nathan, and tell me if anything strikes you as unusual."

He bent over and eyed them from varying perspectives. "They just look like old pots. I don't see anything unique about either one."

"That's what he wants you to notice," said Raúl. "The two are identical. One of them is a copy. He forged it."

They stared at me. Their new teacher—the short guy who couldn't talk if they were texting—could make an exact copy of a thousand-year-old pot. Some of them had grudging admiration in their eyes.

The frail white student at the back of the group said, "Copying that pot is disrespectful."

"Your name, please?"

"Apache."

"Did you ever hear the expression 'Imitation is the sincerest form of flattery'?"

"That doesn't give you the right to copy work from another culture." He had a reedy voice and jumpy eyes. "You should have included a trigger warning in the description of this class."

"Is that like cautioning you to get out of the way of Roy Rogers's horse?"

No one laughed. Too young, I guess, to know who Roy Rogers was.

"A trigger warning is a statement in the course announcement listing any materials or topics that might trigger an adverse reaction from a student."

"Like I said, I'm not a teacher. I don't know about these things. I didn't write the course announcement. And even if I did, how would I know what might trigger an adverse reaction from any of you?"

"It's not that hard," Apache said, "if you're empathetic. But obviously you aren't, because you disrespect other cultures."

"No. I copy these pots precisely because I respect them and the people who made them. I keep their traditions alive. That's what this course is about. The traditions of the ancients—how they made their pottery, how they decorated it, how they used it."

Bruce seemed interested in the exchange, so I asked him what kind of art he made.

"Metal sculptures."

"Would you object to me copying one of them?"

"Give me an A for this course, and you can copy anything you want."

Everyone laughed except Apache.

I held my fake aloft. "The only way any of you are going to get an A in this course is if you learn to do this. But to satisfy Apache, you'll have to get the permission of the potter whose work you copy."

"Why should we have to get permission?" asked Apache. "You didn't have permission to make that copy."

"Actually, I did."

I put down the fake and picked up the original. "I received permission from the woman who made this one."

"How could you get permission from a potter who lived in the eleventh century?" asked Raúl.

"Her spirit gave it to me."

"Whoa," said Alfred.

"Sweeeet," said Nathan.

Aleesha rolled her eyes and said, "Right."

I told them to show up on Thursday dressed in old clothes. We were taking a field trip to dig clay.

4

My class was scheduled for Tuesdays and Thursdays from two to four.

Milton Shorter was waiting for me after the first session.

Shorter was both name and description. He was four inches shorter than me. That and his delicate features and easy smile made him seem childlike.

His handshake was warm but weak. "I don't have time right now to give you a guided tour of the entire department, but I'll give you the nickel tour of this hall."

It started with his office, big desk with a view of the mountains out the window. A silver coffee table with fossil designs etched onto its surface. View of an art gallery on a small television screen. Some paintings with pale diaphanous images. I had seen some like them but couldn't remember the artist's name.

We went from Milton's big office to the small metals studio and the aqueous-media studio, which were between the pottery studio and my office.

"It used to be the slide library," he said of my office, "but all the images are digital these days, so we converted it to an office for adjuncts."

The slide collection must have been tiny. The room was about four by six with a metal desk and a beat-up ladder-back chair.

He made a sweeping gesture worthy of pointing out the Grand Canyon, the effect of which was blunted somewhat when he banged his knuckles against the doorframe.

"It's all yours for four hours a week," he said. "I've reserved it for you one hour before and one hour after each of your class meetings. You might want to use the hour before as prep time and the hour after for office hours in case any student needs to meet with you. The department requires adjuncts to keep two office hours each week. And the bottom-right drawer is also yours."

Wow. Four hours and a drawer.

I decided to use the hour prior to the class for office hours and one after as travel time to Dos Hermanas.

I've been making pots for over twenty years. I didn't need any prep time.

I stayed in the office that afternoon so as not to offend my new boss. He brought me a blank ID card programmed to open the pottery studio, a green spiral-bound grade book and a red pencil. I put the ID card in my wallet and the grade book and pencil in my drawer.

I don't know what he expected me to do with the pencil. I was teaching my students to make pots. There would be no papers to grade.

Maybe I could pencil a red-letter grade on the side of their pots.

Claustrophobia set in when I closed the door. When I opened it, agoraphobia replaced the claustrophobia. I'm not usually nervous about being in public, but the office was so small that it was like being in a display case. And I was the display.

Which reminded me of Susannah dragging me last year to a traveling show of the work of Duane Hanson, an American sculptor known for his startlingly realistic figures. Unlike the sculptures we expect in museums—idealized bodies such as the *Venus de Milo* or Michelangelo's *David*—Hanson fabricates people you would be more likely to encounter on the crosstown bus.

They are creepily real, right down to every eyelash and freckle. Perhaps you've seen his famous one titled *Tourists*—a couple on vacation, overweight, unattractive and badly dressed. She in stretch pants, a scarf over her head, an oil slick of sunblock on her arms.

He in Bermuda shorts, a camera around his neck, flip-flops on gnarled feet.

Susannah makes me nervous because she gets so close to the art that I fear she may be reprimanded by the guard. I violate ARPA with impunity (and a shovel and piece of rebar), but I'm otherwise a rule-following sort of fellow. As Susannah and I moved from one piece to the next, I avoided eye contact with a museum guard stationed in the corner. Although I didn't look directly at him, he was in my peripheral vision, and I could tell he was staring at us.

I distanced myself slightly from Susannah. *Let him scold* her, I thought. She's the one who keeps leaning into the pieces as if she's about to touch them.

The closer we got to the guard, the harder it was for me to keep up the pretense that I hadn't noticed him. So when we reached the piece immediately next to him, I turned and smiled at him.

He glared back at me.

I swallowed. "Nice exhibit," I squeaked.

He continued glaring.

Then there was laughter.

Not from the guard. From Susannah.

"You're talking to an artwork, Hubie."

"I know that. I was just trying to be funny."

"Right." She moved to the first piece on the next wall.

I continued to stare at the guard. He was totally lifelike. Like one of those buskers downtown who dress up as Elvis or George Washington and stand motionless hoping passersby will drop a dollar in the box at their feet.

I wondered how hard it is to hold a pose and appear to be a statue. My picture-frame-size office seemed like a good place to find out. I looked around. The hall was empty. I took a deep breath and held it. I struck what I thought of as a pose—hands clasped on the desk, head slightly tilted, eyes fixed on the ceiling.

I had been holding my pose and my breath for perhaps fifteen seconds when I heard the footsteps. Had someone been watching my ridiculous performance?

Then I saw her from the corner of my eye. I decided to avoid embarrassment by just ignoring her. What did I care if she saw me lost in thought? Or if she thought I was posing? Let her just pass by.

But she didn't pass by. She eased toward me warily, wide-eyed, bent at the waist.

I looked up quickly and said, "Hello."

"Aaack," she chirped, and jumped back. "You scared the hell out of me."

"Sorry."

"What the devil were you doing?"

"Sorry," I repeated. "It was stupid of me. I felt weird in this small space, like being on display. So I was trying to see if I could look like a Duane Hanson sculpture. You know who he is?"

"Of course I do. I teach him."

"Duane Hanson is one of your students?"

"Don't be ridiculous. I discuss his work in my classes. I teach 3-D."

"Do you use those glasses with one green lens and one red one like in the movie theaters?"

She suddenly became quite stern. "Who are you, and what are you doing in the adjunct office?"

"I *am* an adjunct. I'm teaching ART 2330 this semester."

"The one where the students are supposed to learn how the Anasazi made pottery?"

"Right."

"Well, I wish you luck. The reason they hired an adjunct is neither of the pottery professors was willing to teach it."

It seemed suddenly cold in my office. "Why not?"

"Afraid of being politically incorrect, I suspect. Hell, that's what art is all about. If you don't offend people, you aren't making art. But the Tweedle Twins can't grasp that."

"The Tweedle Twins?"

"That's what I call them—Tweedle Dumb and Tweedle Dumber. Their real names are Melvin Armstrong and Junior Prather, and they look nothing alike except for the beards. But creatively, they're clones. The Smith Brothers, except they make coffee cups instead of cough drops."

"I gather you aren't fond of their work."

"Their work belongs in Dollar General, not art galleries. I suppose I should introduce myself—I'm Helga Ólafsdóttir."

Of course I didn't know about those marks over the *o*'s. I learned about them later. But I could hear them even then, although it was not an accent I could name.

She was tall and sinewy with pale blue eyes. Her hair fell loosely to the middle of her back, gray strands mixed with flaxen. Her handshake was firm.

"I'm Hubie Schuze."

"Oh my God! You're the guy who sent Freddie Blass to prison."

And I was so naive as to believe no one would remember.

"I didn't send him to prison. A judge did that."

"Yes, but you're the one who proved he murdered Gerstner."

"It wasn't anything personal. I actually liked Freddie."

"Don't apologize. What I know about Gerstner, he probably got what he deserved. Too bad Freddie had to go to prison. He was a good department head."

"What about Milton Shorter, the new department head?"

"*Acting* head. He doesn't have the job yet, and I hope he never does."

"Why?"

"He's compulsive. The first thing he did on becoming acting head was develop a calendar of when everything is due—course requests, annual activity reports, syllabi, midterm grades, attendance reports, final grades, committee minutes, et cetera. And he sends notes at the end of each month summarizing which things you turned in on time and which ones were late or not done. Artists don't function well under bean counters. Of course, Milt is no longer an artist. But that shouldn't mean the rest of us have to be as organized as he is." She shrugged in resignation. "He must think he's going to remain head. He ordered a big desk."

"He seems nice."

"He's good at that. It's how he manipulates people. Right now, he's in campaign mode. He wants your vote for him as department head."

"I don't think adjuncts have a vote."

"You don't know this department."

"You're right," I said, and seized on that comment to change the topic. "I don't know much about art, but—"

"I know, I know," she said, exasperated. "You know what you like. I hate when people say that, because they do *not* know what they like. You have to understand art before you are entitled to an opinion. Even your own."

"Interesting point. But that wasn't what I was going to say. I was going to say I don't understand the terminology in the department. For example, what is aqueous media? It sounds like underwater television stations."

She had an easy laugh. "It's watercolor. But the Gnome doesn't like that word because it sounds like something children can do. And they can. Better than she can, in fact."

First the Tweedle Twins and now the Gnome. I wondered what derogatory nickname she would hang on me.

"I take it the Gnome is the watercolor teacher."

"In title, yes. But she is no teacher. She wants to teach painting, but Wiezga won't allow it."

"Jack Wiezga? I thought he retired."

"Yes. Five years ago."

"And he still decides who teaches painting?"

"Remember what I just told you? Welcome to the art department, where adjuncts vote and retired people control who teaches. Here's my advice—say little and pay attention to which way the wind is blowing. Any questions?"

"Yes. *Small metals* sounds like the ones you get if you fail to win gold, silver or bronze. But I suppose that isn't what the small metals studio is for."

"No. Small metals is what we call jewelry these days."

"Ah."

In most ways, the University of New Mexico is not your traditional college campus. The climate is too dry for ivy-covered walls and too hot for tweedy-jacketed professors. One thing it does have in common with other universities is the shared delusion that you can change reality by changing labels.

5

After Helga left, the Tweedle Twins arrived. I recognized them by their beards. Melvin Armstrong had a frizzy Vandyke that did a poor job of what I assumed he grew it for—hiding his pointed chin.

Junior Prather's red beard appeared not to have been trimmed since the first term of the Reagan presidency. He was wrinklier than a shar-pei. A lot taller too.

"I'm Assistant Professor Junior Prather," he announced, "and this is Full Professor Melvin Armstrong. We came to tell you we decided not to speak to you."

"Why did you change your minds?"

His wrinkles increased, especially on his forehead. "I beg your pardon?"

"You said you decided not to talk to me, but you just did. So I wondered why you changed your minds."

Junior opened his mouth, but Melvin raised a hand to silence him. "We did not change our minds. Our decision not to talk to you stands. We are not here to talk to you. We are here to tell you we are not going to talk to you."

I couldn't stifle my laugh. "Did you also decide not to listen to me?"

They looked at each other, perplexed. Evidently, they hadn't discussed listening, only talking.

"Because if you haven't ruled out listening to me, I have a suggestion. The next time you decide not to talk to someone, send them a note. That way you won't have to talk to them."

"We are not talking to you," Melvin insisted.

I remembered what Helga had advised. "Do you know which way the wind is blowing in the art department?"

"We do. But we are not going to talk to you about it."

"So you'll talk to me about not talking to me but not about which way the wind is blowing?"

"Yes," said Junior.

"Goodbye," said Melvin.

Tweedle Twins indeed.

My next visitor was not the Gnome. I deduced that from the fact that it was a man and he was six feet tall.

"Harte Hockley, painter," he said, extending his hand.

His smile was genuine, his grip somewhat limp. Maybe because he never grasped anything heavier than a brush.

"Hubie Schuze," I said. "I take it *painter* is not your family name nor *Hockley* your middle one."

His laugh was as winning as his smile. "I don't know why I always introduce myself that way. Perhaps a vain attempt to distance myself from the artisans. No disrespect intended."

"None taken. I'm proud to be an artisan."

"Will you submit for the student/faculty show?"

"I'm not familiar with it."

"Each year in the fall, the John Sommers Gallery has a juried show of works by our own students and faculty."

"Is that the gallery I saw on the TV screen in Professor Shorter's office?"

"Yes. That's a closed-circuit feed we installed after the gallery attendant position was cut. And no offense, but some of the faculty wonder why we hired you when we don't have funds for the gallery attendant."

I didn't comment on the budget issue. "I'm just an artisan. I doubt my work would be worthy of a gallery."

"Acceptance into the show depends more on departmental politics than artistic merit."

"Which way the wind is blowing?" I hazarded.

"You're a quick study, Schuze. One day on the job and you already understand us. Can I see your work somewhere?"

I handed him my copy of the Tularosa black-on-white *olla*.

He held it toward the light. "Nice work."

I showed him the original. "It's just a copy."

He placed the pot gently on the desk. "When my students ask why I require them to make precise copies of paintings by Cézanne and Rothko, I tell them, 'If you can't copy, you can't paint.' Copying is how we develop the eye."

Since I didn't understand that, I merely nodded and asked him if he planned to submit work for the student/faculty show.

"My agent won't allow it. Says it would look ridiculous if I was rejected by my own department. There's another reason. Come with me."

I followed him down the main hall. I heard humming noises as we turned into a smaller hall and approached a pair of metal doors, one of which he opened to reveal a room full of drill presses, grinders, and tanks of oxygen and acetylene.

I spotted Bruce Slater's iguana T-shirt under a welding hood. He flipped up the hood and gave me a thumbs-up. I waved back at him.

Hockley gestured toward the equipment. "Looks like the mechanic's shop where I have my Bimmer repaired," he said, and laughed. "I don't display my paintings next to wrought-iron gates. Any questions?"

"Yes. What sort of art does Milton Shorter do?"

"He does therapy."

"They appointed someone from another department to head this one?"

"Unfortunately, he is from this department. He teaches art therapy."

"Like if a painter develops carpal tunnel syndrome, he can help them recover use of their hand?"

"No. It isn't physical therapy. It's more psychological."

"He counsels artists who are afraid of their brushes?"

He laughed and shook his head. "He teaches people how to use art as therapy for the depressed. The theory is that if you give a canvas and a brush to people who sit around drooling on themselves all day, they will find inner peace. And maybe even learn to breathe through their noses."

"So you are not a fan of his discipline."

"It isn't a discipline. He doesn't impart skills or knowledge. He simply indoctrinates students with the idea that they should use whatever artistic talent they have to cheer people up rather than create art."

"But doesn't he have to be an artist to teach art therapy?"

He shrugged. "He was an artist at one point."

After Hockley left, I returned to my office and rewrapped the Tularosa pot and my copy of it and replaced them in the box. I couldn't leave them in an unlocked office I shared with . . . how many other adjuncts? There were seven drawers in the desk, three on each side and one shallow one in the middle. If we each got one drawer, I might have as many as six fellow adjuncts. All the more reason not to leave anything in the office.

I picked up the box and closed the door.

"What did he tell you about me?"

She seemed to have materialized out of nowhere.

"And you are?" I asked.

"Jollo Bakkie. I'm a painter."

"And who is the *he* you are asking about?"

"Harte Hockley, of course. The guy you were just talking to."

"He didn't mention you."

"I'm surprised. He never misses a chance to undermine me. See those paintings," she asked, pointing to the wall opposite my office.

"Yes, I've been admiring them. Did you paint them?"

She looked like she had just sucked on a lemon. Which went with her wide face, oval body and stubby legs. She had to be the Gnome. I realize unwanted nicknames can be cruel, but it was easy to see why Helga tagged her with that one.

"I did not paint them. Hockley did. And if you admire them, you don't know much about art."

"I admit that. But I know what I like." I couldn't resist.

She gave me the you-are-stupid look and said, "They don't look like anything."

"I thought art had moved beyond representation," I replied, feeling myself drifting into uncertain territory.

"Paintings don't have to look like a photograph, but they have to look like *something*. There is no such thing as purely abstract art. That's why a simple horizontal line on a canvas is classified as a landscape."

"It is?"

"Yes. And any blob with protrusions is a human figure."

Only if you were the model, I thought but didn't say.

I don't like insulting people even when it's done silently in my head. But someone whose first words to a stranger are "What did he tell you about me?" has already rent the cloth of civility.

To atone for my insult, I asked her if any of her canvases were on display.

Her eyes narrowed. "He *did* talk about me. You knew those were not my paintings. Well, mine will be up there soon enough. I know which way the wind blows."

She waddled away.

I locked my office and left the Art Building. Which was like passing back through the looking glass into the real world.

6

My margarita had no salt on its rim because I had rotated the glass with each sip to balance the salt with the tequila, lime juice and triple sec. I was admiring my handiwork after asking Susannah about art therapy. And also feeling lucky that my best friend knew something about the department I was temporarily a small part of.

Her margarita also had no salt, because that's the way she orders them.

"Art is not the only discipline used for therapy," she said. "There's dance therapy, drama therapy, equine therapy—"

"They have therapy for horses?"

"No. It's therapy *using* horses."

"So you ride around on a horse until you feel better?"

"Basically, yes. Florence Nightingale was one of the persons who invented it. The idea is that the natural bond between humans and horses is nurturing."

"So do the horses charge by the hour like a regular shrink?"

She squinted at me. "Do you want to hear about these therapies or not?"

"Sure."

"Okay, the other ones I can think of that are offered at UNM are music therapy, poetry therapy and sand-tray therapy."

"I'll probably regret asking, but what is sand-tray therapy?"

"The patient constructs her own microcosm using miniature figures and colored sand. The construction sums up the patient's life, and by seeing it displayed in 3-D right in front of her, she can resolve conflicts."

"You have got to be kidding. What department teaches that?"

"I'm not certain. It's one of the departments in the college of education."

"I might have guessed."

She ignored my comment and asked why I was interested in art therapy.

"I'm not interested in it. I just wondered what it is because the acting department head teaches it."

"Are you having fun yet in the art department?"

"Not so far. The faculty are a weird bunch, and I had to take away the students' cell phones to get them to pay attention."

"Why not just tell them to turn off their phones?"

"I did. But Aleesha picked hers up when it wiggled."

"They don't *wiggle*. They vibrate."

"Whatever. She started texting, so I decided the only way to get their attention away from the phones was to get the phones away from them. Turns out I didn't need to do that. Telling them I forge pots got their attention."

"I'll bet they like having a criminal as a professor."

"I'm not a professor," I said, and helped myself to some of the pico de gallo, leaving the criminal issue dangling. "I tried to be clever and justify my forgery by using the example of Manet's *Olympia* being a redo of Titian's *The Venus of Urbino*, but a kid named Raúl Zamoria said that was an 'appropriation,' not a copy. Then he said Manet's version was appropriated by someone named Morimoto."

"Morimoto is one of those iron chefs. The artist is Morimura."

"Sounds the same. Another kid named Alfred said Makimori's version of *Olympia* is his favorite painting."

"Maki Mori is a Japanese opera singer."

"That probably explains why I've never seen any of her paintings."

"Sheesh. Morimura inserts his face and sometimes his whole body into famous historical paintings."

"Like the *Mona Lisa*?"

"Right, and self-portraits of Frieda Kahlo and photographs of Marilyn Monroe, Audrey Hepburn and Ingrid Bergman."

"There seems to be a pattern here."

"Yep. All women."

"So he's a drag queen?"

"It's a bit more complex than that, Hubert. His art deals with cultural and sexual appropriation."

"So all I have to do to make my fakes politically correct is call them *Appropriations of the Anasazi*."

"I like that. I can see it being the title of a display of your work. But you couldn't use exact copies. You'd have to change them in such a way that they broach important cultural themes."

"If I made a crude handmade pot and decorated it with an image of a modern potter's wheel, would that be art?"

"Sure. It forces the viewer to think about the artistic effects of mechanization."

I think of Susannah as a rancher girl, and not just because she grew up on the Inchaustigui Ranch near Willard. She's fresh, energetic and blunt, with the kind of outdoorsy beauty you expect to see on the face of someone who rides a horse named Buttermilk. So it's somewhat jarring when she displays mastery of convoluted intellectual theories. Which just proves that men always underestimate the complexity of women.

"It just occurred to me that Alfred may be gay," I said.

"Just because he likes Morimura's *Olympia*?"

"That and the fact that he wears Elton John glasses. And when he cuddled the Anasazi pot I took to class, Aleesha said he would make a good mommy."

"That wasn't very nice. I'm not surprised you don't have gaydar. You totally missed Chris being gay until he kissed you."

"Gaydar?"

"The ability to spot a gay person."

"That's a word?"

"I rest my case."

"Wait—*you* were the one dating him. You're the one with no gaydar. You didn't know he was gay until I told you he made a pass at me."

"I had an excuse. He asked me out, so I assumed they were dates. Besides, he was so drop-dead handsome, I was totally not paying attention to anything else."

"So I have the same excuse you do. He was asking you on dates, so I assumed he was straight."

She laughed and said we should call it even. "So Alfred is the possibly gay guy. Who is Aleesha?"

"She's tall and black with a great smile and a bit of attitude."

"Black attitude?"

"Is that like gaydar? Because I don't think attitude has color."

"Of course it does."

"Sharice is black, and she doesn't have attitude."

"She's from Canada."

"So black attitude can be frozen off like a wart?"

She dipped a chip into the metate of pico de gallo. "You really are lost in space when it comes to popular culture."

"Happily so."

She ate the chip and changed the subject. "So there's Raúl, Alfred and Aleesha. You know the names of all your students after just one meeting?"

"Of course."

"I'll bet you used the memory walk technique you taught me at the Lawrence Ranch."

I admitted my memory isn't as sharp as it used to be. The slight decline is not due to age. I'm only in my forties.

Okay, late forties.

Susannah's memory is almost perfect. But how much do you have to forget when you're only in your twenties?

A memory walk is a method for remembering a list of things like names by placing them along an imaginary walk or journey. I explained to Susannah how I used towns for my students.

"I start walking in San Francisco, where I run into Alfred Caron."

"Profiling, Hubie."

"It's a memory technique. It doesn't have to be politically correct."

"Okay. Then what?"

"I walk to Salt Lake City, where I see Nathan Lake. Then Chicago, where I see Aleesha Jones, because she has a Midwestern accent. Next I go to Mescalero, New Mexico, where I see Apache Fire."

"You have a student named Apache Fire?"

"His name on the official role from the registrar is Larry Smith. When I asked him about that, he said he asked the Registrar's Office to change it, but they refused because he never had his name legally changed."

"I can see where if he thought Larry Smith was a boring name, he might choose Apache Fire to *kindle* a new start."

"Groan. He said he didn't choose Apache Fire—it chose him."

"Did you ask him to explain that?"

I shook my head.

"Probably a good decision," she said. "Tell me the rest of the walk."

I did, but I'll spare you and just give you the cast of characters.

You already know about Alfred Caron, Aleesha Jones, the reptile pair (Nathan Lake with his snake tattoo and Bruce Slater with his iguana T-shirt), Raúl Zamoria the intellectual and Apache Fire the crusader.

The other ones were a giant black guy named Marlon Johnson, a comely brown-skinned lass named Mia New, a white nontraditional student with the alliterative name of Carly Carlisle and the mysterious Ximena Sifuentes. Her deep-set eyes were like black holes capturing any light that came too close.

After everyone else had spoken and been identified during that first class meeting, I looked down at the roll, looked up at Ximena and said, "There is only one other name on the roll, so by process of elimination, you must be Ms. Sifuentes."

She opened her mouth to answer but closed it quickly and sneezed. Then she handed me a paper and a pen. The paper was a form each of her instructors had to sign for her to receive her financial aid. When I returned the form to her, she sneezed again.

I said, "*Gesundheit.*" She smiled.

7

Because we are the same height, neither Sharice nor I have to crane our neck to kiss.

We were engaged in that pleasant activity at her door. Benz looked bored. He had seen a lot of it the past few months. Geronimo looked nervous.

Benz is Sharice's savannah cat, an exotic cross between an African wild serval and a domestic cat. He looks like a cheetah and fetches like a dog.

Sharice is equally exotic, her sepia skin proof that she shares Benz's African roots, and her green eyes evidence of European interlopers during her family's diaspora in Jamaica. She was born in Montreal and ended up in the United States because she wanted reconstructive breast surgery after her mastectomy, and the wait time in Canada was too long.

We dated quite a while before finally having sex. She had a list of things she needed to tell me about herself, one of which was that she'd had the mastectomy. Before I moved in, I asked if there were any other revelations I should be alert for. She replied there was one more thing she had to tell me, but it was not about her. It was about her father.

I didn't see how anything about her father could affect how I feel about her, so I wasn't bothered when she said she would tell me in due time. What's the worst-case scenario? Her dad is a serial killer? Maybe that's why she has a picture of her mother on her desk, a beautiful woman with Sharice's fine features but much darker skin, but no picture of her father.

Oh well, being a serial killer isn't hereditary. And I doubted it could be that serious, since she told me she had a typical if somewhat straight-laced upbringing.

Because of her lithe muscles, Sharice somewhat resembles her cat. And like Benz, she has been known to fetch. In her case, a glass of Gruet, New Mexico's contribution to the world of champagne.

Even though he is only a mutt, Geronimo is also exotic in his own way. My best guess is a mix of collie, chow and anteater.

Sharice likes the old joke that Canada should be a perfect country because it could combine British government, French food and American know-how. But unfortunately, it ended up with British food, French know-how and American government.

Geronimo suffered an analogous fate. He could have inherited the graceful neck of a collie, the bear snout of a chow and the thick coat of an anteater. Instead, he has the auburn fur of a chow, the wispy tail of a collie and the neck of an anteater. Like the camel, Geronimo looks like an animal designed by a committee. But he's good company.

After Sharice and I finally unlocked our lips, I tossed a piece of chicken jerky toward Benz. He batted it in midair and it flew across the room. Geronimo retrieved it and dropped it in front of Benz, who began chewing on it.

I rewarded Geronimo with a Milk-Bone Brushing Chew.

"How embarrassing is it that my dog fetches things for your cat?"

"Benz is the alpha male, Hubie."

"What about me?"

"You're *my* alpha male."

"And Geronimo?"

"Well . . . he's cute. In an odd way."

We moved from her doorway to her dining table. You can see the polished concrete floor through the glass top of the table and the Sandia Mountains through the floor-to-ceiling glass wall.

I told her about Helga Ólafsdóttir recognizing me as the person who, in her words, "sent Freddie Blass to prison."

"Did it bother you that she knew?"

"Yes. I was hoping no one remembered."

"I love your naïveté, but having their department head sent to prison is hardly something they'd forget."

"I guess. But couldn't they at least forget I was involved?"

I looked at the table. Two Champagne flutes and a bottle of Gruet Blanc de Noir shared a Nambé ice bucket. A cutting board was arrayed with sliced cheeses, smoked salmon, olives, roasted artichoke hearts and fennel wedges.

"Let's change the subject," I said.

"Okay. What do you want to talk about?"

"This," I said, pointing at the spread.

"Hope you don't mind a snicky-snacky meal. It was so hot walking home that I didn't want to use the cooktop."

The cooktop is stainless steel. As is the refrigerator, the door handles, the spigots and the railing around the balcony. If there were a bathtub, it would probably be stainless steel. But there is only a shower. The showerhead is stainless.

The place is so sleek, it's almost clinical.

Spirits in Clay, on the other hand, has no stainless steel. It doesn't even have steel that *can* be stained. It occupies the east third of an adobe built by Don Fernando Maria Arajuez Aragon in 1683 and is mostly adobe and pine.

When the middle part of the building came on the market, I had only a few years left on my mortgage, so I leased the middle third with an option to buy. I was thinking I could exercise that option after my mortgage was paid off.

I initially expanded my shop into the new space, but the additional space was more of a hassle than a benefit. It sat empty until a couple of years ago when I leased it to an Englishman named Gladwyn Farthing. He goes by Glad, and I chuckle when I say that because when I told Susannah about him, she quipped that it was a good thing he didn't also shorten his *last* name to its first four letters.

Glad bargained a reduction in his lease payments in exchange for his minding my shop when I'm not there. Now that I'm a full-time resident of the glass-and-steel condo, the reduction is larger because I frequently stay in the condo rather than walking to Old Town to mind a shop that has little traffic.

I admire Sharice's loft-style condo with its hard-edged industrial look and spare, clean feel. But a life spent between adobe walls didn't prepare me for concrete floors and steel-beamed ceilings.

Nor did enchiladas and tacos prep my tummy for a meatless diet.

Being in Sharice's condo is like being on vacation. It's fun, but it doesn't feel like home.

Lately, I'd been thinking home is overrated. Why not a life spent on vacation?

I'd proposed to her twice, both times in the spirit of banter, and she had responded in kind. When I finally asked her in earnest what she thought about the proposals, she said this was her first courtship and she wanted to prolong it.

Evidently, her mastectomy chased away other suitors. Those shallow twits unwittingly did me a great favor.

I'd told her about my new colleagues, my new office and how I felt I couldn't quite settle in there.

"I hope you eventually settle in here."

"I already have."

"You have exactly three shirts and two pair of pants in the closet. That's hardly settling in."

"You forgot I also have a pair of boots in there. The only things left in Old Town are a jacket and a sweatshirt I won't need for a few months. We just happen to be different when it comes to clothes."

"Yeah, that's an even bigger difference than black and white."

"Which reminds me that the new-faculty orientation last spring included a workshop on diversity."

She shook her head slowly as I told her about the event.

"I don't get this country," she said after I finished telling her about the orientation session. "Martin Luther King is a hero. You have a national holiday named after him. A major street in every city. Just last week you took me to see *Selma*, and the theater was packed. But none of you remember what he stood for. His most famous line is 'I have a dream that my four little children will one day live in a nation where they will not be judged by the color of their skin, but by the content of their character.' But Americans are obsessed with judging everyone by color."

"We are?"

"Yes. At last fall's annual meeting of the Association of Southwestern Dental Hygienists, a speaker at the session on diversity claimed you need to adjust your approach for each patient based on their ethnicity."

"That's bad?"

"I don't want my dental hygienist treating me as a black patient. My teeth are just like yours." She took a pause from her serious self and gave me the smile she reserves for ethnic humor. "They just look brighter because of my skin color."

"And also because of your great smile," I added.

"I also don't want my manicurist typecasting me. The first one I went to spent the whole session talking about how black women have special nails. Rubbish. Nails don't have ethnicity. They're just keratin. I changed manicurists. The new one was white like the first one, but the only people she talked to me about were Oprah Winfrey, Gabby Douglas and Kerry Washington, like I'm too provincial to be interested in anyone who's not a black woman. I didn't even know who Gabby Douglas and Kerry Washington were. Then she asked me if I like the songwriter Ne-Yo."

"Ne-Yo?"

"I'd never heard of him either. I told her the songwriter I like is Giacomo Puccini. Then I canceled the next appointment."

"How many manicurists have you gone though?"

She giggled. "Just the two. I do my own nails, now. I've felt pigeonholed and profiled ever since I came to this country. If I join a group of men talking about sports, they change the subject because they assume I'm not interested because I'm a woman. You can't believe some of the dumb things American men say about hockey. Two minutes after I meet people, they steer the conversation to race because they want to make me feel comfortable. It doesn't make me feel comfortable. It makes me feel like I'm not wholly human, like I'm fenced off from anything that isn't feminine or black. All these workshops and sensitivity sessions just make it worse. Americans are so sensitized that they don't see individuals as humans."

She exhaled and shook her head. Then she smiled at me and said, "One of the many things I love about you is that you never pigeonhole me."

"Well," I said, "maybe a little."

"Like what?"

"I admit to thinking that your love of clothes is sort of a woman thing."

"Okay, I'm guilty too. I see your lack of interest in clothes as a man thing."

"I may not be interested in my clothes, but I'm interested in yours."

"Yeah, getting me out of them."

"True."

"Glad you like it." She poured us some Gruet. "Enough social criticism. Tell me about your class."

"The students talk incessantly."

She shrugged. "It's a studio class. You won't be lecturing. So if they want to chatter while they work, why not."

"They chatter while I'm talking."

She laughed. "Stop talking."

"Okay. But tomorrow we're going on a field trip to dig clay. I'll be stuck in the Bronco with most of them, and I'll have to listen to their chattering."

"Tune them out."

"How?"

She brushed her lips across my left ear and whispered. "Just think back on the evening we're about to have."

Sharice never got the reconstructive breast surgery. She saved money for it but decided to spend it on those designer dresses instead.

She looks spectacular in those dresses. And even better out of them. No surgery could increase her sex appeal.

I looked at her and thought of a quatrain from Byron:

The smiles that win, the tints that glow,
But tell of days in goodness spent,
A mind at peace with all below,
A heart whose love is innocent!

8

I don't mind sitting behind the backseat," said Nathan. "I'm moderately autistic. Small spaces keep me calm."

"I'm an ACOA," said Mia.

When I frowned, she said, "Adult child of an alcoholic."

I doubted the *adult* part.

"I'm sort of bipolar," said Apache.

Bruce said, "I'm double-jointed in my wrists, but it's a good thing. Helps me work on my hog."

Raúl said he had attention-deficit disorder, and Alfred volunteered that he was lactose intolerant.

We had gathered in front of the Art Building at two on Thursday. I waited for a few seconds. When no one else volunteered information about their psychological, physical or nutritional condition, I said, "Okay, now that the public-service-announcement portion of today's program has ended, let's talk about the plan. Two of you will have to ride behind the backseat. Nathan has volunteered, so I'll assign one more person to that area. And two in the front and four in the second row."

"That's only eight," said Aleesha. "There are ten of us."

"Bruce is taking his motorcycle. Someone can ride on the back of it."

"I'll ride with him," said Mia.

"I figured you'd volunteer," said Aleesha.

Mia made a face at Aleesha but said nothing.

Bruce handed a helmet to Mia. "Hop on."

She did. And wrapped her arms around him as they sped off.

"I'm too big to fit in back," said Marlon.

"Okay," I said, "you get shotgun. Apache, you sit between me and Marlon."

"There's no seat belt. There isn't even a seat."

"You can sit on the console. I can't put Marlon there. He would crush it."

"You're trying to give me a substandard seat because I complained about you disrespecting Native Americans."

"Oh, for heaven's sake. Anyone want to volunteer?"

"I'll ride on the console," said Alfred. "But if it gets scary, I may shriek like a girl."

They all laughed.

I assigned Aleesha, Raúl, Apache and Ximena to the middle seat and told Carly to ride in back with Nathan. She was mature enough to handle a troubled child.

We drove to the Rio Grande Nature Center State Park, a preserve on the east side of the Rio Grande less than a mile southwest of Bookworks, a high-traffic indie bookstore. Unlike the nature preserve, which gets little traffic at all.

Unless you count roadrunners, sandhill cranes, great horned owls, ring-necked pheasants, bull snakes, long-tailed weasels, beavers and pocket gophers. All of whom fondly remember Edward Abbey.

No critters eat roadrunners, because nothing can catch them. Everything else is likely to become a meal. Beavers are slow, but that's not a problem because their prey can't run. Gophers are fast, but not as fast as the bull snakes that eat them. Owls speed out of the air to eat the snakes. The snakes get revenge by eating bird eggs. One big happy family.

Bruce was still astride his Harley when we arrived. Mia was still clinging tightly to him even though they were parked. He didn't seem to mind.

I opened the console after Alfred dismounted. "All cell phones in here."

"Uh-uh," said Aleesha. "I'm not going out in the wilderness without my phone."

"It's not the wilderness. We're in the middle of Albuquerque. There are joggers passing behind us right now on the Paseo del Bosque. One of them is even pushing a stroller."

"I'm from Chicago, and I'm telling you it looks like wilderness to me."

So she *is* from Chicago. I knew she was from the Midwest, but I didn't realize I had pegged the city.

"No phones," I said.

"I'll wait here."

"Okay, but that counts as an absence, which is five points off your grade."

"That's not fair."

"Come on, Aleesha," said Bruce. "Forget Chicago and just go with the flow. I promise to fight off any bears we run into."

"There are bears out there?"

"No. Can't you tell when I'm kidding?"

She glared at me and tossed her phone in with the others.

We didn't actually enter the Nature Center. We just used their parking lot and followed the fenced path that extends west from Candelaria Road to the Paseo. We crossed over that, over the irrigation canal that parallels the river, through the low-lying bosque and finally descended to the water's edge.

I suspect it is forbidden to traverse the path for the purpose of digging clay from the Rio Grande. I don't know that for sure, because I employ the philosophy that if you suspect you won't like the answer, don't ask the question.

I gave each student a bucket and a shovel. I took off my shoes, rolled up my pant legs and waded into the river. I plunged my left hand deep into the riverbed and came up with a fistful of clay.

"Even though this is a studio class, you'll have to endure a few lectures. This is the first one. Pay attention. The earth's crust is mostly stuff spewed out by volcanic activity. After it cooled and hardened into rock, it got cracked by frost, worn down by erosion and trampled on by mastodons. After a few million years, two of its major components—alumina and silica—ended up as clay."

Raúl stared at me. "Stuff spewed out? Trampled on by mastodons? Are you serious?"

"Completely. I'm not a geologist, so don't look for technical terms, because I don't know them. I know clay. When clay is moved along by water flows, it can pick up other minerals, like iron and mica."

I removed a shard from my pocket and moved it slightly from side to side. "What do you notice about this piece of an old pot?"

"It glints in the sun," said Carly.

"Right. It's from Taos, where they use clay with mica in it. Mica reflects light. There are many variations in clay. What it all has in common is particles so small that they adhere to each other and can be shaped. Open your hands."

I gave each of them a bit of the clay I had scooped from the river. "Squeeze it between your fingers, get the feel of it."

After they had done that, I scooped up some sand from the bank of the river. "Feel this."

"It's sand," said Marlon.

"Yes. Easy to identify, right? And obviously useless for making pottery. The grains are too large. Now feel this."

I dredged up some silt.

They handled it for a few moments then all agreed it was clay.

"Wrong. It's silt. Its mineral particles are smaller than sand. They stick together but not strongly. Your assignment is to find a bucketful of clay."

"We have to wade into the river and get all yucky?" asked Aleesha.

"Not if you don't want to. There is clay along the banks in certain spots and even out in the bosque we passed through. I don't care where you get it. But you have to make sure it's really clay."

"How can we do that?" asked Nathan.

"Find something that feels a bit like melted chocolate. Form it into a ball. Then roll it between your hands until it's like a short rope. Wrap the rope around your finger. If it stays there, it's clay."

Bruce took off his boots and socks and waded in. Marlon shrugged and did the same. Carly followed them in.

Mia took off her jeans and waded in wearing just panties and a T-shirt.

I wondered about the propriety of a coed in class with nothing below the waist except panties, but no one seemed concerned and we weren't on campus, so I decided to ignore it.

"I haven't had this much fun since my son was little," said Carly.

Everyone got into the spirit, even Aleesha. First they just slapped the water. Then they cupped their hands and tried to splash one another. I didn't notice who threw the first mud, but they were soon all covered with it. They made halfhearted attempts to wash it off as they emerged from the river.

Thanks to Albuquerque's low humidity, we were all dry by the time we reached the parking lot.

"Someone else want to risk riding with me?" asked Bruce.

Mia looked rejected.

"I'll do it," said Alfred.

"Hop on, honey," said Bruce, and everyone laughed, even Alfred.

Once the rest of us were in the Bronco, Aleesha said, "It's hot in here. Turn on the AC."

"It doesn't work," I said. "Roll down the windows."

She said . . . well, you probably know what she said.

Carly's suggestion to get ice cream garnered a chorus of endorsements.

"Gelato is even better," said Nathan. "Let's go to Itsa Italian Ice."

They liked that idea, and since it's on the corner of Phoenix and Second, it was on the way back to campus.

I returned their cell phones, and Nathan used his to call Bruce and tell him to meet us there.

To keep things simple, I volunteered to pay.

Who knew a small cup of gelato was $2.50?

I didn't like shelling out $29.43 (including tax) for eleven paper cups of ice and flavoring, but the green chile gelato I ordered was good enough to justify the price.

Yes, green chile. Hey, it's New Mexico.

My charges were comparing flavors, telling embarrassing stories (at least they *should* have been embarrassed by them) and laughing. They glanced at their cell phones when they heard a ring tone, but they just pushed buttons instead of talking.

They were bonding.

9

I plopped down my margarita. "Ten thousand dollars?"

"Yep," said Susannah. "Of course, he doesn't get the whole ten thousand. His agent gets ten percent and the gallery gets maybe forty percent, so he only gets five thousand for each painting."

"Only?" said Martin, who had joined us for the cocktail hour. He was having his usual Tecate. Martin's uncle is a skilled potter, whose work is rooted in their pueblo's ancient traditions.

"White people are weird," he said.

"We are?" asked Sharice.

Everyone stared at her.

"It's your fault," she said, evidently meaning Susannah, Martin and me as representatives of New Mexico.

We continued looking at her, waiting for an explanation.

"Well," she said, "maybe not totally your fault. It started at home. Montreal is less than ten percent black. Most of them are from Haiti and speak Creole, so I didn't identify with them."

"Were they your neighbors?"

"No. All our neighbors were white. I was the black kid in the white neighborhood. Then I moved to New Mexico, where you have three cultures—Native American, Hispanic and Anglo. I know very little about Hispanic culture and even less about Native Americans. So in New Mexico, I'm culturally white."

"So that makes you sort of the black counterpart to that white woman, Rachel Dolezal, who identifies as black," said Susannah.

Sharice smiled and said, "Yeah. But I have a mirror in my house. I may fit in with the white majority, but I know what I look like, and I'm happy with it."

"Me too," I said.

"New Mexico has blacks," said Susannah.

"Yeah, about two percent," I noted. "The three-culture thing is official. New Mexico State University's triangle logo represents the Native American, Hispanic and Anglo cultures that define the state."

"So in New Mexico, I'm white," Sharice said, and flashed her searchlight smile.

"Makes sense," said Martin. "If Jews can be gentiles in Utah, I guess blacks can be white in New Mexico."

Sharice frowned. "Jews can be gentiles in Utah?"

Susannah said, "Mormons call anyone who isn't one of them a gentile."

"Hmm," said Sharice. "So why are we whites weird?"

Martin said, "Because you pay ten thousand dollars for paintings by a guy using a style invented last week doing paintings that don't look like anything, and my uncle who incorporates a thousand years of tradition into his pots gets one fourth that much."

He looked at me accusingly. Spirits in Clay is the only outlet for Octavius Seepu's work.

"You should be grateful I don't charge forty percent, Tonto."

He laughed. "Thanks for that. And for the Tecate."

"I'm buying again?"

He nodded.

Martin Seepu is my height but thicker. His hundred and seventy pounds is mostly muscle. He was a fourteen-year-old dropout when I met him through a program in which UNM students were paired with reservation youth. There was probably an official reason for the pairings. Mentoring? Tutoring? Counseling?

Neither of us knew, so we jokingly refer to it as the "put a white kid from the city with an Indian kid from the rez and see what happens" program.

What happened was I taught him math and he taught me how to draw horses. He started out like a kid brother and ended up a friend. When I was booted from graduate school, he helped me refurbish my dilapidated building into a shop and residence.

During over twenty years in the pottery business, I've met hundreds of Native American artisans. Like Martin's uncle, most are quiet. All are scrupulously honest, which makes transacting business a pleasure. But I rarely feel I truly know them.

One exception was a young lady. I think the normal expression is smitten, but that sounds like it just sort of happened. She was much more proactive. So instead of smitten, I'd have to say she smote me.

But that sounds like what David did to Goliath. The verb *to smite* is difficult to conjugate. Must be from Old English. Maybe she smited me?

She had a round face and a small mouth with a slight overbite. Her coarse hair was clipped short. Her clear eyes peered out over prominent cheekbones and seemed to be looking into my mind.

Which made me blush because of what I was thinking.

Like most of my encounters with women, nothing much came of our flirtation, but I remember her fondly. Maria moved comfortably in both her tribal world and the larger society.

So does Martin. He and Maria have somehow mastered the ability to be equally at home on the rez and in the middle of Albuquerque.

Or the middle of nowhere. Now that I think more about it, where Maria and Martin are most at home is in their own skins. Something that transcends specific cultures. I guess that's why Sharice joked about being white. Her sense of self transcends artificial boundaries.

I'd told Susannah about meeting Harte Hockley, and she'd told me his paintings are on display at major galleries in SoHo, Santa Fe and Los Angeles. He sells about twenty paintings a year. So what if he gets only half the money? That's a hundred thousand, much more than he makes as a professor.

"Two of his paintings are on the wall across from my closet. Isn't it risky to have twenty thousand dollars' worth of art just hanging in an unguarded hallway?"

She smiled. "You thinking about stealing them?"

"I steal only pots."

"Who else did you meet?"

"Helga Ólafsdóttir, the 3-D person. She was a bit peeved when I asked her if she used those glasses with one red lens and one green one."

"I don't doubt it. She does terrific weavings based on the traditional patterns used in Iceland, where she's from."

"She told me her family is from Iceland, but she actually grew up in the Faroe Islands."

"They're in the Nile, right?"

Sometimes I can't tell if she's kidding.

"Helga once explained the Icelandic naming system to me," Susannah said. "The family name is the given name of one of the parents combined with the word for son or daughter. So I would be Susannah Hilargisdaughter."

"Or Susannah Hilargisdóttir."

"That's what I said."

"I added the mark over the ó."

"I thought you had a chip caught in your throat. If we used that system in Euskara, I would be Sorne Hilargisalaba."

"*Alaba* is the Basque word for 'daughter'?"

She nodded.

Sorne (the Basque word for 'conception') is the first name on Susannah's birth certificate. Her mother's Basque name is Hilargi, but she goes by Hillary.

I said, "I've been telling everyone I don't know art—"

"But you know what you like."

"No. Although I did say that to the Gnome just to irritate her."

Martin frowned. "The Gnome?"

"Her real name is Jollo Bakkie."

"With a name like that, I can't blame her for adopting a nickname," he said. "But I don't think I'd pick *the Gnome*."

"She didn't pick it. Helga hung it on her."

"That's an insult to gnomes," said Susannah. "They're cheerful little fellows. Jollo's an insect."

"What I was about to say is that I don't know art terminology. Jollo told me a simple line on a canvas is a landscape. But how can a weaving be 3-D?"

Susannah said, "Helga pours sand on the floor and mounds it into interesting contours. Then she lays the weaving over the sand and coats it with spray-on starch. When she hangs the weaving on the wall, it keeps that shape, so it's a 3-D work."

"All work is 3-D," said Martin.

We stared at him.

He looked at me. "Remember that book *Flatland* you made me read?"

"I didn't *make* you read it."

"When a white college student visits a fourteen-year-old dropout on the rez and suggests a book, that's the same as making me read it."

"But you liked it, right?"

"Yeah, because it made me feel smarter than the guy who wrote it."

"How so?" asked Sharice.

"He says the men who live in Flatland are polygons. The fewer sides a man has, the lower he is on the social scale. So triangles are the lowest level, squares are higher, pentagons higher and so on. But he also says they can see each other and interact, which is impossible. Because if they were truly two-dimensional, they would have no sides, so there would be nothing to see."

"You could see them from the top," said Susannah, "and from that vantage point, you could also see how many sides they have."

"No. To see them from on top, you'd have to be above them. But there is no *up* in Flatland. And there is no down. There is only north, south, east and west. So they wouldn't even know other men existed."

"They would when they bumped into them," she said.

He shook his head and placed two pennies on the table, sliding them until they touched. "These pennies can bump into each other because they have sides. But imagine them without sides. I don't mean just really flat. I mean no side dimension at all. The men in Flatland can't bump into each other because they have no sides."

"Why do you keep calling them men? Aren't there women in Flatland?"

"Sure. The author says they are straight lines."

She shook her head. "Sheesh. I might have guessed. The women are the lowest life-forms because they have only one dimension."

"Right. And he makes the same sort of mistake in describing them, saying that seen from straight-on they look like a point. But you can't see the end of a line because that would require that it have some height. Lines have only length. You could see them from below or above but not in a world that has only two dimensions."

"He says something else about women," I noted. "Because of their lack of intelligence, they accidentally pierce and kill people without even knowing it. But ten minutes later they can't remember it happening."

Sharice stared at me. "And you made him read that?"

"For the math part. I knew he was smart enough not to believe the stuff about women."

"He was also smart enough not to believe the stuff about math. A guy who thinks you can see something that doesn't have sides . . . wait, they can't *see* anything anyway. If they had eyes, they would have to be on their surface, because they have no sides. So the only direction their eyes could look would be up. But there is no up."

"See," I said, trying to move beyond my having forced a misogynist book on Martin, "You're also smarter than the author."

10

This is the second lecture."

It was our next session after the field trip.

They brought their clay. I collected their cell phones.

At which point Aleesha announced that she was attending the class under protest.

I didn't know what that meant and didn't want to inquire, so I said, "Okay."

"You can't count this against me," she said.

"The thought hadn't even occurred to me."

She started to say something else, but I cut her off by directing my attention to the class. "You found the clay. Now you have to get it ready to use. First, you need to press it through a fine screen to remove twigs, rocks and other impurities. We saw out at the river that clay can be molded and manipulated by hand. We call that plasticity. The second important characteristic of clay is that if you heat it to around twelve hundred degrees, it becomes more vitreous."

"Heating me to twelve hundred makes me *less* virtuous," said Mia, and everyone laughed.

Except me. I blushed. "It's vitreous—V-I-T-R-E-O-U-S."

"What does 'vitreous' mean?" asked Nathan.

"Basically, it means glasslike. But what it means in practical terms is it will hold water. The heat fuses the clay into a surface with no pores to absorb water. So it's important that you find your clay's exact maturing temperature. A pot that absorbs liquids obviously has limited uses."

"Why not just fire it a lot higher than twelve hundred? You could be sure it was fused and wouldn't have to waste time finding the exact temperature."

"Sounds like a good plan. But firing clay too high can cause it to deform. I've given each of you a set of pyrometric cones. With this brand, the size indicates the temperature. The smallest will slump at about eleven hundred and fifty degrees, the others at progressively higher temperatures. When the first cone slumps, start paying attention."

"This could take longer than the class time," said Marlon.

"I've ordered pizzas."

"How about beer?" asked Bruce.

"Sorry, not in the studio. Maybe after the semester is over and we can leave the campus for an end-of-the-course party."

"I can't stay after class," said Carly. "I have to pick up my son from day care."

"Could your husband pick him up today?" I asked.

She swallowed hard. Then she started crying. "Sorry to be emotional. The divorce isn't even final, so I'm struggling . . ."

Ximena walked over and hugged her.

What an idiot I am, I thought. I wished I had remembered my pompous lawyer telling me he never asks a question until he has laid a foundation for it.

"How old is he?" asked Bruce.

"Eleven."

"Would you let him ride on a motorcycle? I'd be real careful, and I have an extra helmet."

"He would love that." She turned to me. "Is it okay?"

"Sure. Maybe he'd like seeing the pottery studio in action."

I gave Carly her cell phone. She called the day-care center and talked to her son, then to the staff to tell them Bruce would be picking up Luke.

"Does he like pizza?" I asked.

They all stared at me.

"I retract the question."

It took longer than anticipated for them to screen the clay and make test pieces to the dimensions I specified.

I set up Bruce's kiln for him so that the time it took him to pick up Luke wouldn't prevent him from completing the test firing.

The back of the ceramics studio had a glass and aluminum accordion wall facing a courtyard surrounded by a fence made from concrete blocks with a lattice pattern. I slid the accordion wall open to let the heat escape. Some of the students passing by stopped to peer through the openings. Maybe they wondered where the heat was coming from. Or maybe it was the smell of the pizzas.

"Is this a cooking class?" one of them asked.

"Yeah," said Raúl. "We're learning how to bake pizzas in a kiln."

"I wish I'd known about this class. My elective this semester is a stupid archery class."

Bruce's test piece was the first to reach the perfect temperature, perhaps because the person who set up his kiln was an expert. The other students argued that since all the clay was from the same place, we could use Bruce's result.

"Nice try," I said, "but you learn by doing. And anyway, there may be slight variations. You guys waded all over the river."

"Not me," said Aleesha. "I was right close to the shore in case I saw any shark fins."

Everyone laughed.

Bruce said, "The only shark in that river was you," and she stuck her tongue out at him.

Luke Carlisle was tall for his age and skinny, evidently owing to a rapid metabolism. It certainly wasn't for lack of appetite. He ate three large pieces of pizza, all from the green chile, onion and mushroom combo. He wouldn't touch the anchovy and olive deluxe, and I can't say I blamed him. But Bruce and Ximena loved it.

Marlon was right. It was almost five when we left the studio, an hour over the scheduled time. But there was no class after us, so we could stay as long as we needed to. And the students seemed to enjoy it.

I saw Luke huddling with his mother. Then he approached me with a look on his face that I suspect pediatric dentists often see.

But he did a good job of reciting the speech his mother had instructed him to give.

"Thank you for inviting me here, Professor Schuze. I enjoyed seeing the studio. And thanks for the pizza."

"You're welcome, Luke. How was the ride on the motorcycle?"

He glanced at his mom.

"Better than being in a pottery class, right?" I said.

He nodded.

I was feeling good about the class until I saw the guy in the suit. He was grasping a clipboard with one hand and knocking on my closet/office with the other.

A suit and a clipboard. Never a good sign.

My first inclination was to leave. Maybe he was seeking one of the other vagabonds who used the adjunct office. If he had business with me, it could wait. Susannah was at Dos Hermanas.

But he had a determined knock and a humorless face, and something told me it was me he sought. Better get it out of the way now rather than worry about it all night, I figured.

"Can I help you?" I asked.

"Are you Hubert Schuze?"

"I am."

"My name is William Hughes, assistant director of the Office of Compliance with the Equal Educational Opportunities Act."

"An impressive title," I said, and smiled at him.

He did not return my smile. "I am here to inform you that a complaint has been filed with my office by a student who alleges that you violated the Equal Educational Opportunities Act."

He handed me a sealed envelope. "This is a copy of the complaint."

He handed me another envelope. "This is a copy of the procedure you are to follow in responding to the charge. Please note that neither the director nor the staff of the Office of Compliance with the Equal Educational Opportunities Act forms an opinion about any allegation until all parties have completed the required procedural steps."

It has been my experience that people say they have not formed an opinion only when they have in fact done so. Because if you really haven't formed an opinion, there is no need to say you haven't.

He thrust the clipboard at me. "Please sign here to acknowledge receipt of the complaint."

"No."

"No?"

"No."

"You aren't going to sign the form acknowledging receipt of a copy of the complaint?"

"I am not."

"Why not?"

"Because I don't know for a fact that I have received a copy."

"I just gave it to you."

"You gave me an envelope. I don't know what's in it."

"Open it."

"I'm already late for an important meeting. I'll open the envelope when I have time to do so."

"I can't let you keep a copy of the complaint unless you sign for it."

"Excellent," I said, and returned the envelope to him. "I didn't want it to begin with."

I turned to leave.

"Wait," he said. "If you refuse to sign, the complaint process will go forward without your participation."

"Also excellent. I have no desire to participate."

"How can you know that if you don't look at the complaint?"

"Mr. Hughes, both your suit and your clipboard are spiffy. I'm confident you can handle the complaint without my help. I really do have to leave."

"Failure to cooperate could prejudice the outcome," he said as I walked away.

So much for the director and staff not forming an opinion until the process was complete.

It's only three miles from the Art Building to Old Town, but the downtown traffic is bad at rush hour, so I decided to make a bathroom stop in case I got stuck in traffic.

Luckily, I had zipped up before Ximena Sifuentes walked into the men's room.

"You have the wrong restroom," I said.

She looked me in the eyes, shook her head and walked past me.

"This is the men's room," I said to her back. But she just sneezed and headed into one of the stalls.

11

I arrived at Dos Hermanas with *Desert Solitaire* in one hand and a pizza box in the other. No one wanted either of the two leftover slices.

Susannah signaled Angie that I needed a margarita. Sharice was still at work, helping Dr. Batres fix poor people's teeth.

I didn't know Martin and Glad would be there, but I wasn't surprised to see them, the former at the table with his Tecate at hand and the latter at the bar, no doubt ordering his usual pink gin, a drink consisting of a few ounces of gin with a dash of bitters. No ice.

Not that ice would improve it.

I *was* surprised to see Miss Gladys Claiborne, the owner of the west third of my adobe and the eponymous shop therein, Miss Gladys's Gift Shop. I'd invited her to our cocktail hour dozens of times during the first years of our acquaintance and finally quit doing so because she always politely declined. I know she tipples at home on occasion, but I guessed she might not think it genteel for a widow to visit a bar. As you might imagine, gentility is important to anyone called *Miss*, a title she held even during her long marriage to the late Mr. Claiborne.

Although she never before joined me at Dos Hermanas, she often comes to Spirits in Clay to deliver one of her casseroles, fascinating ventures into factory-made cuisine. In the age of Whole Foods grocery stores, farm-to-table restaurants, organically grown produce and free-range chickens, Miss Gladys remains steadfast in her devotion to ingredients that can be purchased in cans, jars and plastic bags. Indeed, these are the measurements in her recipes. Mix a jar of this with a can of that, cover with a bag of grated cheese, bake and serve from the casserole dish. The stockholders at Kraft, Campbell's and Del Monte offer daily prayers of thanks for Miss Gladys.

Although some of her casseroles are tasty, it is best not to read the nutritional labels on the component jars, cans and packages, which reveal that salt and hydrogenated oils are abundant. I don't know what happens to oil when it is hydrogenated, but it sounds like a process for generating electricity in a dam.

I had been spared the casseroles ever since she and Gladwyn became . . . I don't know what to call it. Friends? Companions? An item?

Glad raves about Miss Gladys's casseroles. Of course, he comes from England, the land of spotted dick, toad-in-the-hole, Cullen skink and bloaters. There's also one called bubble and squeak, which sounds like what happens to you if you eat any of those.

The last dish on that list sounds like what happens to you when you eat any of the other ones.

Gladys's blues eyes sparkled. "I can tell by that look on your face, Mr. Schuze, that you are shocked to see me here."

"That's not shock you see. It's delight. And since you have finally consented to join my circle of drinking buddies, I hope you will call me Hubie."

"Thank you, Mr. Schuze," she said, and we all laughed.

I offered to buy her a drink.

"Gladwyn is ordering my favorite—bourbon and branch."

"What sort of branch would that be, Miss Gladys? Olive?"

"Now, don't tell me that you don't know what branch water is. It comes straight from the limestone over which any quality distillery sits. Bourbon is too strong for me to drink straight, so I like a little water in it. Mr. Claiborne always said adding anything except branch water adulterates the bourbon." She blushed. "I think he used that word just to agitate me."

"And where would you get branch water in New Mexico?"

"At the Don Quixote Distillery," said Glad as he handed the bourbon and branch to Miss Gladys. "They tell me water from the Frijoles Mesa seeps through basalt on its way to the Rio Grande. Fortunately, the distillery gets it before it enters the river. I can't imagine what whiskey made from Rio Grande water would taste like."

"Probably like gin made from the water of the Thames," I said, and he chuckled.

"How was your class?" Susannah asked.

"Bizarre as usual. It started with Aleesha announcing she was attending under protest."

"Did you ask her what that means?"

"No."

"Why not?"

"Because I didn't want to know."

"Makes sense," said Martin.

"But I think I found out anyway. After class, a guy in a suit showed up carrying a clipboard."

"Not a good sign, kemosabe," said Martin. "An official, no doubt."

"Right. The assistant director of something with a name like Bureau of Men in Suits Who Make Sure We Provide Equal Opportunity Education."

"And you figure his visit was prompted by Aleesha," Susannah said, "and that's why she was attending class under protest."

"That would be my guess."

She continued, "You do something to upset her?"

"I took away her cell phone."

"You took away everyone's cell phone. You're an equal-opportunity cell phone taker."

"Maybe I did something else to upset her without knowing it. My nontraditional student, Carly, said she couldn't stay after class to test fire her clay because she had to pick up her son from day care. So I asked if her husband could pick him up instead, and she burst into tears."

"Oh, no. Let me guess. She's a single mom, right?"

"Not quite. She said the divorce isn't final yet. So if I'm insensitive enough to upset Carly, maybe I also upset Aleesha without knowing it."

"I have always found you to be a sensitive person," said Miss Gladys.

"Thank you. I try to be." Angie arrived with my margarita, and I took a sip. "There was another weird thing that happened. I was in the men's room when one of my female students came in."

Susannah laughed. "That's easy to do. You're in dire need of a restroom and don't pay attention to whether the icon has pants or a skirt. The next thing you know, you're in the men's room. The urinals are the tip-off."

"Evidently, they weren't a tip-off to her. I told her she was in the wrong restroom, and she shook her head as if I was the one who got it wrong."

"Oh my God," said Susannah. "She's probably transgender."

"I don't think so. She wears very girly clothes."

"Jeez, Hubert. Don't you know about LGBs and such?"

"I do, in fact. I was just reading about them in *Desert Solitaire*."

Her brow furrowed as her head tilted. "Edward Abbey wrote about LGBs?"

"Yeah." I pulled the book from my pocket and read: "They flitted around Arches National Monument, where he worked as a park ranger."

"Hmm. I would have thought them more likely to frequent urban settings."

"Pigeons, maybe. But not little gray birds."

"Little gray birds?"

"Right." I thumbed to page seventeen and read. "'What the ornithologist terms l.g.b.'s—little gray birds—they flit about from point to point on noiseless wings, their origins obscure.'" I looked up. Everyone except Miss Gladys was laughing.

Susannah said, "LGB stands for lesbian, gay and bisexual, Hubie."

"Oh. Well, Ximena may be lesbian for all I know, but I already told you why she probably isn't transgender."

"That's because you're confusing transgender with transvestite."

"They're not the same?"

"No. A transgender person is a woman trapped in a man's body or a man trapped in a woman's body."

"When I was thirteen, I would have given all my allowance money to be trapped in a woman's body," I quipped.

"I don't understand any of this," said Miss Gladys.

"You're better off not understanding it, dear," said Glad.

Dear?

I guess that answered my question as to whether Gladwyn and Miss Gladys were friends, companions or an item.

"There are no transgender people in my tribe," said Martin.

"Sure there are," said Susannah, "just like there are gay men in ranching communities like Willard, but they stay in the closet because they don't want to be outcasts."

"Transgenders are not outcasts in my tribe. We are all transgender."

"You just said there aren't any."

He nodded. "It amounts to the same thing. Since we are all transgender, no one is transgender."

"That doesn't make sense," I said.

"Sure it does. Legend tells us we were created when Mother Earth mated with Father Moon. Our bodies are male or female, but our spirits are half woman and half man because they came from Mother Earth and Father Moon. No one cares if a young boy plays with a doll or a young girl plays with a spear. But if they do it too much, their mother may gently scold them. When I would draw pictures for hours, my mother would say, 'You are listening too much to Mother Earth. Go outside and listen to Father Moon.' But we children all knew we had both sides and could express them both. So we are all transgender. And since we are all that way, no one sees it. You would only be labeled different in my tribe if you *weren't* transgender, if somehow you never showed your Mother Earth spirit or your Father Moon spirit."

There followed a silence as we each considered his explanation.

Susannah was the first to speak. "I like that legend. The world would be a better place if more men listened to their Mother Earth side."

"Why?" I asked, just to challenge her.

"Because women do everything better than men. If we could get more men to do things like women, we wouldn't have to carry the whole load by ourselves."

"There are some things men do better than women," I said.

She challenged me. "Name a couple."

"Burning things down and growing beards."

"Hear, hear," said Glad.

After our bar session ended, Glad pulled me aside. "I don't wish to be impertinent, Hubie. But as a bloke who's been around longer than yourself, I have to tell you that some folk may consider it odd that you are having cocktails with Susannah and Sharice isn't here."

"That's because she's working tonight."

"You miss my point. It isn't that Sharice is absent. It is that she and you are in a domestic relationship and yet you are having cocktails with another woman."

"Susannah isn't *another woman*. She's a friend."

"So you say. But appearance and reality often diverge."

He was right about that. Susannah's younger brothers seem to believe she and I are a couple. At least, I think they do. Susannah says I've simply misconstrued their words.

I appreciated Glad's concern but had weightier matters to worry about. Like whether violating the Equal Education Opportunity Act (commonly called EEO) could get me fired.

Or land me in jail.

12

Octavius Seepu cut an impressive figure in a buckskin shirt with turquoise buttons. His red headcloth was knotted at one side, its two ends falling over his left ear, each trailing a feather.

His broad face was the color of Chinle Cliffs and about as animated.

He grasped a pot between gnarled hands and raised it above his head. I had no idea what he was going to do with it, but I did recognize it. After Octavius had agreed to speak to my class, Martin asked me to make a quick-and-dirty Anasazi fake. It was now being lofted by Octavius.

"Okamo te leka o keowaa te nilil."

My students were wide-eyed and—for once—completely silent.

Martin translated for his uncle. "He has asked the ancient potters for permission to copy their work."

"Pi ah olleko te wah."

"They have granted it," Martin translated.

Octavius raised the pot even higher. He loosed his fingers. The pot hitting the concrete floor was followed by the sharp crack of shattering clay and a collective gasp from the students.

"Te kio te mato, ne rah tao."

"Those who accept a piece of this pot may make a new one."

When no one moved, Martin picked up a piece and handed it to the closest student, who happened to be Ximena. She closed her hand around it and looked down. Her lips moved as if in silent prayer. Then she hugged Martin.

"You can each have a piece," Martin said.

Bruce bent down for one. "Can I hug you too?"

"Why not?" said Martin, and opened his arms.

Bruce gave him a man hug. "Thank your uncle for us."

All the students took a piece, even Apache.

While the students compared their shards, I walked Martin and Octavius back to my office and said to Martin, "You know I understand a bit of the Tanoan languages."

"And you know our language isn't in that group."

"Right. But neither is yours a language isolate, like Zuni. So when you and your uncle talk, I sometimes pick up a word or two. Today I didn't understand anything."

"Neither did I. He was faking it."

"Why?"

"Because our words are never spoken for outsiders."

"Then why did he agree to speak at all?"

Octavius spoke and Martin translated.

"He thinks you honor the ancient ones by copying their work. He wanted to help you teach the students how to do pots the ancient way."

"So the words were just gibberish?"

"Yeah. But he sounded good, don't you think?"

"Yeah. Even Apache was eating it up."

Octavius said, "Apache easily fooled."

I couldn't tell if he was joking. The Pueblo peoples historically had a low opinion of the Apaches.

Octavius took off the buckskin shirt and put on the blue cotton one he had arrived in. Then he took one of his own pots from a bag and handed it to me.

I looked at Octavius. "How much do you want for it?"

He didn't answer. He almost never does. But it would be impolite not to ask him directly.

"Five thousand," said Martin.

"I never should have mentioned Harte Hockley."

Martin smiled. "Just kidding. But he would like to get more than the usual twenty-five hundred."

"How about three thousand?"

Octavius nodded.

"You gonna price it at five thousand? That would give Uncle Octavius his three thousand, and you would make forty percent like Hockley's galleries."

I shook my head. "Don't want to be greedy. I'll price it at four and make twenty-five percent."

Octavius handed the buckskin shirt to me.

"How much you give us for the turquoise?" Martin asked.

I examined the buttons. "These are not real turquoise."

"I know. Got them at Hobby Lobby. Got the feathers there too."

"And the shirt?"

"Goodwill."

"You going to keep it?" I asked.

Octavius shook his head. "Too hot."

Then he said something in his own tongue.

Martin translated. "He says he is worried about the silent one."

13

Another suit was waiting. He was standing in the hall next to the door.

At least he wasn't carrying a clipboard.

"Are you Hubert Schuze?"

Now what? I thought.

He introduced himself as Garrett Stevens and told me he was from the Office of Environmental Health and Safety.

The card he gave me listed his particular duties as outdoor fire procedures, dry-ice usage, fluorescent lightbulb safety, tent policy and field-trip safety.

A true Renaissance man.

It was that last one he wanted to talk about.

"It has come to our attention that you used your personal vehicle to take students on a field trip."

"I sure did. The place we were going is about six miles away, too far to walk."

"You should have used a university vehicle."

"I didn't know there were university vehicles available."

"You should have asked."

I decided to take the offensive. "Or maybe someone should have told me. It would have been a good thing to include in the new-faculty orientation I attended. But instead of useful information like university vehicles being available for field trips, I learned that the Counseling Assistance Resource Center is called CARS and the Sexual Assault Nurse Examiner is called SANE."

He chose not to comment, handing me some papers instead.

"Please distribute these to your students. They are forms releasing the university from responsibility for any harm they may have suffered on the unauthorized field trip."

"That won't be necessary. No one was harmed. We even stopped for Italian ice on the way back to campus."

"Nevertheless, they need to sign the forms. They may have suffered some harm that has not yet manifested itself."

"Good point. Perhaps one of them might have a delayed allergic reaction to the pistachio gelato."

He evidently missed the humor.

I took the papers and entered the studio.

"Wait," said Aleesha after I explained the forms to the class. "You refused to sign the form saying you had received a copy of a complaint filed against you for violating the Equal Educational Opportunities Act, but you want us to sign a form releasing the university from any liability for that field trip?"

"*I* don't want you to sign it. I'm just the messenger. The person who wants you to sign it is Garrett Stevens from the Office of Environmental Health and Safety."

"Forget the field-trip form," said Bruce. "I want to know about the EEO violation."

I shrugged. "Someone filed an EEO complaint. The office that deals with that wanted me to sign a form acknowledging I had received a copy of the complaint, and I refused to do so."

"Why?"

"Because I didn't know for sure if I had received a copy. It was in a sealed envelope."

"All you had to do was open it," said Aleesha.

"I didn't want to open it."

"Why not?"

"Because I was in a hurry. And frankly, I didn't want to see the complaint."

"Why not?" she insisted like a cross-examining attorney.

"Mainly because I wanted the office that handles those things to just do what they do and not bother me. But also because . . . well, I didn't want to know who filed it."

"You know who filed it," she snapped.

Marlon glared at her. "You did, didn't you?"

"Why you asking? It's none of your business." She looked back at me. "I'm not signing that release."

"Fine," I said.

"Are we going to do anything else today?"

Between the twenty minutes of aimless conversation that started the class, Octavius's performance and my explanation about the release forms, most of the class time was gone.

"Nothing else. Next time, I'll show you how to shape a pot without using a wheel."

"I'm leaving," Aleesha said, and stomped out.

"What did you do to her?" asked Apache.

"I have no idea."

"You must have done something."

"It sure looks like it, but I can't think of anything I've done or said to upset her."

"Then why didn't you read the complaint?"

"Because he didn't want to know which student filed it, Apache," said Carly. "He doesn't want to risk having the complaint subconsciously influence his grading."

She looked at me. "Am I right?"

I nodded.

"And it's just a coincidence that she's black?" said Apache.

"I'm black," said Marlon, "and I haven't seen or heard anything that would justify an EEO complaint."

Apache turned and left.

"I guess you didn't convince him," I said to Marlon.

His casual slap on my back almost knocked me down. "Don't worry about it, Mr. Schuze. We'll all stick up for you, won't we?" he said as he looked at the others.

They all said yes. Of course, given his size—about six-seven and pushing three hundred pounds—who's going to argue with him?

"See?" he said. "It's unanimous."

"That's because neither Aleesha nor Apache is here. I do appreciate your support. But let's not let this EEO thing get in the way of the class. We spent the first Tuesday getting to know each other and talking about what the class entails. We spent the first Thursday gathering clay. We spent the second Tuesday test-firing the clay, and today we had a little ceremony to put us in the right mental and spiritual frame of mind to make some kick-ass pottery!"

I felt awkward using the slang, but Nathan said, "Sweet," Carly said, "Right on," and Marlon fist pumped.

Yet another stranger was waiting at my office.

He introduced himself as Buddy Keys. Both his handshake and his smile made me realize he had not come to scold me for some transgression of university policy.

"I'm the offensive-line coordinator for the Lobos," he said. "I'd like to know how Marlon Johnson is doing in your class."

I pictured Marlon lined up with some wolves and Mr. Keys being offensive to them. It made about as much sense in my imagination as it makes in words.

He must have seen the confusion on my face. "I'm his coach," he said.

"What do you coach him in?"

"Blocking schemes."

I pictured Marlon using toy blocks. Maybe it's another form of therapy like riding horses or playing in a sandbox, although Marlon didn't show any signs of needing therapy.

"I don't understand," I said.

"Marlon is on the football team. He's an offensive lineman. I just need to know how he's doing in class."

"He's doing fine," I said. "And he's never been offensive. Quite the opposite. He is cheerful and cooperative."

"Great to hear it," he said, and handed me his card. "Call me if there's ever an issue."

14

I was back in the Art Building the next day even though it was a Friday. It was the first departmental meeting of the semester.

I grabbed a chair next to Helga, who smiled at me and asked if I enjoyed circuses.

There was a table at the front of the room. It held a large urn, a cooler of ice and Styrofoam cups with straws inserted through plastic lids.

Milton Shorter's desk was to the left of the table. It was large enough to be visible from outer space. I wondered if the desk was some sort of subconscious compensation for his diminutive stature.

Then I remembered Sharice saying she was profiled and pigeon-holed. And here I was doing it to Shorter. Height, skin color, gender. Why do we obsess over things we don't control?

We demand diversity in everything from Supreme Court justices to UNM cheerleaders. But diversity has no intrinsic value.

The Lobos men's basketball team sorely lacks diversity. They are all over six feet tall and all athletically gifted. The team would be more diverse if they put me on it. I'm short and can't dribble, much less shoot. But the point of basketball is not to have diversity. It's to win games.

UNM has a Division for Equity and Inclusion. They were responsible for the workshops I attended as a new teacher. One of their stated functions is "bringing together diverse world views."

Importing a few Taliban to campus would add a world view we don't currently have. But I don't think anyone in the Division for Equity and Inclusion really wants people on campus who think it's a good idea to throw acid in the faces of little girls who dare to attend school.

When it comes to ethics, I don't want diversity. I want everyone to refrain from violence and assist people in need.

I suppose the faculty at the meeting would qualify as diverse.

Helga Ólafsdóttir added both gender and ethnic diversity because she's a woman and also a Viking or whatever ethnicity hails from Iceland via the Faroe Islands.

Jollo Bakkie is a gnome, a race I suspect is underrepresented in the art world.

The two "small metals" teachers were a Native American man named Fe Solís and a Hispanic woman named Ana Abeyta.

Melvin Armstrong was black, so that added to the mix.

Also in attendance was Jack Wiezga, the retired painting professor who retains a small studio where he paints even though he no longer teaches. He was old. I think old may count as diverse.

I'd met Wiezga several years ago when I was trying to figure out who killed Gerstner. He's a big man with thinning silver hair that he tucks behind his ears in lieu of trimming. At one time, I suspected he might have killed Gerstner.

He returned the favor by suspecting me.

Although there was a perfectly serviceable chair behind his desk, Shorter had done a little hop to gain a sitting position on the front of it, his legs dangling a foot above the floor. A man of the people.

"Thanks for coming. The first order of business is to approve the minutes of our last meeting."

"No," said Armstrong. "The first order of business is to serve tea. According to the rotation, it's Junior's turn."

I whispered to Helga, "Tea?"

She whispered back, "Freddie started the tradition hoping it would foster civility. He wanted it to be like high tea in England."

"But they drink hot tea."

She shrugged. "Too hot for that here."

"What about crumpets?"

"What's a crumpet?"

"I have no idea."

While Helga and I were whispering, Junior was filling the cups with ice, pouring in tea and inserting the straws back through the lids. He delivered the first one to me and said, "This one is yours."

"So you're talking to me now."

"No. I'm just delivering tea."

I sat my cup of tea on the silver coffee table with the designs on it. Milton Shorter jumped down from his desk, lifted the cup and put a coaster under it.

"Can't be too careful," he said.

Junior gave everyone tea. Harte Hockley doodled on his cup. He must have been terribly thirsty. And driven to doodle. He helped himself to a second cup of tea and doodled on that one as well. I suppose the artistic urge can't be stilled for something as dull as a departmental meeting.

After the last Styrofoam cup was delivered to Wiezga, Shorter again asked that the minutes of the last meeting be approved.

"The last meeting was in May," said Armstrong. "No one remembers it now."

"I remember it," said Helga. She looked at Shorter. "It was when you announced you had been reappointed acting department head for another year. I move that we approve the minutes and reject your continuing appointment as acting head."

"I'm the parliamentarian," said Jollo Bakkie. "You can't combine those two motions."

"Okay. I'll make two separate motions. First, that we approve the minutes. Second, that we reject the reappointment of Professor Shorter as acting head." She looked his way. "Nothing personal, Milt. I just think we should have a studio artist as head and some new blood."

He smiled at her and nodded.

"You can't make a second motion until the first one is seconded and voted on or until it dies for lack of a second," said Jollo.

A guy I didn't recognize seconded the motion to approve the minutes.

"Okay," said Helga, "Let's vote."

"First we have to open the floor for debate."

Helga shook her head. "What's to debate? It's just approving the minutes."

"It's required. Any debate?"

When no one spoke, Jollo said, "Now we can vote."

Shorter said, "All those in favor say aye." There were a few ayes.

"All those against say nay." There were no nays.

"Motion carries."

"You can make your second motion," said Jollo.

"I already made it," said Helga.

"You made it out of order. If you want it discussed and voted on, you need to make it now."

"I withdraw it."

"You can't withdraw it until it's officially made."

"Okay, I move that we reject the appointment of Professor Shorter as acting department head."

Harte Hockley seconded the motion.

"Any discussion?"

"Yes," said Helga. "Now that it has been officially made in the correct order, I wish to withdraw my motion."

"You cannot withdraw a motion after it has been seconded. Any discussion?"

This could take forever, I thought.

Milton Shorter said, "I fully understand that some of you would like to see an open search for a new department head. I too would like to see that. But after Professor Freddie Blass was . . . um . . . left the department, the university took his line out of our budget on the grounds we are overstaffed."

My new colleagues turned to look at me. Not only had I sent their department head to prison, I had done something even worse—cost them a position. Many academic departments measure their prestige by how many faculty members they have, especially those departments that lack any more meaningful earmarks of excellence.

"We are not overstaffed," said Armstrong.

"I agree," said Shorter. "But we produce far fewer graduates than the college of business, and their classes are five times larger than ours."

"Can't the bureaucrats who run this place understand that you can't put fifty students in a studio?" asked Ana Abeyta.

"I've explained that to them. But they point out that in some of our studios, only half of the slots are filled. In fact, one of the ceramics courses this semester had to be canceled because no one signed up for it."

"My studios are always full and have waiting lists," said Hockley, smiling broadly. "The only studio courses that don't fill up are watercolor and ceramics."

Armstrong bristled at Hockley's comment. "Blass was a painter. Eliminating his budget line had nothing to do with ceramics."

"It was a target of opportunity," said Helga. "Melvin and Junior are both tenured. The administration can't get rid of either of them. So they eliminated another line that came empty and probably expected us to shift around teaching assignments."

Armstrong asked rather loudly, "Did those Philistines expect Junior or me to suddenly become painters instead of ceramicists?"

"The only reason the *aqueous media* studios are not full," said Jollo, stressing the phrase "aqueous media" and glaring at Hockley for using the word *watercolor*, "is because the students know that is not my medium. If I were teaching oils, my studios would be packed."

"Not going to happen," said Jack Wiezga, causing Jollo to shift her glare from Hockley to Wiezga.

There ensued a long and heated debate about painting, for which I was grateful, since it led them away from discussing ceramics. But the discussion eventually circled back to ceramics, specifically to the lab fee.

Armstrong asked Shorter why the ceramics budget was a thousand dollars in the red.

Given that I had nothing to do with budgets and that Armstrong's question was addressed to Shorter, I wondered why he was staring at me as he asked it.

I found out when Shorter answered. "The shortage results from the fact that none of the students in ART 2330 have paid the lab fee. It's not unusual to have one or two students pay a fee late because they're short of money, but having an entire class fail to pay is unprecedented." He looked at me. "Do you have any idea why no one in your class has paid the fee?"

"Yes. I told them not to pay it. The fee is to cover the cost of clay. They dug up their own clay. So there's no reason to pay the fee."

"The clay is in the storeroom and has already been purchased," said Prather. "We need them to pay the fee to cover the cost of the clay."

"I thought you weren't talking to me," I said.

"I'm not talking to you. I'm discussing a motion."

Jollo noted there was no motion on the floor regarding ceramics.

"Okay," said Prather, "I move that we discuss the matter of the lab fee for ART 2330."

Jollo said, "Robert's Rules of Order do not allow a motion to discuss. All motions must be to take a specific action."

Here we go again.

Prather modified his motion. "I move that we order the students in ART 2330 to pay the lab fee."

Armstrong seconded the motion.

Helga spoke up. "You can't order students to pay for supplies they are not using."

"Of course we can," said Prather. "We are the faculty. It is our right and our duty to direct the students what to do."

"With an attitude like that," Helga said, "it's no wonder one of your classes failed this semester to attract any students."

He clenched his jaw but didn't speak.

To break the awkward silence, I made a suggestion. "Could we send the clay back and get a refund? That would balance the budget without making the students pay for something they aren't using."

"If you hadn't let them dig up their own clay, we wouldn't have this problem," said Junior.

"The title of the course is Anasazi Pottery Methods," I said. "The Anasazi didn't buy clay. They dug it up."

"It's called authenticity, Junior," said Helga. "You should try it sometime instead of constantly copying the merchandise in Bed Bath and Beyond."

Junior was steaming. "I move that Professor Ólafsdóttir be censored," he yelled.

"I think the word you're looking for is *censured*," she replied coolly.

"How would you know? English isn't even your native language."

To which she replied, "*Já, ég lærði í raun það. Of slæmt gerðirðu það ekki.*"

Now, that's a conversation stopper.

After the meeting eventually ended—you should thank me for not telling you about the convoluted steps it took to make, second, discuss and pass a motion to adjourn—I asked Helga what she had said in Icelandic to Prather when he yelled that English wasn't her native language.

"I said he was correct. Unlike him, I actually had to learn it."

By the time I walked from the university to Sharice's condo on Silver Street, I had managed to convince myself that the lab-fee issue would be satisfactorily resolved.

Prather's motion to force the students to pay the fee had ended in a tie vote.

Shorter had declined to exercise his tie-breaking authority, opting instead to see if the bursar would agree to count the expense against the next semester if we told him the clay would not be used until then.

Prather's motion to censure Helga Ólafsdóttir had died for lack of a second. Not even his pal Armstrong would go that far. In a room full of people with loaded guns, no one wants to fire the first shot.

I now understood Helga's question about whether I liked circuses.

15

I am *not* going on another field trip," Aleesha announced at the beginning of the next class.

"It's not a field trip," I said. "We're not even leaving the campus. All we're going to do is walk around and collect dry twigs."

"No way. The class schedule says we meet in this room. I'm not leaving this room, and you can't penalize me for staying here."

Marlon asked, "What's wrong with you, girl?"

She shot back, "Ain't nothing wrong with me. And if there were, it wouldn't be any of your business."

He shrugged.

"Anyone who doesn't want to go can wait here in the studio," I said. "No penalty. But it's a beautiful fall day and we need twigs to make pots, so let's head out."

I donned my Tilley hat for protection from the desert sun, and ten people followed me out of the building.

No, Aleesha did not change her mind. There were ten people following me because Carly had brought her son, Luke. The teachers at his school were having an in-service day. I don't understand how teachers can be in-service only when they are not serving students, but I was glad to have Luke join us.

There are more than five thousand trees on the UNM campus,

all of which had to be planted by the groundskeepers. The campus is, after all, located on what was originally a high desert plain.

The earliest trees, a grove of ponderosa pines, were planted when the first building was constructed in 1892 and are still providing shade, scent, habitat and beauty just to the west of that building, now called Hodgin Hall.

When I attended classes in Hodgin back in the '80s, it was scheduled for demolition. They wanted to tear it down to make room for a loop road around the campus. Given what he said about loop roads, Abbey must have been proud of his alma mater when that plan was abandoned because of protests.

We didn't go to that pine grove, because pine twigs have too much resin. We needed hardwood twigs, preferably from native species since we were trying to replicate the method of the Anasazi.

I had consulted one of the UNM arborists, who told me they use a software program called TreeKeeper, which employs aerial photography software to locate and identify the trees on campus.

I guess walking around and looking at them would be too old-fashioned. But that's what the students and I did.

My students know everything about popular culture and digital gadgets but nothing about the natural world around them. They all claim to be avid environmentalists, but they couldn't identify a single tree. I took *Desert Solitaire* out of my pocket and told them about it.

"You should read this. Learn about the natural world around you. I'm going to give you a guided tour as we search for twigs," I said.

Most of the tress I pointed out were not native species, a fact the students could have deduced from names such as the Kentucky coffeetree, the European linden and the Siberian elm.

It was at this point that Bruce said, "No offense, Mr. Schuze, but could we find some trees we can actually use?"

After searching for another fifteen minutes, I came to the conclusion that there are no native trees on campus.

We passed by Hodgin Hall on the way back to the art department, and I took the opportunity to drop in. Hodgin no longer has classrooms. It houses the Alumni Office. I had my paycheck for the course and handed it to one the staffers, Elaine Chew, who had convinced me that my wages from the course were so small that they weren't worth keeping.

Why do you think universities have alumni-relations offices? It isn't just to keep track of their graduates. It's to raise money.

Her office was like an oven. "The old air conditioners don't work well," she explained.

"It's a beautiful day outside. Why not just open the windows?"

She pinched her nose. "The smell from the Dumpster is worse than the heat."

I looked out the window and smiled at the offending metal container. Cottonwoods had sprung up behind it.

I imagined the TreeKeeper software didn't know about the cottonwoods, called *alamos* in Spanish. They were obviously not part of the landscaping plan. They had probably escaped being chopped down merely because no one goes back there.

I looked inside the Dumpster and saw fast-food containers and some long things that were either cottonwood twigs or petrified French fries. Also some decomposing burgers. No wonder the thing stank. There were also greasy paper bags, plastic forks, straws, broken bottles and a shoe.

I told the students to fill their sacks with cottonwood twigs.

As we walked back to the Art Building, I thought about Faye Po, who buys pottery from me and quotes Chinese proverbs, one of which is, "The best time to plant a tree is twenty years ago. The second best time is now."

I wondered if she might know Ms. Chew in the Alumni Office. Then I realized Sharice would probably accuse me of pigeonholing them simply because they are both of Chinese ancestry.

When we got back to the studio, I told the students I was going to give them my third lecture.

"Fourth," said Alfred.

"No. The first one was about clay. The second was about firing. This is the third one."

He was smiling as I spoke. "The third one was about trees."

I laughed. "I stand corrected. This is the fourth lecture. It's about shaping pots. The Anasazi didn't have wheels. They made their pots from sheets of clay, not hunks of clay like we do today on wheels. In order to form sheets into a pot shape, you need an armature—a framework to hold the clay. They made their armatures from twigs."

"How do you know that?" asked Raúl.

"Obviously, we have no written record, but we do have evidence. The only materials they had access to were wood, stone and animal parts. You could find a rock with a nice shape or even sculpt one into the shape you want, but removing the rock after the pot was dried would be next to impossible. You could use hide or bones, but no pot has ever been found with internal indentations compatible with such materials. What we *have* found are pots with internal charring. They removed the armature by burning it."

"Maybe the internal charring was from burning something in the pot," said Raúl.

"And maybe they used Popsicle sticks," I said, and they laughed. "Burning things in the pot could explain the charring, but it still wouldn't explain how the armature was built. There's another reason to favor twigs. They are flexible enough to be woven into shapes and strong enough to hold sheets of clay while we work with them."

I handed them copies of a paper on which I had drawn some common Anasazi pot shapes. "Choose a shape you like and weave a frame."

I dumped one of the bags of twigs on the table, selected a handful and wove them into a gourd shape. "See? Nothing to it."

In fifteen minutes, everyone except Mia had woven a decent armature. Aleesha had chosen the duck shape and done a good job on the most difficult style.

"Now comes the hard part," I told them. "Roll out sheets of

clay and spread them on the armature. Keep your hands wet as you work. It's sort of like making a pie crust."

"You bake, Mr. Schuze?" asked Marlon.

I shook my head.

"I do," said Carly. She started first and everyone watched. She got the hang of it almost immediately.

Most of the others started while Carly was still working. Only Mia watched until Carly was finished.

Mia returned to her station and made a halfhearted attempt at rolling clay into a sheet. When she draped it over the armature, it didn't reach from top to bottom. When I told her she needed to start with a bigger ball of clay, she said she would just add a seam there.

"The seams should be vertical, not horizontal."

"You didn't tell us that."

That was obvious to all the other students, but I didn't tell her that. She needed encouragement, not criticism. "Sorry," I said. "Give it another try."

She removed the sheet, tossed it aside and started with a new ball of clay—also too small.

"You might want to just add some clay to the first ball you used. You know it was a bit short, so that can guide you as to how much to add."

She shrugged and bumbled forward with too little clay.

The next few class meetings were spent forming armatures and sheathing them with clay. The first day we tried it, I made the rounds of the workstations, giving pointers and doing a bit of hands-on work with a few of them who needed it. As the days went by, I gave less instruction and noticed the students who picked it up quickly were helping their classmates. It wasn't long until almost everyone was producing unfired pots that were C or better, including one by Luke, whom I had invited to join in. Some of the pots were A work.

Only Mia was failing. And she seemed unenthusiastic. When I announced that we had reached the last session of shaping pots and would begin the next time to fire some, she asked if she could see me after class.

We walked to my office. She closed the door. It was awkward because there wasn't enough room for two people and the chair. I sat on the desk to avoid invading her space.

"I don't think I can do this," she said.

"Sure you can. You're an art student. You know how to work with your hands."

She shook her head. "Actually, I'm majoring in interior design. We use software in all our classes. Point and click. Know what I mean?" She held her hand in the air and moved her index finger up and down to illustrate.

I guess my ignorance of computing somehow showed on my face.

"They make all interior-design students take three studio art courses, one in drawing, one in painting and one in 3-D, like ceramics or sculpting. I flunked the drawing class last semester. I'm going to have to take it over. Trying to do something 3-D is even harder than drawing, where at least we had a surface to work on. I think maybe I'm dyslexic."

"How can you use a computer if you're dyslexic?"

She smiled. "Point and click."

I nodded.

"So I need to do something for extra credit or I'm going to fail this class just like I failed drawing."

"It's a studio class in pot making, Mia. I'd like to help, but I can't very well have you do a book report or something like that in a studio."

"I wasn't thinking about a book report. And anyway, I don't read too good. I was thinking maybe something else."

She took a small step toward me. Given the size of my office, even a small step put her too close.

"Like what?" I asked.

"Anything you want." She casually placed her hand on my knee. "I can't afford to fail this class. I'll do *anything*."

I swallowed. "*Anything?*"

She nodded slowly. "Anything."

I thought about it briefly.

"What's your schedule tomorrow?"

"I have classes in the morning, but I'm free after that."

"Okay. Meet me in the pottery studio at one tomorrow."

She brightened. There was no room to move, so I couldn't dodge her kiss on my cheek.

"See you tomorrow," she said, and danced away.

You may recall me saying that the new-faculty orientation sensitized me to sexual harassment, so I was alert when it happened. I did not, however, expect to be the victim. I believe the term is *unwanted sexual advance*.

I hoped I was wrong. But in case I wasn't, I stopped by Tristan's apartment on the way home. He's not actually my nephew. He's the grandson of my aunt Beatrice, my mother's eccentric sister who lives in Tucumcari.

How eccentric? Well, for starters, she named her daughter Beatrice and called her Junior. I suspect eccentricity is not inherited, so the fact that Beatrice Jr. is eccentric no doubt stems from her upbringing.

Beatrice Jr. plays the mandolin, which may explain why she eloped with a touring guitarist. Given that one of his stops was in Tucumcari, you probably realize it wasn't Les Paul or Jimmy Hendrix. All I remember about him was that he drove a rusty Chevy pickup and went by the name Rhino.

Most members of the family gave the relationship three months tops.

Rhino brought Junior back to Tucumcari eight months after they left, one month before she gave birth to Tristan on December 17, 1992. Rhino was so happy after he held Tristan in his arms at the hospital that he stopped in a local bar and bought rounds for the house. And several for himself. Then he ran head-on into a big tree (hard to do in Tucumcari) and died.

Shortly thereafter, Junior decided that her true soul mate was the actor Dana Andrews, who died on the same day as Rhino.

This epiphany came to her when she saw *Strange Lady in Town*, a film about a woman doctor from Boston who comes to New Mexico in 1880 to introduce modern medicine. The local doc, played by Andrews, doesn't think women can be doctors and makes fun of her newfangled device, the stethoscope. But she eventually wins him over, and he even teaches her to ride a horse, telling her as she struggles to "sit up straight and try not to look like a sack of potatoes."

It was this line that brought Beatrice out of her combination of mourning and postpartum depression and made her fall in love with Dana Andrews.

Tristan was probably seven years old before he finally came to understand that Dana Andrews, whose movie posters papered the walls of his home, was not his father.

Despite this unorthodox upbringing, he is a remarkably stable young man.

I found him in his kitchen with the guts of a computer strewn across the table. I knew it was a computer because it had a keyboard.

Sort of.

Diodes, LEDs, resistors, capacitors, circuit boards, chips.

I have no idea what any of those things are, but I've heard him use the words, and I imagine most of the things on the table were also on that list.

"Reverse-engineering an old PET," he answered to my unspoken question.

"I've heard of pet rocks, but I never knew people thought of computers as pets. Is that one you had as a toddler?"

He gave the polite chuckle he humors me with. "PET stands for personal electronic transactor. It was made by a company called Commodore and was the first personal computer. Probably about when you were a student at UNM."

"Why would you want to reverse-engineer a computer that old?"

"I found some old game programs that ran on the PET's eight-bit system. I'd like to see them in action." He looked up at me. "Sort of like the way you enjoy outdated music."

"Frank Sinatra and Count Basie are not outdated. They are classic."

"So is this thing. But I can't use that Chiclets keyboard, so I'm creating an interface for . . . but you didn't come here to talk about computers."

"No. I came for some advice about sexual harassment."

Before I left, he gave me a gadget and showed me how to use it.

I asked if he needed money. He said he was okay, so I gave him fifty dollars.

16

The window in the studio door was covered the next afternoon, so I didn't know if Mia had shown up until I stepped inside and saw her standing there in shorts and a halter top that was not doing much to halt anything.

"I took some of the sketching paper and covered the window so no one can see us," she said. "It wouldn't bother me. I might even get turned on if I knew someone was watching us, but you're sort of a fuddy-duddy, so I figured you'd want the window covered."

Any doubt I had about what she had in mind for extra credit vanished.

"You might be surprised by what I want," I said.

"Something kinky?" she asked.

"Something you've probably never done before," I said.

"Oooh. What is it?"

"You said you would do anything, right?"

"Anything," she said slowly, grinning.

"Okay. Here's what I want you to do." I handed her a tub of clay and an armature for a simple *olla*. "I want you to roll this clay into sheets and spread it over this armature. If it doesn't come out right, I want you to wet the clay and try again. I want you to stay at it all afternoon, over and over, until you get it right."

Her lower lip was quivering.

"I know you can do this," I said, and walked to the door. "Good idea covering the window. That way you won't be distracted by anyone."

I'd told Sharice about it, of course. But reporting it to anyone at the university seemed petty. Why get the girl in trouble? I was saddened by Mia's offer of a sexual favor in return for a passing grade, but I wasn't harmed by it.

So far. But I had a hunch I could be. That's why I had sought Tristan's help. Which turned out to be one of the few good decisions I made during what turned into a hectic semester.

17

Another midlevel bureaucrat was waiting outside my closet/office before class the next afternoon to inform me that a student had filed a complaint charging me with sexual harassment.

Unlike the EEO complaint filed by Aleesha, I accepted my copy and signed for it. As I feared, the complaint had been lodged by Mia.

I was standing there wondering what else could go wrong when I saw six of my students coming toward me. The four missing ones were Alfred, Aleesha, Mia and Ximena.

"Am I late for class?" I asked.

Carly said, "We're not having class, remember? This is the day we're going to the gallery to see the body-cast thing."

I perked up. "Right. Okay, lead the way."

They were so enthusiastic. It felt good following them down the hall. Seeing such an unusual art event would take my mind off complaints about equal education opportunity, sexual harassment, unauthorized field trips and the deficit in the ceramics budget.

As you already know, things did not get better.

The crowd in the gallery was large. We stood in a circle around the model as we watched the artist remove the plaster cast in two large halves like a clamshell. I use the word *artist* only because that's how Junior Prather was billed on the printed program they handed out.

I knew one of his classes was canceled because no one signed up for it. I knew he thought we should force students to buy supplies they didn't need. I knew he had a strange definition of not talking to me. But artists are frequently strange.

Everyone knows Van Gogh cut off his ear. But that act of self-mutilation pales in comparison to the Russian artist Petr Pavlensky, who nailed his scrotum to the cobblestones in Moscow's Red Square.

Sorry, guys. I know the sickening queasiness just hearing that causes in the pit of your stomach. But Petr said it was art.

Another artist, Tehching Hsieh, punched a time clock every hour on the hour for an entire year. I guess the idea was to illustrate ennui.

Jana Sterbak creates sculptures made of meat.

Francis Alÿs enlisted the help of five hundred volunteers with shovels to move a sand dune ten centimeters to the left. In response to people who asked the obvious question—why?—he said, "Sometimes making something leads to nothing, sometimes making nothing leads to something."

Who can argue with that?

In comparison to these nutty activities, covering a person in alginate, gauze and plaster seems as normal as painting a bowl of fruit.

I chose to stand behind the model to avoid seeing frontal nudity in the company of my students. So call me old-fashioned.

I had a good hunch why Aleesha and Mia were not in the group of students who walked me to the gallery.

When we arrived at the gallery, I discovered why Alfred was not with my other students. He was assisting Junior Prather.

After the cast was removed and the model fell backward with a thump, I could see her face. And that was when I realized why Ximena was the fourth student missing from the class.

It was also when I realized calling 911 was pointless. Ximena's failure to move was not from her remaining in the same position for hours. It was from rigor mortis.

I remember screams, gasps, shouted orders, running, crying.

I don't remember sitting down, but I must have done so because I was on the floor with my back against a wall. Or maybe I fell down and then righted myself against the wall. Carly was holding my hand and crying. Alfred was dabbing his eyes with a handkerchief. Nathan looked catatonic. Bruce and Marlon were standing guard over Ximena's body, which had been covered with a canvas from the supply room. Apache was whispering to a student I didn't know. Raúl was staring at the ceiling. I looked up there and saw a security camera. I wondered what the tape would reveal.

Then I wondered if it was a tape. Probably not.

I closed my eyes and thought about Sharice. Because of her, I'm reluctantly weaning myself from red meat. I'm haltingly learning French. I'm trying to enjoy opera. The title of an aria from Smetana's *The Bartered Bride* came to mind—"How dark the day that dawned so bright."

18

The police officers took down the names of everyone in the gallery. They herded us into a classroom and told us we were not to talk among ourselves about what we had seen. We could leave the room only to use the restroom and only one at a time.

It was over two hours before a policeman called my name and led me to a room, where one of the detectives was questioning the witnesses.

The detective was Whit Fletcher. He should have been more surprised to see me than I was to see him. After all, he's a homicide detective. There are only nine of them in the Albuquerque Police Department, so my chances of drawing him were better than 1 in 10.

But there are half a million people in the city, so the chance of him drawing me was a lot slimmer.

He wasn't as surprised as the odds would dictate. "I mighta known you'd be here. What is it about you and dead bodies?"

I shrugged. "Bad luck."

"Nobody has that much bad luck."

"Oh yeah? A park ranger named Roy Sullivan was hit by lightning seven times. And he was attacked by a bear twenty-three times. One of the bear attacks happened right after he was hit by lightning."

"Where do you get this stuff?"

"I read a lot."

Whit and I have known each other for almost as long as I've been in the pottery trade. He doesn't care about my digging up pots.

"So why were you here?" he asked.

"I'm teaching a class this semester."

He gave me a crooked smile. "Teaching them how to steal pots?"

"Teaching them how to *make* them."

"They must be hard up for teachers. Weren't you kicked outta this place?"

"That was a long time ago."

"So you brought your class to see how to cover a naked girl with clay?"

"It was plaster of Paris, not clay."

"Same difference. So you and your students were just spectators?"

My mind flashed back to the image of Ximena on the gallery floor. I took a deep breath. "My class had ten students. Six of them were spectators. Two were absent. One was helping the artist. The other one is the dead girl."

"I'm sorry, Hubert. You know her well?"

I shook my head. "I don't know any of them well. She was the one I probably knew least well." I thought about her. "She seemed shy and sensitive." Then I thought about Whit being a homicide detective. "You think she was murdered?"

"Don't know. The FDMI said he couldn't tell by looking, but the OMI will figure it out."

"FDMI?"

"Field deputy medical investigator. Every county in the state has at least one. They investigate any death that's sudden, violent, untimely, unexpected, or where there's no known cause of death. After the FDMI finishes his work, the body is transported to the OMI—Office of the Medical Investigator—right here at the med school, where they determine the cause and manner of death." He was silent for a moment. "One of the other homicides you were involved with was a guy who died of a poison you were using to paint your pots."

"I wasn't *involved* with that homicide. I just happened to be making plates for the restaurant where the dead guy worked."

"The body was found in your vehicle."

"I didn't put it there."

"Just more of that bad luck?"

"Exactly. And I don't *paint* pots. I glaze them."

"Kinda like that homicide at the restaurant glazed you without involving you."

I resisted the temptation to comment.

"You know anything about the plaster they covered that girl with?"

"Looked like ordinary plaster."

"Could there have been chemicals in it?"

"Anything is possible."

19

"A dentist's worst nightmare is having a patient die in the chair."

"That actually happens?" I asked. Now I had yet another thing to obsess about.

"Infrequently," Sharice answered. "Only about one in every half million people who have general anesthesia in a dentist's office die from it. But the odds of one of your students dying must be even higher."

I had come home late because of the investigation. After telling Sharice about Ximena's death, she was consoling me.

I shook my head slowly. "I still can't believe it."

She held my hand a bit tighter. "Ximena's death hit you hard."

"It did. My parents always kissed and said goodbye even if it was just my dad going to teach or my mom going to her bridge game. They said it was in case anything happened. Eventually, it did."

"But at least he got to say goodbye."

"Yes."

The desert air was dry, but my eyes were keeping themselves moisturized. A bit of the excess lubricant trickled down my cheek.

"It's a silly comparison, of course. I hardly knew Ximena. But that somehow makes it worse. I should have talked to her. Maybe gently pressed her to tell me about herself. Shouldn't a teacher make an effort to know his students?"

"They're not children, Hubie. They're college students. They ask questions if they're unsure or confused. Since she never asked you anything, that means she was comfortable in your class. You should feel happy about that."

"I remember her hugging Carly when I unthinkingly asked about her husband. I remember her hugging Martin when he gave her that shard. She smiled at everyone. Even when I told her she was in the wrong restroom, she smiled."

"What happens next?"

"I don't know. I'm dreading the next class. We should have some sort of . . ."

"Memorial?"

"Yeah. But I don't know what to say."

"Maybe you should just ask any of the students who feel so inclined to say something about Ximena."

"That sounds right."

20

I saw him in an old movie where he played Sam Spade." I said. "The original movie with Bogart was classic noir, but the remake with George Segal was a comedy. I knew he played the banjo, but I didn't know he's also an artist."

"He isn't," Susannah said. "The artist is a different guy with the same name."

She had just told me that George Segal was the first artist to wrap people with gauze and plaster. It was the day after Ximena's death. I was willing to lay part of the blame on the idiot who first came up with the idea of wrapping people in plaster.

I sipped my margarita and said, "I guess it didn't occur to him that there might be a reason why no artists had done that in the fifty thousand years since the first cave paintings."

"That just shows his genius," she said. "Rodin was almost run out of Paris because his statues were so lifelike that people thought he was doing what is called 'casting from life.'"

"Which is what Prather was doing, right?"

"Exactly. But the tradition is for artists to create statues by carving. They might ultimately use casting if the statue was to be in bronze, because you can't carve bronze. But they had to be great artists to carve a likeness of someone in wax."

"Why wax?"

"Because it melts. After they finish the figure, they encase it with plaster. After the plaster is dry, they pour in molten metal. The wax melts and runs out the bottom, replaced by the metal. Then you remove the plaster and *walla*."

"That's pronounced *vwä-'lä*."

"Learning French is making you stuffy."

"Sorry. So Segal wasn't a good carver and resorted to cheating by just making molds from real life?"

"They weren't technically molds because he never filled them with anything."

"His art was just the gauze and plaster?"

"Yes, but he manipulated it. He would smooth it out, add more plaster afterward, paint it, things like that."

"And he became rich and famous for this?"

"He did. He was given a Lifetime Achievement in Contemporary Sculpture Award by the International Sculpture Center. We saw a documentary film about him in my class on controversial art."

"So casting from life is still controversial?"

She shook her head. "What was controversial was a casting he did of two lesbians on a bench."

"Were they doing something lewd?"

"No. One has her hand resting lightly on the top of the other's thigh, but the pose could just as easily be two heterosexual friends. You only realize they're lesbians when you see the other statue nearby with two guys holding hands. Or if you read the plaque that identifies the work as the Gay Liberation Monument."

"So Segal was gay?"

"No. He was married to Helen Segal for over fifty years. She was frequently his model."

"I can understand a wife being willing to have her husband cover her in plaster—"

"Or whipped cream," she said, and laughed.

"Exactly. I mean, they're a couple. So anything goes. But why would Ximena let Prather do that to her?"

"Maybe they were a couple."

"That's a disgusting thought. He's a wrinkly old guy with a scraggly beard, and she was a shy young woman."

"There are lots of couples you would never expect to be together."

"Like Sharice and me?"

"By today's standards, you two are normal." She drank some of her saltless margarita. "I just remembered something Segal said in an interview—'My first models had to be people who were convinced I wouldn't kill them.' He said most models didn't mind having plaster on their bodies. But having it on their head freaked them out. Of course he also noted that he never covered their nostrils."

"Prather put straws into Ximena's nostrils so she could breathe, but he could have come back after the plaster hardened and plugged them up."

"Did he stay in there the whole time just watching the plaster dry? Because if he didn't, anyone could have come in and closed off her air supply."

"I don't know if Prather stayed while the plaster hardened. Fletcher wondered if there might be poison in the plaster itself."

"Yes!" She bolted upright and assumed her Girl Detective face. "There's a classic murder mystery in which the blind victim is killed by poison on her Braille cards. You want to guess the title?"

"*She Never Saw It Coming?*"

"No."

"*She Never Felt It Coming?*"

"No."

"*The Fingertips of Death?*"

"Are you trying to guess or just joking around?"

"Well, you didn't give me much to go on. How about a hint?"

"You were warm with the word *felt*."

"Hmm. Felt . . . touch?"

"Getting warmer."

"*The Touch of Death?*"

"Even closer."

"*Fatal Touch?*"

"You missed by just one word. It was titled *The Fatal Touch*."

"Not bad, considering I don't read murder mysteries."

"You couldn't have read this one. It doesn't exist as a real book."

"It's one of those ebooks?"

"Nope."

"A book on tape?"

"No."

"But you said it's a classic."

"It is. It's the title of a book written by a character in a mystery about three aging murder-mystery writers who become murderers for hire using the classic techniques they wrote about before their books stopped selling because they were too intellectual and puzzle-oriented and everyone had started reading thrillers that don't use poison because the deaths in thrillers have to be gory and noisy."

When Susannah gets excited, she often packs too many words into one sentence. Strangely, they still make sense once you parse them.

"Ximena wasn't blind," I noted, "so the Braille-card method wouldn't have worked on her."

Susannah's eyes narrowed. "Her eyes may have worked, but maybe her voice didn't. You did say she never spoke."

I thought she might be on to something. "You think she may have been dumb?"

"Hubie! That's a terrible thing to say."

"No, it's not. It's only terrible when you use it to describe someone who's stupid. It's okay to use it when describing someone who can't speak because that's actually what *dumb* means."

"It may have meant that at one time, but now it's politically incorrect."

"So what do we now call someone who is unable to speak?"

"Speechless."

"You have got to be kidding. *Speechless* means temporarily unable to speak because you're overcome with emotion. It's not a permanent condition."

"Yeah, but it sounds better."

"It sounds better to call liver 'chocolate ice cream,' but it still tastes awful."

"Just don't use the word *dumb*, okay? People will think you're insensitive."

"I'm a very sensitive guy. Anyone who doesn't think so is dumb."

"Can we get back to Ximena? Maybe the reason she didn't yell out for help was because she wasn't able to."

"More likely it was because her mouth was covered with plaster."

"Couldn't she break the plaster just by opening her mouth? The jaw muscles are pretty strong."

"Remember, she was also wrapped in gauze. If a continuous loop went from under her chin to over her head, that could make opening her mouth difficult. And even without the gauze, it would be hard for her to open her mouth. Jaw muscles are strong when they close because they evolved that way back when we had to crunch bones in the animals we ate when we lived in caves. But jaw muscles aren't strong when they open because there is normally no resistance to that motion."

She tested my claim by first biting on her finger to feel how strong the jaw muscles are when closing and then by opening her mouth while at the same time trying to hold it closed with her thumb under her chin and her fingers pressed across her upper lip to show how little force it takes to keep your jaw shut.

I pretended I didn't know her.

"I think you're right," she said after her experiment was complete. "We need to get a list of everyone who was in the gallery after the plaster was applied and a log of when they came and left."

"We?"

"Well, you probably. As a member of the art faculty, it's easier for you to get that info."

"As a member of the police department, it's even easier for Whit to get it."

"Yeah, but will he share it with you?"

"Why would he?"

"Because without it, we can't find out who murdered Ximena."

"We don't know she was murdered. And if she was, it's Whit's job to figure out who did it."

"But she was your student."

"Yes. And I'm saddened by her death. But it's not my job to find out how it happened."

"Fletcher may need your help."

"If he thinks I know something that might help his investigation, I'm sure he'll ask me. And I will cooperate like any good citizen. But I am not going to try to solve a murder."

She ignored my refusal to play detective and said, "I know there's a security camera in the gallery. If he lets you look at the comings and goings, you may know some of the people."

"If he wants me to look at it, I will, although I see no reason why he would ask."

She looked disappointed.

21

I was happy to get back to the condo, where I hoped to get Ximena's death off the front burner of my overheated mind.

It was not to be.

When I asked Sharice what she had in mind for dinner, she said, "Let's see if you can guess when the scent begins to fill the room."

Shortly after she went to the kitchen, the doorbell rang. I opened the door and saw Charles Webbe.

And very little else. At six-three and two twenty-five, he pretty much fills a doorframe.

He had on his usual dark-blue suit, white shirt and conservative striped tie. The suit was so well tailored that the pistol tucked against his left rib cage was easy to miss.

Several years ago, he ran at me with that pistol drawn. I thought he was going to kill me. In fact, he was trying to prevent my being killed. Obviously, that was prior to my learning that he was an FBI agent. He was working undercover and sporting dreads. When that assignment ended, the dreads gave way to a shaved head and a dark-blue suit.

He is impressive in that suit, his body as hard as coal and just as black.

"The English gentleman at your shop told me you now live at this address. Got a minute to talk?"

I invited him in and we sat on the two Barcelona chairs.

"I was surprised to hear you'd moved," he said. "You had an affinity for Old Town."

"Still do."

"You don't strike me as a condo guy."

Before I could reply, Sharice came out of the kitchen.

Charles stood up. "Good evening, Miss Clarke."

"Please call me Sharice."

"Yes, ma'am," he replied, then looked at me. "Sorry, I didn't realize you had company."

"I don't."

He was momentarily confused.

Sharice said, "It's my condo, Agent Webbe. Hubie lives here now."

He was silent for a moment. Then shook his head. "There goes the neighborhood."

When we stopped laughing, he said, "I can't call you Sharice if you call me Agent Webbe. So it's Charles, okay?"

"Deal. I just opened a bottle of Gruet. Would you like a glass?"

"Why not? I'm not officially on duty."

She asked me if I also wanted a glass. I told her I'd already had a margarita.

"Just one?"

I nodded.

"Good boy. You can have a small glass of Gruet."

She served piñon brittle with the Gruet.

I bit into the brittle and asked if it was approved by the American Dental Association.

"Only if you're living with a dental hygienist who can make sure you clean your teeth properly."

"In that case, I'll have a second piece. So, Charles, are you here as an agent or a friend?"

"Both. I want to talk to you as a friend, but the topic is a case I'm interested in. Well, it's not a case yet, but I think it will be—the death of Ximena Sifuentes. Whit Fletcher told me you were there when they removed the plaster and discovered she was dead."

Sharice asked if she should leave the room while we talked.

"I'd actually prefer that you stay," he said. "Seeing as you two are a couple, you can be helpful recapping our discussion after I leave. Sort of a second pair of ears."

Sharice put her hand on my arm.

I asked Charles why the FBI might be interested in Ximena's death.

"We're responsible for investigating hate crimes."

"Her death was a hate crime?"

He shook his head. "We don't know. We're not even sure it was a crime. The medical examiner's finding was that she died from asphyxiation, but he hasn't determined if it was accidental."

"How could it be accidental?"

"I know someone put straws in her nose so she could breathe. I don't know anything about art, especially weird things like making a mold of someone's body. Maybe the person who put the straws in had a lot of soft plaster on his hands and some of it accidentally got stuck in the straws. Or maybe after they left her, bits of torn gauze were floating in the air. She aspirated some of it, and it clogged her nasal passages. I'm not a forensic scientist, just a flatfooted cop. I'll wait for the lab guys to tell me what happened."

"But you wouldn't already be looking into it if you thought it was an accident."

He nodded. "Those two scenarios I tossed out seem unlikely. I just suggested them because I'm supposed to keep an open mind."

Sharice tightened her grip on my arm and said to Charles, "You think she was murdered, don't you?"

"I do."

"Why would it be a hate crime?"

"Any crime can qualify as a hate crime if it's motivated by prejudice."

"You think she may have been killed because she was Hispanic?"

"I doubt it. Although the prejudice in most hate crimes is usually racial or sexual, I suspect the prejudice in this case was against her disability."

"Which is?" I asked.

"She was deaf."

"Oh my gosh," I said. "Susannah suggested that, but I sort of dismissed it."

"She was in your class," Charles said. "How could you not know she was deaf?"

"It's a studio class. I assign activities. They don't have to make presentations or do book reports. Whenever I gave her instructions, she followed them perfectly. So I assumed she heard me."

"No. She read lips."

The restroom encounter now made sense to me. When I told Ximena she was in the wrong restroom, she shook her head to disagree. She knew what I said. But she didn't respond to my second comment because she was walking toward the stall and couldn't see my lips.

"I know a bit about prejudice," said Sharice, "and I imagine you do too, Charles. But who would be prejudiced against someone just because she couldn't hear?"

"You probably know the federal mint has a program to have a quarter dedicated to each state. When they selected Helen Keller to be the image on the Alabama quarter, someone in Alabama blogged that no one had asked him if he wanted a 'deaf, dumb, blind and ugly woman' on the state quarter."

"That's also awful, but it seems more like hate speech than hate crime. It's not like the blogger attacked someone."

"A few years ago a deaf guy using the Library of Congress was stabbed from behind. When the police screened the security video, they saw the assailant was mocking sign language behind the deaf guy's back immediately before stabbing him. The assailant had never met the deaf guy. He just attacked him because he was deaf."

"That makes no sense."

"Hate crimes never make sense. They arise from a twisted, irrational mind."

He asked me to write down everything I could remember about Ximena. Who she interacted with in the class. Anything she carried with her. What she wore. Anything, no matter how seemingly insignificant.

After Charles left, Sharice asked, "Have you figured out what's in the oven?"

"I smell potatoes, anchovies and nutmeg, but I can't think of any dish that has those three ingredients."

"Wow, your nose is good. It's a dish from northern Quebec called *Les expulser de la maison.*"

"Expel them from the house?"

"I would say your study of French is going well, but that one is all cognates and too easy. Colloquially, it's more like 'kick 'em out of the house.' It stays light in northern Quebec in the summer past midnight, and guests sometimes don't know when to leave. This dish is served as a signal that after you eat it, you should go home."

The anchovies were chopped and spread over thin slices of potatoes. Cream was added to about half the depth of the potatoes and grated Parmesan and nutmeg sprinkled lightly before baking. Sort of scalloped potatoes with attitude. The dressed watercress on the side lent color and a false sense of eating healthy.

The cold Gruet paired perfectly with the hot, starchy russets.

"So I'm supposed to go home now?"

"You are home, Hubie. I'm going to take a shower. Want to join me?"

"You know what happens when I see you naked."

She gave me a lascivious smile. "I was sort of counting on that."

The girl knows how to get my mind off negative things.

I sprang from the table and began unbuttoning my shirt while opening the door to the terrace. When Geronimo hesitated, Benz swatted him gently on the nose and herded him onto the terrace. Benz likes watching the pedestrians below while Sharice and I are otherwise engaged. He also knows we want Geronimo out there as well.

Fast-forward. If it had been an old movie, I'd have lit a cigarette and passed it to Sharice. It should have been a perfect moment. A sexy woman under the covers. Something by Puccini playing on Sharice's computer.

But my bliss had turned to panic as I held her in a postcoital embrace.

I'd felt a very small lump in her breast.

Every thread of my emotional fabric urged delay. Think about when and how to break it to her.

My conscience was unmoved. The *when* is now, it said. And the *how* is straightforwardly.

I returned my hand to the locale in question and tried to ban any tone of concern from my voice.

"I think I felt a small lump here."

She was on her back. I felt her muscles tighten and still as she stopped breathing.

She slowly exhaled.

She slid her hand under mine. I moved it around and pressed gently upon it.

When she remained silent, I said, "Maybe I was mistaken."

"No. I feel it."

"It's very small."

"Yes. But it's there."

Neither of us spoke for several minutes.

She finally turned on her side and cuddled against my chest. I felt her warm breath and the rise and fall of her breathing.

"You're going to stay with me, right?"

"*Toujours.*"

She giggled. "I never should have suggested you learn French."

"I said it wrong?"

"No, you said it right. Even your accent is getting better. It just seems silly hearing French from you. It should be Spanish."

My relief that she could giggle and then joke about my French was short-lived.

She started sobbing.

I held her close and waited. It must have been a full five minutes.

She pushed her head up and looked at me. "I'm not going through that again."

I swallowed hard. "Don't get ahead of yourself. It's tiny. Probably nothing to worry about."

She nodded.

But I knew what she was thinking.

22

As she does every morning, Sharice roasted green coffee beans when she awoke. She ground them up and brewed them in her compact espresso machine.

The roasting part was my alarm clock. I arrived at the table in time to see her stream heated milk and espresso into two mugs I'd made. The black one has my name written in white letters in my handwriting. The white one has Sharice's name in her handwriting.

I never thought I'd stoop to making mugs, but romance has a way of undermining previous attitudes. She liked writing on the unfired clay and then seeing the results after I fired the mugs in my kiln.

"You want breakfast?" she asked.

"How would you like a picnic brunch instead?" I countered. I figured a picnic might lessen her apprehension.

We walked to Old Town, where I gathered supplies and put them in the back of the Bronco. We crossed the Rio Grande on the Alameda Bridge into the suburban wasteland on the west side of the river, passing a Sam's Club, then the big Intel plant before veering westward on Southern Boulevard until we passed the last of the homes.

Beyond the homes, a grid of roads has already been graded out for the next building boom.

I recalled Abbey writing, "Growth for the sake of growth is the ideology of the cancer cell."

When scientific studies in the early '90s showed that Albuquerque's aquifer was not being replenished as fast as it was being pumped, no one suggested limiting growth. Instead, Albuquerque turned to the Bureau of Reclamation.

A misnomer. The Bureau of Reclamation doesn't reclaim things. It destroys them. In this case, the San Juan River that flows through northwestern New Mexico. The San Juan passes less than a mile from Four Corners and used to feed clear, cool water into the Colorado River. Their confluence is now a waterfall because the level of the Colorado is so low. And the water falling from the San Juan is no longer cold and clear. It's warm and muddy. Like Mark Twain said about the Mississippi, it's too thin to plow and too thick to drink.

Why has the San Juan been reduced in places from a mighty river to a muddy stream? Because much of its water is now diverted into tunnels that carry it to the Rio Grande so that the desert city of Albuquerque can continue to grow beyond what its natural water supply will support.

The San Juan–Chama Project takes water out of the San Juan River and pumps it into the Chama River, which flows into the Rio Grande. An impressive engineering feat when you consider that the San Juan and the Chama are on opposite sides of the continental divide.

Who says water doesn't run uphill?

In fact, it runs toward money, something that Albuquerque and the Bureau of Reckless Reclamation have a lot more of than the small villages that depended on the San Juan for drinking water, agriculture and fly-fishing.

Albuquerque's suburbs across the Rio Grande creep like a fungus, eventually covering everything. The only thing standing in the way of farther westward expansion is the Tohajiilee Indian Reservation, a small noncontiguous section of the Navajo Nation, which is now only ten miles away. It's less than 1 percent of total Navajo land, and the sixteen hundred people who live there are less than 1 percent of the Navajo population. Let's hope some backroom deal doesn't result in the redrawing of boundaries.

I've never set foot on Tohajiilee, but I like knowing it's there. The Navajo phrase *tó hajiileehé* means "where people draw up water by means of a rope one pot after another."

No wonder the Japanese could never decode the Navajo language during WWII.

Sharice and I were looking at Tohajiilee from the west side of Mesa Prieto, which is home to hundreds of petroglyphs. Efforts are under way to protect the entire area, so I resisted the temptation to climb and get a closer look.

But even from a respectful distance, we could see images from the Archaic period, some as old as 5000 BCE.

One was a six-point star. One was a single-pole ladder. Wood is scarce in the desert, so why have a pole on both sides when one in the middle will do?

There are more images from the Ancestral Pueblo period, which runs up until the arrival of the Spaniards.

"You see the armadillo playing the flute?"

She turned her head and located it. "Amazing."

"It's one of a series of fifteen animal flute players. The animal next to the armadillo must be mythical."

"If not, then it must be extinct," she said. "I've never seen anything like it."

"Or maybe it's actually just a rabbit, but the painter took lessons from the Gnome."

She laughed. "Why are you and Susannah so down on her?"

"Susannah said Jollo is so jealous of Harte Hockley that she gives bad grades to any student who likes him."

"That's terrible."

"Yeah, but it doesn't happen often, because they're smart enough never to praise him in her presence. For my part, I don't like her because she started quizzing me about him before even introducing herself, and her behavior as parliamentarian is the academic version of the reign of terror."

"Without the beheadings, I hope."

"So far."

We spread an old blanket in the shade of a slab of igneous rock protruding like an awning between two layers of coral-colored sandstone. I fired up my propane-fueled mini-grill and placed a cast-iron skillet over the fire. When it started smoking, I poured in some corn oil and seared two trout filets. I slid those onto plates and dumped the New Mexico trinity—chopped green chiles, onions and garlic—into the still-smoking skillet. When they began so soften, I cracked in four eggs, did a five-stir scramble and dumped the results over the trout.

"Why is it that food cooked outside tastes so good?" Sharice asked after mopping her plate with a corn tortilla.

"Maybe it's an evolutionary thing—some part of our brain recalls when all eating was outside."

"And it's special to us because you never knew each morning whether you would have anything to eat that day. Especially in the desert."

"Food is plentiful in the desert. You just have to know how to find it."

"This from a guy who found our food in a picnic basket."

"I could forage if I had to."

"Uh-huh. Your last attempt at foraging ended with you in a dental chair and me helping Dr. Batres repair the tooth you chipped trying to open piñon nuts."

I reflexively slid my tongue across the tooth in question.

We lie silent on the blanket.

The air is cool, still and dry. Asters are blooming between the rocks, their yellow centers like small suns in the blue sky of their petals. The popcorn scent of chamisa wafts from a clump in a wash. In the Jemez Mountains to the north, I see patches of gold. The aspen are beginning to turn.

Sharice is sleeping.

I hear the *brt-brt* call of a scaled quail, followed by his second call, a short screech. I scan the area and find him under a juniper. He repeats the calls several times and then begins foraging. I don't think they eat juniper berries, but they do like tumbleweeds, several of which are tangled against the juniper.

A red-tailed hawk circles above. Maybe he's spotted the quail. Or maybe he's just enjoying the freedom to soar up where the air is clean and cool.

I could live here. Build a one-room adobe house. Get water from the spring at the head of the wash. Dig clay for pots. Go to town once a month to sell pottery and buy victuals. Come home to find Sharice arranging wildflowers.

The desert is clean, open and honest. No concrete and glass buildings. No bureaucratic university. No weird faculty artists.

No cancer, I think.

I say a prayer to that effect, dispatching it to the Great Spirit at the heavenly GPO address rather than attaching any of the many names we humans have tried to pin on the deity.

Sharice awakes. "Sorry I fell asleep."

"I'm glad you did. You didn't get much sleep last night."

She is silent for a moment. "I was worrying."

"I know."

"If it turns out to be—"

I place a finger on her lips. "Don't speculate."

"You're right. I'll see if I can get in to see Dr. Rao on Monday. Can you go with me?"

"Of course."

She cants her head. "What's making that sound?"

I point. "There's a quail under that juniper."

"He's so cute."

"Tastes good too."

She pokes my arm. "You hunt those?"

"I don't hunt. But I used to eat them before we started dating."

"You don't have to change your diet because of me."

"I didn't change it because of you. I changed it because of us. I like that we eat the same things."

"You always say the sweetest—eeeek!"

She jumps up and grabs my arm.

I look down to see a whiptail lizard leaving the edge of our blanket and heading down into the wash in the frenetic style of her breed, tail lashing and legs wheeling. Then just as suddenly as she appeared, she is gone.

I don't mean out of sight. I mean dead. Speared by the beak of a roadrunner who, deftly using claw and beak, turns the lizard laterally so that she can be swallowed.

"What was that thing?" Clarice asks as she tightens her death grip on my arm and shudders.

"Just a whiptail lizard. They're harmless and sort of cute."

"Yuck. They are *not* cute. He looked like a baby alligator on meth."

"She."

"How do you know it was a she?"

"All the babies are clones of their mothers. Whiptails reproduce asexually."

She releases her grip on my bicep, places her arms around my waist and says, "I feel sorry for them. They miss all the fun." She kisses me.

After she releases me from her embrace, I glance down at our blanket. She follows my eyes and says, "Forget about it. No way I'm taking my clothes off with those little devils scurrying around."

On the way back to the Bronco, we saw more recent rock art made during what is called the historic period—after the arrival of the Spaniards.

As if the natives had no history before then.

I ask her if she can guess when they were made.

"Must be after the Spanish came. There's a man on a horse. Who is the other guy with the feathers?"

"Some people thinks it's Po'pay, the leader of the 1680 Pueblo Revolt."

"What caused the revolt?"

"The Spanish priests tried to prevent the tribes from practicing their traditional rites. After the revolt, the priests stopped interfering with pueblo religious ceremonies provided that the puebloans observed the outward forms of Catholicism. That's still pretty much the case today. Many of the Pueblo residents practice both Catholicism and traditional rites."

"Can't hurt to cover your bases," she said.

That's why I prayed to the nameless Great Spirit about your cancer, I thought.

God, Yahweh, Jehovah, Jesus, Mohammed, Gautama, Mary Baker Eddy, Confucius, Joseph Smith, the Dalai Lama. There's a lot of holiness swirling around the universe.

And not a few charlatans.

23

Weekends in Sharice's condo usually pass too quickly. A good woman, an exotic cat, a weird dog and a view of the Sandias are things worth holding on to.

But when you discover a small lump on a Friday night, Monday seems a year away.

The picnic filled most of Saturday. We took Geronimo and Benz for a long walk on Sunday and laughed as people stared at the mixed couple with what looks like a cheetah on a lead and another animal of indeterminate species plodding behind. We played Scrabble. We read.

But mostly we vacillated between saying there was no reason to talk about it before seeing the doctor and talking about it anyway because even though it was a very tiny lump, it was the elephant in the room.

We showed up at the doctor's office Monday morning at eight with no appointment. When Sharice told the receptionist the reason for the visit, she said she was sure Dr. Rao could squeeze us in, but it might be a long wait.

To pass the time, Sharice taught me a new game called, for no evident reason, Ghosts. "One of us chooses a letter," she explained. "The other one adds a letter before or after. We take turns adding letters before or after so that the string of letters gets longer. The first person to spell a word loses."

"That's too easy. All you have to do is keep adding *q* or *x* and you'll never spell a word."

"You haven't heard the rule."

"I should have known there's a rule. Just one?"

"Two actually. The first one is you must have a word in mind every time you add a letter. If I think you don't have a word in mind, I can challenge you. If you don't have a word, you lose. If you do have a word, I lose for challenging you. The second rule is that not spelling a word only applies after the third letter."

"Because otherwise, we'd spend all our time avoiding 'it,' 'at,' 'on,' et cetera."

"Exactly. Let's try a game."

After she won the first five games, I was trying to decide if I should challenge her after only two letters into the sixth one. It seemed like my first chance at a victory. I had gone first and chosen *z* to give myself what I hoped would be a competitive advantage. I once spent a full day at Spirits in Clay—not a customer in sight—reading the *z* section of the unabridged edition of the *Oxford English Dictionary*.

Tristan tells me everyone looks up words on their phones now and paper dictionaries are obsolete. But I love my *Oxford English Dictionary*. All thirty-five pounds of it. In addition to its primary function, it makes a great doorstop when the New Mexico winds are howling.

There are almost two thousand words that start with *z*, from *zabaglione* (an Italian custard) to *zyzzyvas* (a tropical beetle often found in palms). *Zyzzyvas* would score a zillion points in Scrabble, but there's only one *z* tile, so it's not possible.

Sharice appended a *v* behind my *z*.

Zv?

Surely, no word contains those two consonants back to back. "Ozvoi"? "Azvight"? "Uzvacate"?

She was bluffing. Trying to get me to add a letter so she could challenge. And she would win because I had no word in mind.

So I took my only option. "I challenge you. What word do you have in mind?"

"Rendezvous."

Oops. Tripped up by the silent *z*.

"That doesn't count," I said. "It's French."

"Its origin is French, but it's been adopted into English."

"Adopted words don't count." I was grasping at straws.

She laughed. "In that case we can't play this game in English, because all your words are adopted."

"My words?"

"Well? You're the native speaker here."

"Then why can't I win at least one game?"

"You're new at it. I've been playing for years. Let's try another round."

We didn't because a nurse arrived and led us to an examination room, where she pulled one of those one-size-fits-none gowns out of a drawer. It was a shade of blue you can get only after a hundred launderings. One of the ties was missing.

The nurse thrust the gown toward Sharice.

I took it instead. "I can't let her wear this."

The nurse frowned. "The doctor will need to examine her."

"I know that. But she can open her blouse as easily as this gown."

"She will have to remove her bra."

"She isn't wearing one."

The nurse stared at me.

"Trust me," I said. "The blouse won't be an issue."

She shook her head at my idiocy and left.

Sharice hugged me. "Thanks."

"I love your sense of style. You are not wearing one of these until Vera Wang starts designing them."

Dr. Rao showed up a couple of minutes later. She said hello to Sharice, then turned to me.

"Hubie?"

"Hi, Linda." I turned to Sharice. "We graduated from Albuquerque High School the same year. She was the valedictorian."

"Are you here in some official capacity?" asked Linda. "Counselor? Case worker?"

"Fashion consultant," I said, and held the gown aloft. "I saved her from the indignity of wearing this."

While she and Sharice were laughing, I put the gown on and did a pirouette. "Good thing I have my pants on. Otherwise you two would be looking at my backside. Now you know why you hear 'ICU' so often in hospitals."

Linda laughed some more. "So you're here as a comedian?"

"Actually, we're a couple."

Her laugh stopped in mid *ha*. "Oh." She covered her surprise more deftly than most people do and said, "Good. Having a partner present during a visit helps put the patient at ease. It can also help afterward, since she has someone to talk to who saw and heard what was going on—sort of like a second set of eyes."

Sharice took my hand and looked at me. "Just like what Charles said I could do for you."

Dr. Rao asked Sharice if she was ready. Sharice nodded, unbuttoned her blouse and touched her right breast. "Right about here."

The doctor felt around for the lump. Then she poked around in Sharice's right armpit.

The doc relocated the lump with her hand. "Does it hurt?"

"No."

"What about when I press on it?"

"Nothing. All I feel is the pressing."

"Okay. You can button up. The lump is very small, and I couldn't find any other abnormality. About ninety percent of all lumps located solely in the breast with no other indications are benign. Normally, I'd just give you a date to come back and see if it's changed. But given your history, we need to err on the side of caution."

Sharice nodded again.

"I'm going to give you a diagnostic mammogram. We can do it now, here in the office. Unlike a screening mammogram, a diagnostic mammogram gives us views from different angles and at a higher level of magnification. Which is good because with a lump this small, it's sometimes hard to see enough to make a judgment. Since it isn't painful, I'm surprised you found it."

"I didn't. Hubie . . ." Her hand went to her mouth.

I blushed.

The doctor laughed. "See? Contrary to popular belief, it is sometimes useful to have a man around. The radiologist will be here in a few minutes to take you to the radiology lab." She turned to me. "It's good to see you after all these years. I think I've read about you in the paper a few times. Are you in some newsworthy profession?"

"Just a merchant. I have a shop in Old Town."

After Linda left, Sharice mimicked me. "Just a harmless merchant."

"I didn't say *harmless*."

"You said it with your tone. But it won't work. She'll probably Google you and discover you're a notorious pot thief."

"No, the only people doctors Google are patients. They want to make sure you have enough money to pay them."

24

I've never worried much about what people say about me. Which is beneficial for a guy who's been in the paper a few times as a murder suspect.

So it surprised me that I felt apprehensive when Susannah and Sharice went to the restroom together at Dos Hermanas just after we all arrived Monday a little after five.

A crazy thought popped to mind. Maybe they were talking about what Glad had cautioned me about—the appearance of impropriety, living with one woman and having cocktails with another.

I banished the thought. This is America in the twenty-first century, not Victorian England or Saudi Arabia. Men and women at a bar together is not scandalous.

I assume women escape to the restroom to talk woman-to-woman.

When they returned from the restroom, Susannah gave me a kiss on the cheek.

"What's that for?"

"Sharice told me about the gown episode."

Angie arrived to take our order. "Two margaritas, one without salt, and a glass of Gruet?"

"Do you have pomegranate juice?" asked Sharice.

"Yes. You want a Pomarita? We make them with agave syrup. They're delicious."

"That does sound good, but I don't drink spirits. I'd like a Kir Royale with pomegranate juice instead of cassis."

Susannah ordered a Pomarita.

I ordered a margarita with extra salt on the rim.

"Boring," said Susannah.

"Predictable," said Sharice.

"Hey, I got extra salt. Why this sudden urge to change drinks?"

"Pomegranate helps prevent breast cancer," said Sharice.

"A girl needs to use all the arrows in her quiver," said Susannah.

I guess I knew what they were talking about in the restroom. It wasn't me.

The whizzbang special mammography machine with all its multiple angles and special magnification had failed to produce an image clear enough to determine the nature of the lump.

Lump.

An ugly word.

My *Oxford English Dictionary*/doorstop says it derives "from a Germanic base meaning shapeless" and is something with an "indiscriminate mass shape." It is sometimes used to describe a "heavy, ungainly, or slow-witted person."

Neither Sharice nor any of her parts can be described as indiscriminate, and she is certainly neither heavy nor ungainly.

I don't like the word *lump*. I don't even like words that rhyme with it: *chump, dump, grump, rump, slump.*

I decided to bump *lump* from my vocabulary.

"To your health, ladies," said Angie as she placed the Pomarita and Kir on the table.

She looked at me. "Here's your standard margarita with too much salt." Then she flashed that lightning-bolt smile and swirled away in her broomstick skirt.

"So what's next?" asked Susannah.

"I'm getting an ultrasound tomorrow morning."

Susannah looked at me. "You're going with her, right?"

It was more a command than a question.

"Absolutely," I said, and turned to Sharice, "I know you're having an ultrasound. What I don't know is exactly what that is."

"It's like an X-ray," said Sharice, "except it uses sound waves instead of radiation."

"Will we need to wear earplugs?"

"No, silly. The sound waves are called *ultra* because they're very high-frequency. A dog might hear them, but not a human."

"Good thing Geronimo isn't going with us. He'd probably howl."

25

After the ultrasound Tuesday morning, Dr. Rao told us the image was just as inconclusive as the mammogram and decided to do a fine-needle aspiration, which she explained involves inserting a very slender needle into the area of concern and drawing out a small amount of tissue, which is then examined under a microscope.

Forget the phrase *very slender*. Having a needle of any size plunged into your breast cannot be pleasant. I got woozy just thinking about it.

I didn't tell Sharice I hate needles. I held her hand while Dr. Rao did the needle biopsy, but I didn't look.

If someone stuck a needle that deep into my chest, I'd go home and curl up in the fetal position under my blanket.

Sharice went to work.

I went to class and was surprised to see Aleesha, who had not been coming to class. Her first words were, "What are you going to do about Ximena?"

The whites of her eyes were as cold as alabaster, but the pupils burned like lava.

"My suggestion would be to have a memorial of some sort, but each of you should have a say in what we do."

"A memorial is okay," said Aleesha, "but if I was dead, I'd want someone to do something about the person who killed me."

"It was an accident," said Carly.

"No. It was Prather. We all know how bad he is with clay. That's why nobody takes his classes. Evidently, he's just as bad with plaster as he is with clay. We know he's got no talent. Now we know he's got no common sense. You can't cover someone up with plaster and expect them not to suffocate."

Raúl said, "George Segal covered scores of people with plaster during his career, and not one of them ever suffocated."

"That's because he never covered their entire body."

"He sometimes covered their heads, and they were still able to breathe."

Carly said, "Prather left straws in Ximena's nose so she could breathe."

"You're all missing the point," said Aleesha. "You don't breathe with your nose. You breathe with your diaphragm. Take a breath and feel your muscles move."

Most of us did as she ordered.

"She's right," said Nathan.

"I think so too," said Carly.

"Yeah," said Bruce. "It's like a boa constrictor. They don't suffocate you by covering your nose. They do it by preventing you from expanding your diaphragm."

Although Aleesha's theory made sense and everyone agreed with her, I wondered if she was right. The medical investigator had ruled that Ximena died from asphyxiation. The simplest explanation was someone deliberately clogging the straws or maybe holding them closed.

I understand you can't breathe if a big snake compresses you into the diameter of a garden hose. But having your diaphragm simply restricted but not compressed is a different matter. You might be able to take enough small breaths to stay alive. In that case, it wouldn't be Prather's fault except insofar as he was the one who put her in a position to be murdered by anyone who wandered into the gallery and cut off her air supply.

I was determined not to be pulled into the investigation. I reminded the class that it was a police matter. If they determined simply being encased in plaster was the cause of death, Prather would likely be charged with something like involuntary man-slaughter. Meanwhile, the best thing we could do was some sort of tribute.

"Won't her family do that?" asked Marlon. Then he added, "And should we do a memorial without consulting them?"

"The *Journal* ran an article about her death," said Carly. "I was surprised it didn't contain any information about her. It didn't even say where she was from."

I thought about the times when I was arrested for murder and released the same day only to hear that it was already in the news. "They probably didn't have time to get that information and were just rehashing the police reports. Reporters hang around the police department to get all the bad news fast."

"You should know since you been arrested so many times," said Aleesha.

I winced. Even I knew everything could be searched online.

"It's been five days since her death," Raúl noted. "And today's story still didn't have any info about her."

"Neither did the one in the *Daily Lobo*," said Bruce. "You'd think the student paper would know something."

"Maybe they're withholding the information because they haven't been able to notify the next of kin," said Alfred.

"If they haven't notified the next of kin, dummy," said Aleesha, "they wouldn't have put her name in the article."

"Oh," he said. "Right." Then he started crying.

I thought it was because of Aleesha's insult and was about to demand she apologize when Alfred spoke. "She insisted I be Prather's helper. I normally avoid him like a biker bar. But when she explained why she wanted me to do it, I couldn't say no." He stopped to wipe his eyes. "If I had refused, she would still be alive."

Carly hugged him. "You don't know that. Prather would have found someone else to assist."

Alfred shook his head. "No. She wouldn't have done it unless I assisted."

When I asked him how he could be sure of that, he reached into his backpack and handed me a note that read:

I'm willing to be the model because I need the money. And because that stupid Helen S. asked me to. Even though we don't get along, she seems to think I owe it to her. But I don't want Prather touching me. I don't want him wrapping gauze on me. I want you to do that. And I want you to make sure there's no monkey business.

"What's it say?" asked Aleesha.

I looked at Alfred. "You can read it to them," he said, and lowered his head.

After I did so, I asked if any of them knew her well.

"I never heard the girl say a single word," said Aleesha.

"Come to think of it, neither did I," said Bruce.

Raúl said, "I had another studio with Ximena. Studio classes aren't normally like this one. They don't involve weird field trips, twig gathering and eerie Native American pot-making chants. Mostly you just work on your own project. Some students are talkative. Others concentrate on their work. She seemed absorbed in her art."

Aleesha looked at Alfred. "I still think Prather killed her. Why else would she write down that stuff about him not touching her? She wanted a written record. If she wasn't suspicious, she would have just told you."

"No," he said. "She wrote it down because she couldn't speak."

"She was deaf and dumb?" Aleesha asked.

"That's hate talk," said Apache.

"What do you know about hate talk?" she shot back at him.

"More than you, evidently."

Aleesha started to reply, but I interrupted. "No arguments. I knew Ximena even less well than all of you did. But I'm sure she wouldn't want us bickering. For your information, she was in fact a deaf-mute."

"Why didn't she have a signer with her?" asked Aleesha. "The university provides them free of charge."

Raúl said, "My guess is she didn't want one."

"Why not?"

"She was obviously great at reading lips. None of us even realized she was deaf. When a teacher gave her instructions, she was always able to follow them. And the few times I asked her some-thing, she always responded appropriately—nodding yes, shaking her head no, shrugging, smiling, whatever. I thought she was just shy. Now that I think about it, the only noises I ever heard her make were sneezes."

"She had allergies," said Alfred.

Raúl said, "She hid her muteness perfectly. She probably didn't want anyone to know she was mute, so she didn't ask for a signer."

"That's ridiculous," said Aleesha. "Being deaf is nothing to be ashamed of."

"I didn't say she was ashamed," said Raúl. "My guess is she was proud of being such a proficient lip reader."

Speculating about Ximena's attitude about being deaf and mute was getting us nowhere, so I said, "Let's get back to the topic of what to do."

"A scholarship," said Carly. "Let's start a scholarship in her name."

"Where are we going to get enough money to fund a scholar-ship?" asked Aleesha.

"Have an art sale," said Bruce. "Maybe Mr. Schuze can put the pots we make this semester in his shop. When they sell, we can donate the money for a scholarship."

He looked at me.

"I'd be happy to sell them."

"But would anyone buy them?" asked Aleesha.

"They would if some of the pieces won prizes," I said. "Let's work on making great copies of ancient pots. Then let's enter them in the student/faculty show. If some of your pots win prizes, that will be great publicity for the work we'd be selling. I know a few wealthy collectors who might buy some of your work. But it's got to be first-rate."

"That's a great idea," said Nathan.

"It is," said Bruce. Then he looked at Alfred. "But before we talk about that, I want to know why you avoid biker bars."

Alfred dried his eyes, smiled, took a couple of illustrative steps and said, "The customers would probably beat me up just because I walk funny."

Bruce lifted his right forearm and flexed his bicep. "Don't worry, little buddy. I'll make sure they leave you alone."

He sounded like the captain on those reruns of *Gilligan's Island*. But Alfred didn't look like Bob Denver, the actor who played Gilligan. He looked more like Mitzi Gaynor.

I thought about Charles Webbe asking for information. "The note tells us why she wanted someone to assist Prather," I said to Alfred. "Do you mind telling me why she selected you?"

He shook his head. "I can't talk about it."

I didn't want to press him. "Okay, is everyone agreed about selling your pots to get money for a scholarship?"

They were all in. They had become proficient at forming armatures and draping them with clay. If they could master glazing with traditional designs, I thought we might create enough saleable merchandise to fund a small scholarship.

Turns out I was wrong. Not about the scholarship. About the size.

26

After Sharice left for work on Wednesday, I spent the morning cleaning the condo and rereading *The Monkey Wrench Gang*. It's the most famous of Edward Abbey's twenty-one books because it was made into a film and also because it spawned the radical environmental movement.

A widowed surgeon, his receptionist/mistress, a Green Beret freshly returned from the Vietnam War and a polygamist Mormon river guide find they all have two things in common: a deep-seated love of the Southwest and a willingness to stop the rape of the land they love by any means necessary short of murder. They wage war on the machines of destruction. Road graders, coal trains, power plants and logging trucks are sabotaged, crashed, pushed over cliffs and set ablaze.

Desert Solitaire is a love story between a man and the high desert, the sort of book you find yourself finishing at two in the morning because you can't put it down. *Monkey Wrench* has a great premise and became a successful film, but I couldn't stay with the book for long stretches. After about the third explosion, you want to move on to something else. I'd finish one chapter then do the windows. Read another then do the floors. Then read about three chapters because the next task was cleaning Benz's litter box.

Whit Fletcher showed up after lunch and walked in when I opened the door.

"So you and the dental woman have shacked up. Can't blame you for choosing her place. It's a lot fancier than yours."

"Her name is Sharice, Whit."

"She know about your bad luck?"

"She knows I'm a treasure hunter, if that's what you mean."

"I mean like that guy you told me about got hit by lightning seven times. Except in your case, it's dead bodies. Maybe you been struck again. Seeing as you and me are friends, there ain't no need to haul you downtown." He looked around. "Hell, we are downtown. Well, no need to take you to the station. I can get a set of your prints right here."

I felt a twitch between my shoulders. "Why do you need my prints?"

"Same reason any cop wants prints. To see if they match some we already got."

"Why would you think any prints you have are mine?"

"You gonna cooperate or not? I'm doing you a favor, Hubert. You give me your prints. They don't match, no one even knows I asked you."

"Yeah. But you don't just go around asking random people for their fingerprints. There must be a reason why you want mine."

"You gonna give me the prints or you gonna go all ACLU on me? The reason I need your prints is because someone connected with the case told us prints we found might be yours."

"Connected with what case?"

"The Ximena Sifuentes case. Is there another one you're involved in?"

This time it was a full shudder instead of a twitch. "I'm not connected to the case. I just happened to be in the gallery when they discovered she was dead. There must have been a hundred other people there. You planning to get prints from all of them too?"

"If I have to. But nobody has suggested any of them as possible matches."

"Who suggested the prints might be mine?"

"I can't tell you that."

He was silent while I thought it over. Where did the prints he wanted to compare mine to come from? I never touched Ximena. I never touched the plaster around her. I suppose I touched the gallery floor, where I found myself sitting after the shock of seeing her tumble backward. I may have touched the wall because I ended up resting my back against it.

But the gallery is a public space. What would be the point of finding a match for prints taken from its walls or floor?

On the other hand, what would be the point of refusing to be fingerprinted and ending up in the police station?

"You're right, Whit. I haven't done anything wrong, so why not give you my prints? And I appreciate that you came here instead of taking me to the police station. I don't exactly have fond memories of that place."

"Now you're making sense," he said, and reached into his pocket for a fingerprint kit.

Up to this point, I had steadfastly refused to worry about the investigation, much less get involved in it. I wanted to keep it that way. But if I were going to be fingerprinted, it seemed like a good idea to have some sense of what was going on. "Before we do this, I want to ask you a question. I know there's a security camera in the gallery. Can you tell me what it showed the day of her death?"

"Mostly a lot of nothing. She's in the video twice. Once just standing there with the gay kid. The second time is when they take the plaster off and she falls over dead. You're on the video too. It shows you fainting like a girl."

"But if the video shows her—"

He held the fingerprint kit aloft for me to see. "I ain't got all day. You want to know about the security camera, talk to Shorter."

I stuck out my hands.

27

The first thing Sharice said when she got home was, "The condo is sparkling, but it looks like all the dirt you scrubbed off ended up on your fingers."

"That's not dirt. It's ink. Whit Fletcher came by about an hour ago and fingerprinted me."

"Why?"

"The police want to see if my prints match some they found."

She frowned. "Found where?"

"He wouldn't say. But he did say it has to do with their investigation of Ximena's death."

"Why would they think the prints are yours?"

"Someone connected to the case suggested the prints might be mine."

"That's weird. And scary."

"Yeah. And I don't have any answers. Which makes sense, because I don't know what the questions are."

"The first question," she said, "is what does 'connected to the case' mean?"

"Someone in the art department? Someone at the event where the plaster was removed?"

"Did you know any of the people at the event other than art department people?"

"No."

"Then it has to be someone from the department, probably Aleesha."

"Why would she do that?"

"She filed a groundless compliant against you, Hubie. Anyone who would do that might also try to sic the police on you."

"She came back to class and agreed to help in the scholarship plan."

"Is she still pursuing the EEO complaint?"

"I don't know."

Sharice went to the refrigerator and returned with a bottle of Gruet and two coupes. I used to prefer flutes, but the coupes are fun because their wide, shallow shape allows the bubbles to tickle your nose. I needed tickling.

After she filled the coupes she said, "How can Aleesha think you're prejudiced against her? After all"—she flashed her Klieg-light smile—"you are living with *moi*."

"She doesn't know that."

"Tell her."

"I can't do that."

"You don't want your students to know you're living in sin?" she said, and giggled. Then she said, "Seriously, why not tell her?"

I sat my coupe down on the glass coffee table. "When I first met Charles Webbe, he was undercover. I thought his name was M'Lanta Scruggs, pot scrubber at Schnitzel."

"M'Lanta? Why do black Americans give their kids such weird names?"

"It wasn't his real name."

"I know that. But he must have chosen it because he knows that some black parents pick weird names."

"I'm sure he knows that. He knows everything. But he chose it because he thought it was funny. Anyway, he was explaining the menu to me. When I asked him how he knew so much about Austrian dishes, he said, 'You think 'cause I'm black, I don't know nothing?'"

"How did you respond?"

"I pointed out that my question had nothing to do with color. I'm white and know nothing about Austrian food. Then he asked if I knew any black people. I said I dated a black woman named Sharice."

"We weren't dating then."

"I know. But we did have lunch together."

"Yeah. I was hoping it was a date, but you seemed to think it was just lunch. What's so funny?"

"I was hoping it was a date, but *you* seemed to think it was just lunch."

"Drat. Look at all the time together we missed because of tip-toeing. I should have suggested a second date."

"Anyway, I felt like I had used you. Sort of like your manicurist and your hairdressers. Putting the fact that you're black above the fact that you're a person because it was to my advantage to do so."

She scooted closer to me. "You are the most colorblind person I know. I'd be honored for you to get Aleesha off your case by telling her about me."

I just nodded. I had no intention of doing that.

"Where did they find the prints they're trying to match with yours?"

"Whit wouldn't tell me."

"Maybe we can figure it out. Could they be on the dried plaster they took off Ximena?"

"I never touched the plaster."

"Something in the gallery? The door, a tabletop?"

"I may have touched the door, and probably the floor and wall while I was sitting down. But just having prints in the gallery only proves I was there, and they already know that."

"I've got it. Something connected with the plaster. The bucket it was carried in. A spatula or whatever was used to put the plaster on. Do the faculty share brushes and other stuff used in making art? Maybe your prints are on a tool."

Finally, a ray of reason. "You might be right. I passed out buckets from the departmental supply room to the students when we went to gather clay from the river. Maybe one of those buckets found its way to Prather, who carried plaster in it to the gallery."

"Having your prints in the gallery or the studio where you have the class wouldn't be significant. Did you ever interact with Ximena somewhere else?"

"Yes. The men's room, remember?"

"Why was she in the men's room?"

I shrugged. "I don't know. It's next to the studio. More convenient than searching for the women's room?"

"Which is far away?"

"I have no idea. Never been there. Never plan to use it."

"That's my Hubie. You didn't touch her or maybe her backpack or something?"

"I didn't touch anything. Any prints I left were elbow prints, because that's what I used to push the door open."

"That is so you. Did you put disposable plastic covers over your shoes before you walked on the bathroom floor?"

"They make those? Where can I buy them?"

28

I walked to Spirits in Clay Thursday afternoon, my first visit in two weeks. Sharice had instructed me to release Glad from the shops at four and meet her and the rest of the gang at Dos Hermanas at five.

Glad doesn't seem to mind going to and fro between Spirits in Clay and F°ahrenheit F°ashions, his catchily named shop that offers desert apparel—cargo shorts, wide-brimmed hats, sunglasses, hiking boots, sunscreen, et cetera. Also T-shirts with cartoon saguaro cacti, the bubbles above them displaying their thoughts. "Humans are needleless," for example, and "Uh-oh. Here comes a thirsty guy with a machete."

"Good afternoon, Hubie," he said. "I hope I did the right thing providing your current address to Agent Webbe. Seeing him reminded me of the trouble I caused you during that unfortunate episode at the missile range."

"The misfortune was of my own doing. I knew digging for pots inside White Sands Missile Range was risky."

"Is he still tying up the loose ends of that case?"

"It wasn't his case, actually. He was involved only tangentially. What he wanted to talk about was the death of one of my students."

"I read about that in the newspaper. What an odd event." He shook his head. "Covering a girl in plaster. Art seems to have become quite daft."

"Have you heard of Joel-Peter Witkin?"

"No. Is he famous?"

"He is. And he lives here in Albuquerque. He takes photographs of dead people."

"Head shots for the obituary pages in the newspaper?"

"Hardly. The corpses he photographs are naked and often dismembered."

"Crikey Moses! Is that legal here?"

"No. He works mostly in Mexico. Susannah told me he said in an interview, 'In death I find a power of reality that no sculptor or painter could re-create, not even a Michelangelo or a Da Vinci.'"

"What a load of rubbish. Has this Witkin chap never seen Da Vinci's anatomical drawings? Da Vinci could create more power with a pencil than anyone could with a camera."

"I suspect you're right. I've never seen any of Witkin's work and have no plans to do so."

I changed the subject and asked how sales had been the last two weeks.

"Same as usual," he said.

"That bad, huh?"

He gave me the list of sales and showed me a pot he had conditionally accepted on consignment subject to my approval. It was a Zia bird jar with mocha slip and looked to be from the 1930s.

"How much does he want for it?"

"How do you know the seller is a he?"

"Because in twenty years of buying pots, almost all the sellers have been men. My speculation is most women are sensible enough to hang on to valuables and sentimental enough to want to."

"Indeed. It was a gent, and he wants a thousand for the pot."

"Call him and tell him we'll buy it."

I brought up a tented card from the drawer below the counter and penciled in the pueblo name, the estimated date and the price.

"I guess I did well," Glad said when he saw me pencil in *four thousand five hundred dollars.*

He seems to be developing a good eye for pots.

"Sharice told me I'm to relieve you at four," I told him, "and then meet with you and the others at Dos Hermanas, but she wouldn't tell me why."

"Nor shall I." He smiled and looked at his watch. "See you in an hour."

I settled in behind the counter with *The Monkey Wrench Gang* and learned how to start a Caterpillar D8 bulldozer. The diesel engine is so big that there is a small gasoline one called a pony engine that is used to start the diesel one. All you have to do is place the transmission in neutral, pull the master clutch in, set the main throttle to a bit above idle, set the hand brake, pull out the choke, use the hand primer pump to prime the diesel, move the compression release lever into the release position, put the hand crank on the pony engine, turn the crank over a couple of times to get a little oil up and prime the carburetor, make sure the pony is set to the compression stroke, switch the ignition on and firmly pull the crank handle. After the pony starts, let it warm up. After it's warm, throttle it up to a roar, engage the pinion gear lever and pull on the pony motor clutch till the big engine is turning over. Once the diesel is running, shut off the pony.

Now you understand why I didn't mind taking breaks to clean the condo while I was reading *The Monkey Wrench Gang*.

Martin arrived shortly before five with a wide-mouthed clay bowl in his hand. "Susannah told me to meet you here," he said.

"Did she say why?"

"Yes."

If it had been someone other than Martin, I would have asked what the why was. But when Martin stops talking, there's nothing else he's going to say.

"That doesn't look like one of your uncle's pieces."

"Right."

Tristan arrived a few minutes later and said he too was following Susannah's instructions and also had no idea why we were to meet at the shop and then go to Dos Hermanas.

I nodded toward Martin. "He knows, but he's not saying."

"That doesn't look like one of his uncle's pots."

"Yeah. We already established that."

I locked both shops and we headed to the cantina, where we found Sharice wrapped in a Celia Kritharioti sheath dress with a swirl pattern of white and a darker shade that matched her skin so that she appeared to be wrapped in white ribbon.

I know two things about Kritharioti. First, she's Greek. Second, if other Greek products sold for as much as her dresses, they wouldn't be needing a bail-out from the European Union.

Susannah was wearing fancy Levi's and a white western shirt with turquoise and black swaths in what looked like random locations but were no doubt carefully planned.

When I said her blouse looked like it came from a designer, she smiled and said, "It *is* from a designer. Patricia Michaels from the Taos pueblo. Her work is known as Native American haute couture."

Martin shook his head. "I suppose my handmade buffalo-hide boots don't qualify as Native American haute couture."

Susannah looked at his feet. "Since when is Tony Lama Native American?"

She is not easily fooled.

We bantered about clothes and style while waiting for whatever was supposed to happen.

Gladys arrived, radiant in a white cotton dress with white embroidery on the neckline and sleeves. Glad was in a gray suit with a white shirt and blue bow tie.

Tristan and I glanced at each other.

Martin was expressionless.

Angie brought an ice bucket with a bottle of Gruet Blanc de Noir, which she handed to me.

"I believe you are skilled at opening these."

While I was holding the cork and twisting the bottle (one never twists the cork), Glad said, "I have an announcement. Miss Gladys has consented to become Mrs. Gladys Farthing."

His announcement caused me to flub the uncorking. A loud pop was followed by the crack of the cork hitting the ceiling then a loud ding as it caromed off a ceiling light and a boing as it bounced off a tabletop. It sounded like the beginning notes of a John Cage work with one of his crazy titles like "Composition for Tin Can and Two Dimes."

After a couple of additional bounces and caroms, the cork came to rest in what Susannah later explained to me was a mixture of vodka and apple schnapps called an Appletini.

I told the Appletini drinker the cork lent more style to his drink than the slice of apple in it. He told me the thing cost five dollars and held out his hand.

When I finally regained my composure, I proposed a toast. "To Gladwyn. You're a better man than I. Miss Gladys turned me down when I proposed to her."

"He was just jesting," she said.

"I would never toy with your affections," I replied.

"'Toy with your affections' sounds so old-fashioned," she said, "something I might say."

"She must have known I would come along," said Glad.

"Have you set a date?" I asked.

"No. But the place will be the gazebo in the plaza and the officiant will, of course, be Father Groas."

"It's odd," I said, "that you, Glad, are from England and are Catholic, and Miss Gladys is from Texas and is an Anglican."

"Not odd at all. You were our colony at one point so our state religion is part of the legacy. I, on the other hand, am a devout follower of Sir Thomas More, who remained loyal to the pope despite Henry VIII's break from the Vatican."

"As I recall, More lost his head over that."

"Literally, yes. But figuratively, no. He was a true stalwart."

In fact, More was sentenced, "to be hanged till he should be half dead; that then he should be cut down alive, his privy parts cut off, his belly ripped, his bowels burnt, his four quarters set up over four gates of the City and his head upon London Bridge."

The nuptial announcement didn't seem a good time to mention having one's privy parts cut off, so I refrained from sharing what I remembered about More's penalty for remaining faithful to the pope. And thankfully, it never happened. King Henry commuted More's sentence to a simple beheading.

Miss Gladys said, "I may be an Episcopalian, but I live in Old Town and just adore Father Groas."

Susannah, who is also Catholic, asked if Miss Gladys was going to convert.

"I will be married there and attend Mass with Gladwyn. But I will not convert."

"Does Father Groas have any qualms about officiating?"

Gladys's eyes sparkled as she spoke. "He does not. I promised him that if Gladwyn and I have children, we will raise then as Catholics."

This brought a round of laughter as Glad and Gladys are both around sixty years old.

Tristan proposed a toast. "To the patter of little feet."

Martin set the clay bowl on the table and startled me by pouring Champagne into it.

"My people call this a wedding bowl. It is traditionally made by the future husband's parents five days before the wedding ceremony. The husband and all his relatives go to the bride's house. Dos Hermanas is a second home to all of us, so I brought the wedding bowl here. First, the future husband drinks from one side of the bowl. Then the future wife drinks from the other. Then they drink simultaneously. If they can do that without spilling anything, they will have a long and happy marriage because they know how to cooperate."

He handed the bowl to Glad, who took a small sip and handed it to Miss Gladys.

"I'm going to wait just a moment till my hands stop shaking," she said. Then she took a deep breath and a very small sip.

Glad stepped beside her and took the bowl in his hands. They put their faces together, the corners of their mouths as close together as possible. They drank without spilling a single drop.

During the spontaneous applause that broke out among all the patrons, I studied the bowl. I wondered if the two slight indentations in the rim that allowed them to drink without loss were traditional or had been pressed into the wet clay to make sure the happy couple could experience the good omen.

Martin said, "You will keep your wedding bowl as long as you are together. When one of you passes into the spirit world, he or she will take the bowl filled with corn. Corn does not go stale in the spirit world. So when the other one joins you, you will eat the corn together."

After additional toasts, embraces, jests, blushes by Miss Gladys and funny stories about how Glad had courted her, everyone finally left except for me and *ma femme*. The first bottle of Gruet had been followed by three others. Even though six of us were sharing, Sharice and I were both a bit tipsy.

"Maybe we should have a coffee to brace us for the walk downtown," she suggested.

"Good idea. I'd hate to be ticketed for walking under the influence."

After Angie brought two black coffees, Sharice squeezed my hand and said, "Dr. Rao called just before I left work. The needle biopsy didn't capture enough to do an analysis."

"So after a diagnostic mammogram, an ultrasound and a needle biopsy, they still don't know what it is?" I shook my head. "It's like that Higgs boson thing that's been in the news. It's so small that it took them ten years to find one and just like in your case, they have no precise idea what it is. So what's next?"

"She wants to do another needle biopsy, but with a larger needle to capture a larger sample."

My needle phobia conjured up a device manufactured by Caterpillar. Probably a result of reading *The Monkey Wrench Gang*.

"Well, the good news is we know you won't need another mastectomy."

"How do we know that?"

"Because they're going to remove your right breast bit by bit with a needle."

She gave me a playful poke. "It's not *that* small." She bit her bottom lip. "I told her I didn't want another needle biopsy."

I made no response.

She sipped her coffee. "It's very small. And there appears to be no involvement of the lymph nodes."

I nodded.

"And," she took another sip, "old memories die hard. I feel like I'm being dragged back to something I escaped. I'm not going back."

"So no more doctor visits?"

"I'm not that reckless. I'll go back quarterly to be checked. If anything changes, we'll deal with it then."

"Sounds like a plan."

"You think I'm being irrational? Sticking my head in the sand?"

"Dr. Rao said ninety percent of all lumps like yours are benign. Going with that high a probability is hardly irrational."

"I'll see her in three months. Meanwhile, I don't want to think about it. And I don't want you to think about it, let alone mention it."

"Yes, ma'am."

She changed the subject. "I can't believe Miss Gladys is getting married. How old is she?"

"It's love, Sharice. The heart does not know age. Or color."

We were the only remaining customers. I'd been drinking. Both of which made it easier for me to overcome my inhibitions and slide off my chair and onto my knees.

I took her hand in mine. "Marry me."

"You're just saying that because of Glad and Gladys."

"No. I'm saying it because I love you."

"I know you do. But I suspect you're proposing now because I mentioned the lump and you want me to know you aren't going to abandon me if I get sick."

"You already know I would never abandon you. But it's a moot point. I'm ten years older than you and men usually don't live as long as women. The chances are greater you'll be a widow than I'll be a widower."

"If we don't get married, neither of those will happen."

"Good point. So since one of us will eventually die and the other will be sad, we should make the sadness official by being either a widow or widower."

She laughed. "Marry me so that one of us can eventually be a widow or widower? That's the worst rationale I've ever heard for marriage."

"I'm grasping at straws here, woman! Give me one reason why you won't marry me."

She tugged me back up into my seat. She took a deep breath.

"Remember I told you there was one more thing on my list of things I had to tell you?"

"Yeah. It's something about your father."

She nodded. A few sudden tears ran down her cheek. "I promised him I'd never marry a white man."

"That's a relief. You were so secretive about it, I figured maybe he was a serial killer."

"Be serious."

"Why? Obviously you made that promise before we met. Now that you know how terrific I am, you can change your mind."

"It's not that easy. He's the one who asked for the promise." She took a deep breath. "As I was growing up, he tried to teach me that happiness for a black person can be achieved only by a sort of emotional firewall between yourself and the white world. He interacts with whites, of course. And he is courteous with everyone. But he has never worked for a white man. He would never rent from a white landlord. And most of all, he would never allow his daughter to marry a white man."

"Do you think he's right?"

"If I did, I never would have dated you." She gave me her candlelight smile. "And now I'm hooked. Look, I know prejudice exists. But you can't wall yourself off from all white people just because some of them are prejudiced. You have to believe that prejudice can be eliminated. You believe it not because science or reason proves it. It's more an article of faith. The first requirement for solving any problem is believing it's solvable."

"So how do we solve this problem? How do we get your father to accept us as a couple?"

"I'm not sure we can."

I hesitated then said, "He doesn't know about me, does he?"

More tears. "I'm sorry, Hubie. I hate that I haven't told him. It feels like being disloyal to you."

"It doesn't feel that way to me. I don't want you to hurt your father. But you can't keep us a secret forever."

She wiped her eyes and gave me a smile I hadn't seen before, a little-girl timid one, crooked and beguiling. "You're right. Especially because he's coming here for Thanksgiving."

29

It was late when we got back to the condo, so Sharice threw together a light meal.

Farro—whatever that is—with all manner of plant products thrown in: shallots, tomatoes, parsley, edamame, walnuts and dried cranberries.

I would have killed for some carnitas tacos.

After we loaded the dishwasher and went to the loveseat for a nightcap of Gruet, she said, "We need to talk about my father's visit."

"Now? He won't be here for weeks."

"He'll be here tomorrow."

"Tomorrow! You said he's coming for Thanksgiving."

"Canadian Thanksgiving. Ours is celebrated the second Monday of October."

She must have seen the air go out of me.

"It's only for three nights—tomorrow, Saturday and Sunday. Then he flies back on Monday. Poor Dad. He'll be in the air on Thanksgiving Day, missing the Thanksgiving Classic."

"Which is?"

"Back-to-back games in the CFL."

"Which is?"

"The Canadian Football League."

"They play football in Canada? I thought it was hockey."

"Hockey isn't a sport in Canada. It's a religion. But football is also popular. Dad's favorite team is in the first game, and he'll miss it."

I figured I may as well learn something about the guy now that he was a topic of conversation, so I asked which team was his favorite.

"The Montreal Alouettes, of course."

"What kind of a football team is named after a ballet maneuver?"

"An alouette is a lark."

"Oh. In that case, I repeat the question for a different reason. What sort of football team is named after a songbird?"

"When I was a little girl, they were called the Concordes."

"They were named after a grape? That's even wimpier than a lark."

"They were named after the supersonic jet, not the grape. And you are hardly one to call any football team wimps."

"*Au contraire*. I'm a wimp and know it. But if I were a big, strong football player, I wouldn't want to play for a team called the larks."

She was quiet for a few moments. "You'll—"

"I know. I'll have to move out. You want me to leave tonight."

"Heavens no. That can wait until morning." She gave me her seductive smile. "I'm going to take a shower."

You know the rest of that routine.

30

If you're keeping score at home, your card should look like this:

One EEO complaint
One sexual harassment complaint
One failure to post a trigger warning
One unauthorized field trip
One insubordination for telling students not to pay fees
One request from police for my fingerprints
One forced move from Sharice's condo

They say don't sweat the small stuff. Which is good, because I also had two biggies:

One lump in Sharice's breast, which was evidently going to
    be more or less ignored
One student dead, possibly murdered

After Sharice left for work Friday morning, I packed my belongings. She said I had to get everything out—clothes, toothbrush, razor, dog.

Everything. I knew it was only three nights, but it felt final. And sneaky. Like covering up a crime. Which I guess was the way her father would view me living with her.

As Geronimo and I walked to Old Town, I became angrier with each step. I toyed with the idea of marching back downtown after he arrived and confronting the racist old bastard. I know that's harsh, but it's how I felt. I wasn't a suitable son-in-law just because of my skin color?

Then I thought about all the injustices and slights he must have endured over the years because of his skin color, and I felt guilty.

I decided not to march back downtown.

But you already knew that. I don't do confrontation.

Geronimo was happy to be back at Spirits in Clay. I wanted to be with Sharice. He wanted to be away from Benz.

After sticking his snout in all the nooks and most of the crannies, he took a nap, secure in the knowledge that no felines were within sniffing distance.

I brewed coffee in my old percolator. It was awful compared to Sharice's brew, but the bitter, burnt taste was reassuringly familiar.

I ran my hand across the pine table. Looked up at the crooked vigas.

The chamisa in the courtyard was blooming, the popcorn scent of its slender branches now mingled with the rotting-apple smell of its clumps of yellow fall florets.

The scientific name is *Chrysothamnus nauseosus*. Whoever named it has a different idea of nauseous than I do. I like the smell. Of course, I also like the smell of clay baking in a kiln, so I'd be a poor *parfumier*. "Courtyard, the new cologne from Schuze Scents—hints of a fall afternoon in the desert with undertones of dried fruits and burning brush, attenuated by notes of creosote and coyote."

I was homesick, but I didn't know it until I was home. I wondered if Sharice would consent to move to Old Town. I could volunteer to convert my studio into a walk-in closet for her. I could buy stainless-steel appliances.

Then my thoughts turned from *where* we would be together to *if* we would be together. How difficult would it be for her to break the promise to her father?

I needed to stop digging into the pit of melancholy. I decided to take a walk. Geronimo awoke when he heard the rattle of his leash.

After a dozen turns around the plaza, I crossed to the south side of the plaza and entered Treasure House Books, where I chatted with John Hoffsis before buying another book by Abbey, this one a collection of essays. Hopefully none dealing with earthmoving equipment.

I knew Abbey believed the degradation of the American Southwest was a crime against nature and was being exacerbated by growth. What I didn't know was that this led him to oppose immigration. When the *New York Times* asked him to write an op-ed piece on the topic, the essay he sent was so radical they refused to print it.

So much for airing the full spectrum of opinions.

Abbey's basic tenet was that there were already too many people in our country. Letting in others would only speed up the fouling of our air and the destruction of our forests. To those who sympathize with immigrants fleeing from dictatorial and dysfunctional countries like Honduras, Abbey suggested we stop them at the border, give them a rifle and a case of ammunition, and send them back home to clean up their own country.

He wrote that essay a quarter of a century ago. I wondered what he would think about the 12 million illegal immigrants now in America.

I wondered what I thought about them. I'm not political, so I had to ponder it. Search as I might, I could not find any opinion in my consciousness. I don't know how to have a single overarching opinion that would cover 12 million people.

They are individuals. I know maybe 20 out of that 12 million. One is a mechanic who works on my Bronco in his front yard and somehow keeps the old heap running. Another is the repairman at Tristan's rundown apartment complex near the university. Another washes dishes at Dos Hermanas. One owns a bookkeeping service and does income tax returns.

Yes, an illegal immigrant does tax returns.

I've heard people say we're not supposed to call them illegal immigrants. It might hurt their feelings. Those people obviously know even less about illegal immigrants than I do. Unlike many of today's pampered Americans, illegal immigrants don't have thin skins. They're working like the devil and saving for a better life. They don't have any time to waste worrying about what they're supposed to be called.

Which these days is "undocumented workers."

Nonsense. Melquiades Telles, the income-tax guy, is hardly undocumented. To begin with, he has a New Mexico driver's license. My state is one of only ten that will grant driver's licenses to illegal immigrants. Most of the others are places you expect— California, Nevada, Colorado.

Oddly, one of the ten is Vermont. I guess all three of the illegal immigrants up there have driver's licenses.

Melquiades also has a business license and a tax-preparer number issued by the IRS. The man has more documents than I do.

I know this because he did the tax return for another illegal immigrant—Gladwyn Farthing. Glad is illegal because he entered the country on a tourist visa and is running a business. An illegal immigrant from Mexico filing income tax returns for a tourist from England who is illegally running the business that is being taxed.

Is this a great country or what?

Then I remembered I was living with an immigrant. I was sure she was legal. I was no longer quite so sure about the "living with" part.

31

I walked to the university on Saturday and found Shorter ensconced behind the desk. Department heads work on weekends. He looked as silly behind that hulk as I would in the seat of a Caterpillar D8 bulldozer.

But both his smile and handshake were warm, and I scolded myself for typecasting him just because of his Brobdingnagian desk.

"For what we pay adjuncts," he said, laughing, "we don't expect them to put in overtime. What brings you here on a Saturday?"

"An unhappy errand. I was talking with Detective Fletcher about Ximena. He told me the only two shots of her on the security video are of her standing with Alfred and then when she falls over. When I started to ask how the camera could capture those two things and not capture what came between them, he said I should ask you about it."

The smile evaporated as he sighed deeply. "I messed up, Hubie. I turned off the video camera when Ximena was ready to prepare herself for the plaster. You can't blame her for not wanting to be videoed standing there naked. So I went to the gallery. Ximena and Alfred were there. I climbed up a ladder and switched off the camera."

"Why couldn't Prather turn it off himself? Is he not talking to you?"

He laughed heartily. It was good to see him brighten. "So far as I know, you're the only one he's not talking to." He looked at the door and then back at me before adding, "Lucky you."

He thought for a moment then said, "I passed Prather in the hall as I left the gallery. He told me the plaster would be on in less than an hour, and I could go back then and turn the camera back on. He couldn't do it because the camera switch is operated with a key. Otherwise anyone could turn it off, which defeats the purpose of having it. As department head, I have the only key, and departmental policy is that I cannot loan it out even for a few minutes."

"I wouldn't call what you did a mess-up. I'd call it common decency."

"My mess-up was a delay in turning it back on. I returned to my office where I was ambushed by Jollo Bakkie, who tried to convince me she should be teaching painting. She does that several times a semester with what she seems to think is a new rationale that will convince me. The rationale is never new. It is merely reworded, as if she believes I am too dense to understand, and she needs to find the right words. I tried to cut her presentation short by saying nothing had changed. Hockley is senior. The course is his so long as he wants it. But she launched into her plea anyway. I tried to shoo her out even as she was talking. But she wouldn't budge."

I smiled at him. "I'm going to ask a question you may not want to answer. Is seniority the only reason Hockley has the course instead of Jollo?"

He smiled back at me. He picked up a pencil and wrote on a small pad. He held up the paper, which read, *He is a better painter.* Then he put the paper in his mouth and chewed on it. I thought he might complete the gag by swallowing it, but he took the chewed mass out and dropped it into the waste can.

"Can't be too careful," he said.

"What if you told her she can be the painting teacher as soon as her paintings start selling for ten thousand dollars?"

"She would likely become even more difficult to deal with." He thought for a moment and added, "If that is even possible. At any rate, she stayed so long that by the time I got back to the gallery to turn the camera on, some of the guests had already arrived. At that point, I didn't regret not remembering. I didn't think it mattered. It was only after Detective Fletcher questioned me that I understood the magnitude of my error. Fletcher believes someone went into the gallery and suffocated poor Ximena by cutting off her air supply. If I had done my duty, that would have been videoed and the murderer would be in custody."

I felt sorry for the guy. "You don't know that," I said, trying to console him. "The murderer might have been disguised. Or kept his back to the camera. Having the camera on wouldn't guarantee his capture. And having it off won't prevent it. Very few murders are caught on video, but the police still manage to find the murderer in most cases."

"I hope you're right." He was silent for a moment before asking if there was anything else I wanted to know about the security camera.

"Can I see the video?"

"Seeing as how Fletcher referred you to me, I don't see why not."

He pushed some buttons on a remote and the monitor on the wall flickered slightly then showed Ximena and Alfred alone in the gallery talking. Then Shorter walked in and exchanged greetings with them. He retrieved a ladder from the closet and carried it close to the camera. He pulled a key ring from his pocket and started up the ladder. It was odd seeing his face get larger with each step.

Then the screen went dark.

After a second or two it comes on again. The early arrivers for the event are already there. I watched the top of Shorter's head as he descended the ladder.

"I don't need to see the rest of it," I said. No need to see myself "faint like a girl," as Fletcher so delicately described it.

Shorter nodded knowingly and hit the remote. The current feed from the gallery returned to the monitor. It showed the usual number of people in the gallery. None.

We sat in silence for a few seconds.

32

I returned to Sprits in Clay and entered through the alley just in time to hear the bong that indicates a customer.

That's the problem with bongs. They can't distinguish a customer from a homicide detective.

"So she kicked you out," said Whit Fletcher. "I coulda told you that would happen, Hubert. Dating a white guy was just a fling. Once she found out how the colored community felt about it, I figured you'd be out on your ear." He pulled at the top of his right ear as if trying to align it with the left one. "She must like older men. First you and now a black guy who's even older than you are."

"You went to her apartment?"

"'Course I did. I was looking for you, and that's where you been living."

The panic in my eyes must have prompted what he said next. "Don't worry. I didn't ask for you. Soon as I saw the black guy open the door, I knew the score. No sense letting the cat outta the bag."

"So you said nothing about me?"

"What'd I just say? When I seen him at the door and Sharice there in the background, I showed 'em my shield and made up a story about a tip concerning a suspicious person hanging around the building."

"You lied to them?"

"If *you* gave that story, you'd be lying. When I gave it, it was in the line of duty. To protect and serve."

"Who were you protecting?"

"You, Hubert. You wouldn't want the new boyfriend paying you an unwelcome visit, would you?"

"Tell me about him."

He shook his head slowly. "The less you know the better. Why torture yourself thinking about her with another man?"

"He's not another man. He's her father."

"Hmm. He don't look like her. Big dude. Black as the ace of spades. Sharice is a wisp of a girl and medium-skinned. Must take after her mother. Maybe her mother was white."

I knew that wasn't the case, because I had seen her picture. The only thing I knew about her mother was she was deceased. And for the first time—call me slow-witted if you want—I wondered if Sharice's mother had died from breast cancer.

"So he came to meet his daughter's new boyfriend?"

I didn't want to discuss Sharice's father with Whit, particularly the part about the promise. "He came for Thanksgiving."

"Kinda early, ain't he?"

"The Canadian Thanksgiving is this Monday."

"That a fact? Well, Hubert, I'm afraid you won't be giving thanks for what I'm about to tell you. Maybe you better sit down."

33

Susannah dropped her chip back into the bowl. "A straw? The prints they wanted to compare yours to were on a straw?"

"No. Whit still won't tell me where they found those first prints. Now they have a second set of prints."

"And they're on a straw?"

"Yeah. And both sets of prints are mine."

I'd headed to Dos Hermanas after Whit left at four thirty. I spent twenty minutes resisting the temptation to order a margarita. When Susannah arrived, I told her they found my prints on a straw while she was waving at Angie.

Actually, they found my prints on the straw about two days before Susannah waved at Angie. Whit had come to tell me as soon as he was able and advised me to see my lawyer because he figured I was likely to be arrested.

No, that's not right either. My lawyer didn't figure I'd be arrested. Whit did.

I was so discombobulated by Whit's news that even now I lose track of sequences and people in trying to recall it.

"So exactly how many prints did you leave?" she asked after Angie brought the margaritas.

"I don't know. Here's what I do know. They found one—"

"Wait, let's do this systematically. We can't solve this thing unless we have all the clues lettered. Call the first set of prints Set A."

There's no arguing with her when she wants to use what she calls her police procedural approach, and in this case, I needed a bit of organization anyway.

"Okay. We don't know anything about the prints in Set A except they're connected with Ximena. They found Set B on a straw—"

"No. Set B are the ones Whit made on Tuesday."

"We have to letter those too?"

"Of course."

"Okay. Set C were found on a straw. Which looked like bad news."

She turned up her palms. "So you used a straw because you don't want your lips to touch a glass. All that proves is you're finicky and . . . oh my God, it was a straw from Ximena's nose."

I nodded.

"How do they know it's one of those straws?"

"It had my prints on one end and Ximena's nasal mucus on the other."

"They did a DNA match?"

I nodded again.

"You said you never touched anything in the gallery except maybe the walls and floor."

"Right. And I know for certain I never touched the straws in her nose. I never got closer than ten feet to Ximena in the gallery. I didn't even know it was Ximena until they took the plaster off and she toppled backward."

"So how do you explain the police having a straw with your prints on one end and Ximena's nasal gunk on the other?"

I smiled. "Easy. Junior Prather is trying to frame me."

"Yes!" She said excitedly. "Let me see your hands."

I held them up.

"Shoot. You're not missing a finger."

We've been friends so long that nothing she says surprises me.

"Is that bad?"

"Not in general, but it would have explained your prints on the straw."

"Okay, I'll bite. How would it explain my prints on the straw?"

"Because Prather could have put a print on the straw with your severed finger and you wouldn't know about it."

"I think I would know about it if I had a severed finger. It's not something I'd be likely to overlook."

"You know what I mean."

"Actually, I don't. How could he make a print with a severed finger?"

"Happens all the time. A detective named Keith Gamble had a case that turned on a print from a severed finger. Except in this case the finger was a thumb."

"Someone had a thumb growing where a finger should be?"

"Of course not. The guy who had the thumb was Carson Reno, but it wasn't his thumb. He got it from a delivery guy."

"So this guy named Reno cut off the thumb of a delivery guy?"

"Don't be ridiculous. The delivery guy just delivered it. He didn't know it was a thumb because it was sealed in a package."

"Probably a good idea. Getting out of a UPS truck with a severed thumb in your hand would be bad for business."

"Probably. Anyway, the case had several murders and a bunch of prints and the murderer had cut the thumb off one of the victims and used it to leave a print."

I was surprised to hear myself saying, "I think I understand it now."

She picked up the chip she had dropped into the bowl, loaded it with salsa and nodded encouragingly.

"The murderer kills someone on Monday and cuts off the thumb of the victim. Call the victim John Doe," I said. "Then on Tuesday he kills Jane Doe. He uses the severed thumb to put John Doe's thumbprint on the weapon hoping the police will think John Doe killed Jane Doe."

"How did you know one of the victims was a woman?"

"A lucky guess?"

"Admit it, you read the story."

"The story?"

"Yeah, it's called *The Fingerprint Murders* by Gerald Darnell, part of his Carson Reno Mystery Series."

"Ah. Well, just because it happened once in a book doesn't mean it could happen in real life."

"It didn't happen just once. In another case, Oscar Wilde and Arthur Conan Doyle met by chance at a spa in Germany. Doyle was sorting through letters addressed to Sherlock Holmes."

"People wrote letters to Sherlock Holmes?"

"Sure. Elvis gets tons of fan letters every year."

"I imagine he does. But Elvis was a real person."

"And now he's dead, which makes him fictional in real life."

I had no reply to that and took a sip of my margarita to brace myself for what I imagined was coming next.

"Anyway," she continued with gusto, "one of the letters addressed to Holmes contained a severed finger. Wilde and Doyle set out to discover who the finger belonged to, and they solve the mystery of where the finger came from, plus another murder that happens when they get to the Vatican."

I decided not to inquire about why and how Wilde and Doyle got from Germany to the Vatican and asked instead whether the two actually knew each other.

"They did. They met by chance when J. M. Stoddart, the American who published *Lippincott's Magazine*, went to England seeking writers. They were interviewed by him on the same evening and became friends."

"Stoddart must have had an eye for talent," I said. "Can you imagine interviewing Oscar Wilde and Arthur Doyle on the same evening?"

"Arthur *Conan* Doyle, Hubie. You have to use all three names."

"Why? I don't call you Susannah Dolores Inchaustigui."

"That's because Dolores is my middle name."

"And Conan was Doyle's middle name."

"No. His middle name was Ignatius."

"Really? I never heard that before. Where did the Conan part come in?"

"It must be one of those double-barrel English last names.

Like Olivia Newton-John, Andrew Lloyd-Webber or Camilla Parker-Bowles."

"But it's simply Arthur Conan Doyle, not Arthur Conan hyphen Doyle," I said.

"Well of course not," she replied. "Who would name someone Hyphen?"

I dropped it and moved back to Wilde, telling her he once visited New Mexico.

"Where?" she asked. "Even better, why?"

"He made a tour of the States in the late nineteenth century. He gave lectures in New York, Boston, San Francisco, all the places you might expect people to turn out for an English poet and writer. But one of his stops was in Leadville."

"Leadville's not in New Mexico. It's in Colorado."

"I know that. It was a raucous town with thirty thousand miners and a hundred saloons. For some unknown reason, it also had an impressive opera house, which may explain why Leadville got added to the itinerary. Wilde came out onstage in a purple Hungarian smoking jacket, knee breeches, silk stockings and diamond jewelry. Then he began his lecture, which was titled, 'The Practical Application of the Aesthetic Theory to Exterior and Interior House Decoration with Observations on Dress and Personal Ornament.'"

She shook her head. "To an audience of miners? Can you imagine what they thought of him?"

"I don't have to imagine it. He wrote about it. He said when he read them passages from the autobiography of Benvenuto Cellini, they asked why he hadn't brought Cellini with him. When he told them Cellini was dead, they asked who shot him."

"Well, at least they were interested enough to ask about Cellini."

"Yes, but the stagehands evidently decided Wilde was too 'sissified' and pushed him into the orchestra pit. Then they dragged him back up onstage and announced they were going to get him drunk then hand him over to the ministrations of a local lady of the evening to make a man out of him. Their plan was thwarted when he managed to drink them all under the table. When they passed out, his handlers spirited him south to Antonito, Colorado, where they boarded the Chili Line railroad to Santa Fe."

"The Chili Line?"

"Great name, right? The little village of Tres Piedras north of Taos still has the water tower the train used to top off its boiler when it stopped there."

"Why are we talking about this?"

"Because you were trying to explain how my fingerprints got on the straw that was in Ximena's nose, and you brought up the severed-finger thing."

"Oh, right. So how did your fingerprint get there?"

"You'll be proud of me, Suze. I solved the mystery. See, the important thing is not *how* my fingerprints got on that straw—it's *when*. My fingerprints got on the straw on Friday, September third. That was the afternoon of the departmental meeting. Prather served tea in Styrofoam cups with straws in them. He collected them afterwards and must have saved the straw from my cup. He then inserted one end into Ximena's nose, being careful not to smudge the other end, where my print was."

"Why would he do that?"

"Because he killed Ximena. And then tried to blame it on me so that he wouldn't be charged with murder."

"But why you?"

"Two reasons. First, he doesn't like me. He won't even talk to me."

"But he does."

"Only because he has a strange concept of 'not talking to.'"

"And the second reason?"

"I'm the only one who was expendable."

"Why?"

"Because they're already fuming over the fact that Freddie's position was not filled. If another art professor goes to prison, they'd have two empty slots. That would make art seem like a dying department. But losing a lowly adjunct is nothing."

"Why did he kill her?"

"I have no idea."

"I thought you solved the mystery."

"I solved the mystery of my prints being on the straw. I also figured out who did it. I have to let the police do something, so I'm leaving the motive question for them."

"You tell Fletcher that?"

"Not in those words. But I did tell him I think Prather killed Ximena."

"He agreed?"

I shook my head.

"I bet he also didn't buy your cockamamie story about the straw from the tea?"

"Of course he bought it. It's brilliant."

"More like bizarre. The police find your prints on a straw that was obviously in Ximena's nose and they let you walk because you claim it must be a straw from a departmental meeting that was weeks ago? Why would Prather save the straw?"

"I already told you—to frame me. And there's something else. That's the only straw in the universe that has my print on it, so it has to be the one from the departmental meeting."

"You never use straws?"

"I drink coffee, tap water, Champagne, margaritas and beer. Which one of those would you put a straw in?"

"I see your point. But the cops aren't going to take your word for it. So unless they think Prather has a motive for framing you, you're going to stay on the suspect list."

I shook my head. "There's another reason for them to buy my story. They have only one straw."

"Of course! And Ximena had two nostrils."

"Right. Because she isn't a hagfish."

"What the devil is a hagfish?"

"One of the few animals that has only one nostril."

"You know more useless facts than anyone else on Planet Earth. I suppose you're going to tell me it has a dozen eyes so that its sense of sight can make up for its poor sense of smell, like that baloney compensation theory about people who lack one sense having their others become more acute."

"Hagfish have the usual two eyes. But it doesn't matter because they live down deep where there's not much light. They are disgusting creatures. They bore into big fish and eat them slowly from the inside out."

"Charming. Let's get back to your theory."

"It's simple. If I had murdered Ximena by cutting off her air, there would have to be two straws with my prints on one end and her mucus on the other. And if Prather had them both, he would have given both to the police to make the frame stronger. So the fact that there is only one straw fits my story. Drinking tea results in one straw with prints. Closing off two nostrils results in two straws with prints."

"Prather gave the straw to the police?"

"Who else?"

"What did Whit say?"

"He wouldn't tell me how they got the straw."

"What's your best guess?"

"Maybe Prather mailed it to them via UPS like the thumb that went to Carson Reno."

Angie brought us a second round, which prompted Susannah to check her watch.

"It's past six," she noted. "Where is everybody?"

"Martin just drops in when he happens to be in town. It's Friday night, so Tristan probably has a date. Maybe Glad and Gladys are also on a date. I still can't believe they're engaged."

"What about Sharice?" she asked.

"She's also not married, but not for lack of effort on my part."

"I meant where is she?"

"With her father."

"She's spending the weekend in Montreal?"

"No. He's spending the weekend here."

She brightened. "He's come to meet his future son-in-law."

"No." I hesitated then exhaled. "He doesn't know I exist."

"Ohhhh. So she's breaking the news to him. I guess it makes sense she wouldn't want you there when she says, 'Guess who's coming to dinner!'"

"That was about a white girl who brings home a black guy she plans to marry. This is a bit different."

"Right. You're the remake where a black girl brings home a white guy."

"There was a remake?"

"Yeah, but they changed the title to *Guess Who*. Bernie Mac played the father who was dead set against his daughter marrying a white guy. His attempts to break them up were hilarious."

"Sounds like Sharice's father. But without the humor."

"Since he doesn't know you exist, how can you know he's not like the Bernie Mac character?"

"He asked her to promise him she wouldn't marry a white man."

"And did she?"

I nodded.

"When was that?"

"I don't know exactly, but it was before she came to the States."

She shrugged. "Ancient history. And anyway, you two living together more or less negates the promise."

"More less than more."

"Is that like 'less is more?'"

"More or less."

I ate a chip and slumped back in my chair.

"Don't worry about it, Hubie. Bernie Mac comes to accept Ashton Kutcher as his future son-in-law."

"This is real life. Love stories don't always have happy endings."

"You think I don't know that?"

I winced. The first guy Susannah dated after we became friends turned out to be married. And she was dating Freddie when he went to prison. Or as Helga phrased it, when I sent him to prison.

"Sorry to bring up painful memories."

"You know me. Bulletproof."

"And you're with Baltazar now, so that's good."

"Baltazar and I broke up," she said, and started crying.

I guess she isn't bulletproof after all.

34

Neither am I.

What little sleep I got was marred by fitful dreams featuring a woman who kept morphing from Susannah to Sharice, Sharice to Ximena, Ximena back to Susannah.

I was groggy when the sun finally peeked over the Sandias.

I brewed more bitter coffee. After three cups, my metabolism was on life support.

I couldn't face sitting there thinking about Sharice and her father. I removed my hand from the doorknob and put it in my pocket, where I found the key to the Bronco. Geronimo rode shotgun as we headed down Second Street into the south valley to the little adobe that has been a second home to me since my parents died.

Which is natural, since the woman who lives there is like a second mother to me. Consuela Saenz entered the Schuze household the same year I did. I as *niño*, she as *niñera*.

Almost half a century later, she is now Consuela Sanchez, wife of Emilio Sanchez and mother of Ninfa Sanchez, who continued to be Ninfa Sanchez after she married. Not because of a feminist desire to keep her last name but because she married a guy named Beto Sanchez.

I suspect Consuela and Emilio don't like Beto any more than I do, but they are too proper to say so. I'm not. So I'll tell you he is arrogant and condescending to Consuela and Emilio. And to their neighbors. And to me.

Come to think of it, he's condescending to everyone in New Mexico. He's the Ugly American and we are his Third World country.

Susannah says it's because he's from California. But he lives in Irvine, for God's sake. Not Napa. How can being from Orange County make you haughty?

His other major flaw is that he doesn't want children. Consuela's one remaining wish is to have a grandchild. Or—even better—several of them.

She met me at the front door and took me out the back door to the patio, where Emilio was grilling *arrachera* marinated in smoked paprika and lime juice. The smoke from the barilla went through my nose and straight to my stomach, where it made its presence known audibly. A cold Modelo Especial kept my innards under control while the tacos were prepared.

Consuela asked why I hadn't brought Sharice.

"Her father is here. I think they need some time alone."

Emilio smiled and said, "You have asked for her hand and they are talking of it?"

I hesitated then said, "Yes, I have asked her to marry me. I hope he will approve."

"*Claro*," said Emilio. "He should be proud to have you as a son."

"I hope you are right," I said. Then, to change the subject, I told Consuela she seemed to be getting younger.

She blushed and said, "Is because of the new kidney."

The kidney came from Ninfa. The cost was shared between Medicaid and Hubieaid. I earned my share by selling a pot. The same government that runs Medicaid would have jailed me for digging up that pot. Doesn't bother me. I have the satisfaction of knowing the potter likes her work being admired. And she's glad it saved Consuela's life.

Emilio said, "It seems to me a *milagro*, Uberto, that they can take the kidney from one person and put it in another."

"Yes. That's why they call it a miracle of modern medicine."

"But I worry about Ninfa," said Consuela. "She has now only one kidney."

"Millions of people have only one kidney and lead perfectly normal lives."

"So you have told me, but—"

"Let us eat," said Emilio.

He sliced the *arrachera* and covered it with grilled onions and Serrano peppers in the folded corn tortillas.

We were sitting on homemade lawn chairs made from woven willow branches. Sunlight filtered through the pecan trees, which still had most of their leaves. A faint breeze carried the smell of dry grass.

Consuela reminded me that Día de Muertos was only a few weeks away by asking, "You will visit the grave of your parents?"

"Of course. And I will take *cempasúchil*."

Cempasúchil is the Náhuatl word for marigolds. The Aztecs called them the flowers of death.

I wondered if anyone would visit Ximena's grave. I doubted she had one. I feared her mortal remains were still in a refrigerated drawer at the medical school awaiting the possibility of further examination if there was a murder trial.

I passed from my former residence through my pottery workshop into my store to see something I rarely see. A customer. This was one of the rarest. He was black.

35

I've been in business for twenty years and had maybe ten black customers. One every two years qualifies as rare.

But the oddest thing about this particular man was that I knew who he was. And when I realized that, I also realized he wasn't a customer.

He was carrying something I had made, a black coffee mug with my signature in white letters.

"Are you Hubert Schuze?"

"I am."

He held the mug up for me to see.

"I believe this belongs to you."

Drat. She told me to get everything out, and I was scrupulous about it. Toiletries, clothes, even Geronimo's leash. I hadn't looked in the kitchen cupboards because all the dishes were hers.

Except for the mugs.

"You are mistaken, sir. That does not belong to me."

He was tall and gaunt. I could see where Sharice got her long limbs and lithe muscles.

"It has your signature on it," he said.

"The Declaration of Independence has John Hancock's signature on it, but it doesn't belong to him."

When his eyes narrowed, I could see Sharice's almond eye shape. "This is hardly a joking matter."

"It was an analogy, not a joke. I formed that mug. I signed it. I fired it. Then I gave it to your daughter. It belongs to her."

"What is your relationship with my daughter?"

"Would you like a cup of coffee? I have some New Mexico Piñon Coffee you might enjoy."

"This is not a social call. I repeat the question. What is your relationship with my daughter?"

"I am in love with her."

"Are the two of you sleeping together?"

There was no way in hell that I was going to answer that question.

"Mr. Clarke, you and your late wife did a terrific job raising Sharice. She is intelligent, inquisitive, kind, quick-witted, focused and free of the psychoses and neuroses that seem to plague so many people of her generation. You must know what a sound person she is. If she has decided or ever does decide to sleep with a man, she will do so for reasons that even a father could not object to."

"That's a nice speech, Mr. Schuze. But it is not an answer."

"It's the only answer you will get. And the only one you are entitled to. Sharice is a grown woman. If and when she is ready to tell you about her love life, she will do so." For some reason I cannot fathom, I took a step toward him before continuing. "And neither you nor I have the right to deprive her of her right to handle that information on her own terms."

His jaw was clenched so tightly that he seemed to have grown muttonchops.

He finally loosed his muscles enough to speak. "Can you at least tell me what your intentions are?"

"I have asked Sharice to marry me."

"I feared as much. You two are making a grave mistake."

"She's your daughter. Your only child. You should be able to read her better than anyone. Does she seem to you like a woman who's making a mistake. Is she unhappy?"

"It's not the present I'm worried about. It's the future. Neither of you has any idea what you're letting yourself in for, what it's like to be a mixed couple."

"No disrespect sir, but we know more about it than you do. You and your wife were not a mixed couple. My parents were not a mixed couple. Sharice and I are a mixed couple, but we are not fools. We know some people will dislike us merely because we are together. We've already experienced that. But why should we care about the opinions of bigots?"

He was silent, his countenance not quite so knotted. "Sharice will decide whom to marry. I understand that. But I will not give my blessing for her to marry you."

"I think you will."

He bristled. "You doubt my word?"

"No. I doubt your ability to stick to your word. I think you will discover that you love her too much to withhold your blessing."

"Perhaps she will reject your proposal of marriage."

"I acknowledge the possibility."

"I will take my leave."

I offered my hand. He hesitated then shook it.

As he turned to go, I said, "Have a good flight tomorrow. I hope the Alouettes win the game."

He said thank you, but it didn't sound like he meant it.

36

Instead of going to La Hacienda, I went to bed. The drumming of the rain stopped in the middle of the night, allowing me to hear the rumbling of my stomach.

I made a mental note to store some canned goods for emergencies.

At 6:00 a.m., I was at the door of the Blake's Lotaburger on Rio Grande Boulevard a few blocks north of my residence. Blake's is a New Mexico chain with about seventy locations across the state. You used to be able to spot one from five miles away because of their distinctive signs, a tall stick-figure man dressed in red, white and blue with a matching top hat. His legs were the poles supporting the sign, his fingers held the sign and his cartoon face looked a bit like Curious George.

The Blake's on Rio Grande has the strip-mall look. Sadly, New Mexico's kitschy architecture is disappearing.

At least the menu is the same. I ordered the #7 from the breakfast menu. Most New Mexicans know that's the Southwest Burrito with fresh egg, tomatoes, onions, Hatch Valley green chile and cheese.

Then I ordered two more, one more for me, since I had fasted all day Sunday, and one for Geronimo since he was tired of the canned dog food.

Despite the double breakfast, I was still hungry at lunch. I walked over to La Placita, passed among the Indians plying their turquoise and silver wares under the restaurant's covered portal, slipped past the staircase imported from Spain by the family patriarch for his daughter's wedding in 1872, and chose the table closest to the ancient cottonwood tree that was planted in the courtyard and still lives there even though the courtyard was converted years ago to an enclosed dining room.

I chose the table by the tree because it's one of the tables covered by Susannah.

"I guess your future father-in-law is still in town," she said, "or you wouldn't be here."

"He left town about thirty minutes ago on the United flight to Houston."

"Houston's on the way to Montreal?"

"Only if you're flying."

The historic Casa de Armijo that houses La Placita is fascinating, but the best feature about the restaurant—aside from Susannah—is the salsa that makes your eyes water even before you taste it. It is best to have a cold *cerveza* at the ready before eating the fiery concoction.

Susannah brought me a Corona and said, "Have you heard the news about Harte Hockley?"

"I'm back at Spirits in Clay. Where would I hear news?"

"It's good news, Hubie. You're off the hook. Harte Hockley was arrested this morning for the murder of Ximena Sifuentes."

I dropped the tortilla chip back into the bowl and placed the beer glass back on the table. "Why would Harte Hockley kill Ximena?"

"I have no idea. I'm just telling you what I heard on the radio on the way to work. You remember radios, right? Little boxes with voices coming out of them."

My only radio is a satellite model and the only thing that comes out of it is swing music from the '40s. It's what my father listened to. I remembered how he exercised exclusive control over what records were played on our old hi-fi and what channel the television was tuned to. I was probably five or six before I realized there was any other sort of music. David Bowie sounded so odd to me that I stuck with the stuff that had been imprinted on me. And now David Bowie is dead. Where did the years go?

I pulled myself out of the reverie and thought about Hockley. A successful painter. A good-looking and charming fellow. Why would he kill anyone?

For that matter, why would anyone kill anyone?

Susannah brought my lunch, but my appetite was gone.

37

I was longing to see Sharice, but she was at work.

We hadn't discussed my return to the condo. I'd assumed I would go back after her father left, but my insecurities were making an unwelcome house call. Why did Mr. Clarke say, "Perhaps she will reject your proposal of marriage"? Did he think he had made progress in convincing her to keep the promise not to marry a white man? Was she upset that I accidentally left the mug? Did she think I left it on purpose? Had she and her father quarreled about the mug and what it meant?

The phone rang.

"Hubie," Sharice said when I answered, "will you come home, please?"

"As fast as I possibly can."

She opened the door to the condo while staying behind it. Good idea, since she was naked. Benz was on the balcony. I shoved a reluctant Geronimo out there. We sprinted to the bathroom. The shower was running. The room was full of steam.

It got steamier.

We'd been apart only four days. It's not like we can't go four days without making love. We're not sex maniacs.

Our passion wasn't fueled by the lapse of time as much as by the uncertainty.

Did she want me back after her father's visit? Would I come back after his visit to me?

At some point after our heart rates dropped below three figures, she put her head on my chest and said, "He likes you."

"He managed not to show it."

"I was mad at him when he told me he'd gone to see you. And I was a bit peeved at you for not remembering to take the mugs."

"Sorry."

"But after he told me, I was glad he did it. Now everything is out in the open."

"No more things on your I-have-to-tell-you-these-things-one-at-a-time list?"

She gave me a coy smile. "Maybe. You want to know something he said that's really neat?"

"What?"

"He said if I insisted on dating a white man, you were a good choice."

"Isn't that like saying 'Since you insist on dating a fat girl, it's good the one you chose doesn't sweat much?'"

She gave me a love bite and asked about my conversation with her father.

"He asked blunt questions, and I gave him blunt answers."

"No wonder he liked you. He likes straightforward people."

"I'm not all that straightforward," I admitted.

"What were his blunt questions?"

"He asked if we were sleeping together."

"I figured as much. What did you say?"

"I said, 'Twice every day, seven days a week.'"

"Seriously. What did you say?"

"I said if you had decided or ever did decide to sleep with a man, you would do so for reasons that even a father could not object to."

"Perfect. What did he say?"

"He said that wasn't an answer. I told him it was the only one he was going to get and the only one he was entitled to."

"That is blunt."

She lifted her head off my chest and gave me a look that said, *Now you have to ask me the same question.*

So I did. "Did he also ask you if we were sleeping together?"

"Yes. After he told me he had searched you out and you hadn't answered the question."

Her pause prompted another question.

"So, what did you tell him?"

She scooted up closer to me, our faces inches apart. "I told him you are the first man I've ever slept with." She kissed me. "And I told him you are the last man I'll ever sleep with."

I jumped out of bed and yelled, "Yes!" I looked at her and said, "Does that mean you'll marry me?"

She looked down and then back up at my face. "Are both of you proposing?"

Okay, I probably should have gotten dressed. Or at least stayed under the sheets. But it wasn't the first time I'd asked her, so it hardly needed to be formal. And standing in the nude is about as informal as you can get.

"I don't want this ever to end," she said. "But I still have some thinking to do about the marriage part."

"Remember when you tricked me into telling you about my history with women?"

"I didn't trick you into it."

"Yes, you did. You said it was one of those things on your I-have-to-tell-you-one-at-a-time list, and you made me go first. But you didn't have anything to tell, so it was a trick."

"And why are you bringing this up?"

"You remember my last girlfriend before you was Dolly Aquirre?"

"Did you propose to her?"

"No. You're the first person I've ever proposed to. And like you said to your father, you are the last person I will ever propose to."

"That's sweet, Hubie. But my question still stands. Why bring this up?"

"Because she told me she wanted to be my girlfriend but didn't want to marry me. So I'm wondering why it is that girls hesitate to marry me. Am I like the convertible Hertz rented to you one weekend? It was fun to drive but not practical to own?"

"Don't be silly. You're more of a compact car than a convertible."

"Thanks."

She kissed the frown off my face.

38

The next few weeks were uneventful. I began to think life would return to normal.

You already know it didn't, because otherwise why mention it?

It was a lazy Saturday. I was on a bench in Old Town, about to nod off when I heard, "Gud marnink, Youbird."

"Good morning, Father," I answered.

I didn't have to look up to know it was Father Groas, the priest from Old Town's San Felipe de Neri Church. He's the only person in Old Town with an eastern European accent. It is less noticeable when he speaks Spanish because the vowel sounds and extended *s*'s of his native tongue fit better than they do with English.

When I mentioned that theory to the good father, he said, "Is true. Wass easy to learn Spanish bot difficult to learn Anglish."

"It was a snap for me."

He laughed. "Wass easy for me to learn Rusyn."

Not Russian. Rusyn. The Rusyns consider themselves to be the indigenous inhabitants of Carpathia, part of which is in Ukraine. The official Ukrainian position is that the Rusyns are Ukrainians and the Rusyn language is a merely backward dialect of Ukrainian. Sort of what we in America think of people from Boston. It sounds funny when they add an *r* to the end of Cuba, but they are not speaking a foreign language. It is merely a dialect of English.

He sat next to me. "I think Got plan this meeting, Youbird. I wass trying to find you to suggest you attend this year's Día de Muertos tomorrow."

"I'm not Catholic, Father."

"Yass, you always say so. But am I not your priest?"

"I am proud to claim you as my spiritual adviser. But I seldom attend Mass."

"Tomorrow is special, Día de Muertos. I wass told one of your students died. The Holy Sacrifice of the Mass will be offered. The names of the dead will be written on luminarias, which will line the steps in front of the nave. You would like to add a name?"

"Yes. Ximena Sifuentes."

I walked with Father Groas back to the church. After he entered his office, I went to the parish gift shop next door and bought a Calavera Catrina carved by a *santera* named Marie Romero Cash.

My official class roll included an email address for each student. Tristan gave me a laptop, but its sole duty is security. It maintains the pictures snapped automatically when anyone enters or exits the shop. And even if I knew how to send an email, I couldn't do so because the laptop is not connected to the Internet.

Which seems to me a great advantage. Susannah's email address was recently hacked, which resulted in her friends receiving messages that purported to be from her but were actually viruses.

Not surprisingly, Tristan gets most of his email from women. They fall into two groups: attractive coeds who are hoping for a date and Nigerian widows whose husbands were bank presidents, a job that must be highly stressful considering how many widows it has created.

I'm not opposed to the Internet. I'm just waiting until they get it debugged.

I knew Tristan sleeps late, so I walked at a leisurely pace, composing an email in my head.

I committed a misdemeanor by letting Geronimo off his leash. No one complained. He knows the way to Tristan's apartment and is disinclined to explore unfamiliar territory.

Tristan answered the door in his underwear.

"Sorry. Just got out of the shower."

I sniffed the air. "You using mothball-scented soap?"

"New underwear. Mom sends me a package of new briefs four times a year. She always packs them with mothballs."

"That's a lot of underwear."

"Yeah. She says I need to have new underwear each time the season changes."

Nothing she does surprises me, so I didn't respond to that.

"I think you forgot to pull off one of the labels on that pair."

He looked down and retrieved a white slip of paper protruding from near his hip bone. Then he read it to me.

"'You may not have everything you want. But you have everything you need.'" His face was red. "She sends little notes in each pair. Sort of underwear fortune cookies."

"You have a great mom, Tristan. Look how good you turned out."

I handed him the napkin with my draft email. It read:

I hope you can join me tomorrow morning at San Felipe de Neri Church in Old Town at 10 a.m. for a Mass celebrating the Day of the Dead. There will be a prayer for Ximena, and a luminaria will be lit with her name on it. I will give extra credit to all who attend. I suspect God may do the same.

"You want to leave in the part about God?" Tristan asked when he got to the last sentence. "Some people are sort of touchy on the topic of religion."

"Who would object to saying God might give you credit for going to church?"

"The Church of Euthanasia might."

"Is that a joke?"

"No, there's actually a religion with that name. They believe the earth is being destroyed by humans because there are too many of us. Instead of ten commandments, they have only one: Thou shalt not procreate."

"So they want to save the planet by having humans become extinct?"

"Exactly. And since the Catholic Church is against birth control, Church of Euthanasia members would especially not want to go to Mass."

"I think Edward Abbey might have joined that church had he known about it."

39

I awoke at nine the next morning to the sound of rain and the silence of anxiety.

Albuquerque gets afternoon thunderstorms, not morning drizzle.

I showered and shaved. Ironed a pair of chinos and a blue shirt.

Using my Tilley hat as raingear, I trotted to the Bronco, drove to Old Town and trotted again to San Felipe de Neri Church.

It was dark and smelled of candles and wet wool. My students were huddled on the rearmost bench. The looks on their faces seemed to say they were happy to be near the door in case they had to beat a hasty retreat. Probably not regular attendees.

Susannah, Aleesha and Carly had brought scarves. I sat next to Mia and handed her my handkerchief.

"Put this on your head."

"Why?"

"Because I say so."

She did.

Father Groas introduced himself to each of them after the service. If any of them were unhappy about the Catholic doctrine on birth control, they kept it to themselves.

He was a hit with my charges. With his Transylvania accent,

bushy black beard and outsize robes, he is something of a spectacle. He is also a raconteur.

Raúl challenged him about the day of the dead. "Shouldn't modern churches reject pagan beliefs?"

"Do you study art history?"

"I do."

"And do you not begin your study with such things as the cave paintings of Lascaux?"

"Yes."

"Why?"

"Because they are the earliest evidence of human creativity."

"Just so," said the good father as he stroked his beard. "Pagan beliefs are the earliest ahvidence of human awareness of a greater power. Chust as the seed of the great painters of the Renaissance can be seen in cave paintings, so too can the seeds of modern religion be found in our pagan past."

Raúl nodded.

Father Groas turned to the parishioners now gathered on the steps in front of the nave. "The luminarias khave the names of our brothers and sisters who went to the Lord this year. Regrettably, the lighting must be canceled becoss of the rain. But the light of those we honor today can naaver be extinguished." He thrust his hand forward and made the sign of the cross. "Go in Peace to love and serve the Lord."

My students located the luminaria with Ximena's name on it. They encircled it silently, rain dripping from their eyebrows and noses.

Except for Mia, who remained next to me.

"Here's your handkerchief back. Thanks for helping me not look so stupid. But it doesn't change anything."

I handed her the gadget Tristan had given me after the class when Mia had requested extra credit. "There's something on this you need to listen to."

I punched the button and handed the miniature recorder to her.

She placed it against her ear. Then she looked down. She handed it back to me.

"What are you going to do?" she asked.

"Nothing."

"What do you want me to do?"

"I want you to come to class. I want you to learn how to handle clay. I want you to make a pot and sell it as part of our fund-raiser for Ximena."

"That's it?"

"That's it."

She walked away.

A couple dressed in black approached Father Groas. He read the paper they handed him then led them to Ximena's luminaria. The students moved away discreetly.

The woman began to cry. The man put his arm around her shoulder.

Susannah stepped forward and signed to them. They smiled at her and signed. The conversation lasted ten minutes. Then she called me over and introduced me to Señor and Señora Miguel Sifuentes.

40

Susannah handed me the notebook Señora Sifuentes had given her. It was six by nine, bound in black leather and had a red ribbon connected to its spine. I opened the notebook to the page marked by the ribbon and read out loud.

Your words are temporary
mere ripples in the air
betraying your thoughts to strangers

My words are forever
curves and lines on a page
cloaked in the silence of my life

I see your every word
You know none of mine

"Ximena wrote this?"

Susannah nodded. "Her mother said she loved writing poetry."

The Sifuenteses had accepted my invitation to have coffee. They and Susannah signed. I brewed coffee and watched. There was a lot of finger spelling.

I read another poem.

I decline the offer of an interpreter
interpretari – from the Latin – *understand*
Lips and ears are not required
Only mind

"So what did you learn?" I asked.

"They live in Gallinas Canyon north of Montezuma. They work for a wealthy woman who owns about a mile of riverfront full of plants and animals."

"The river is full of plants and animals?"

"The land next to it is. Señora Sifuentes is the housekeeper. Señor Sifuentes is the farmhand. Mows the fields. Feeds the animals. The woman was visiting her daughter on the island of Majorca when Ximena died, so they only learned of it a few days ago."

"Do they have other children?"

"No. After Ximena was born, their employer paid for them to get DNA testing. They both tested positive for GJB2 and GJB6 mutations."

"In English?"

"Any child they have will almost certainly be deaf."

"And you know this because Mark had those mutant genes?"

"He had only one. My parents had neither, so their having a deaf child was just random. But if both parents have mutations of both genes, any child they have is almost certainly going to be deaf. They said they didn't want another deaf child."

"Ms. Nose might be very angry with them. She'd say they're rejecting their own culture."

"That wasn't the reason they decided not to have another child. They aren't ashamed of being deaf. But they know the challenges being deaf presents and wanted to concentrate on helping Ximena. They are so proud of her. Did you know she was an honor student?"

I shook my head. "It's hard to tell when you're teaching a studio class. Although it's pretty obvious that Raúl is brilliant and Mia is not."

"Why did you hand Mia a cell phone?"

"It wasn't a cell phone. It's a small recorder."

I retrieved it and handed it to her. She listened to the recording.

"She offered sex for a grade? That is so sad. Why did you record this?"

"To protect myself in case she gave a different version of what happened."

"And she did?"

"Yes. She filed a sexual harassment complaint about me."

"First an equal educational opportunity complaint, then a sexual harassment complaint. What's next? A violation of the Americans with Disabilities Act because you didn't recognize that Ximena was disabled?"

"Ms. Nose certainly wouldn't think she was. And I bet Ximena didn't think she was."

"But Ms. Nose might think Ximena was a traitor to the cause because she read lips. Some deaf people think that's a form of linguistic colonialism—being forced to use a language that is not your native tongue."

"*Native tongue* is probably the wrong phrase to use when describing sign language."

"Oops. But you understand what I'm saying, right?"

"Sure. But if deaf people don't learn to read lips, how can we communicate with them?"

She signed.

"Okay, we could all learn to sign. But only about one in a thousand people is deaf, so although it would be great if we could all sign, isn't it more practical for the one in a thousand to learn lip reading than for the other nine hundred and ninety-nine of us to learn signing?"

"Some deaf people would say it doesn't matter. They don't want to communicate with us anyway."

"Sounds a bit extreme, but I suppose everyone has the right to determine who they interact with."

"That's fine for adults, but what about children who have that decision made for them?"

"Are you saying some parents of deaf children won't let their kids play with hearing kids?"

"Yes. And some refuse to authorize medical procedures that would allow the child to hear."

"Wouldn't that fall under some child welfare law like those current cases where states are prosecuting parents for child abuse for refusing medical care to their dying children because of their religious beliefs?"

"Being deaf doesn't kill you, Hubie. Look at it this way. Suppose there was some sort of high-tech headphone thing that would filter incoming sounds and only accept English words. And suppose someone had made Martin wear one of those from the time he was born. He never would have learned his tribe's language. Letting a deaf child have an implant so that he can hear reduces the likelihood that he will learn to sign, so it's like taking away his natural language."

"Signing is not a natural language."

"You said anthropologists think we signed before we spoke. So signing is more natural than speaking."

"Hmm. Maybe so. Why didn't your parents have Mark get a cochlear implant?"

"The Food and Drug Administration didn't approve cochlear implants for children under two until 2000. Mark was already four and progressing brilliantly in oral training."

We were silent for a minute or two.

I asked Susannah if she thought Ximena would have wanted an implant.

"Maybe. She liked poetry. Maybe she would have enjoyed hearing it."

41

An hour after Susannah left, someone knocked hard on the door.

I buzzed in Charles Webbe with the fancy gizmo Tristan gave me. I asked him if he was looking for Native American pottery.

"No. I'm looking for you. You hear that Harte Hockley was arrested for the murder of Ximena Sifuentes?"

"Susannah told me she heard it on the radio, but there were no details."

"There's one detail you'll find interesting. The primary evidence is his fingerprints."

"Let me guess—on a straw."

"On two straws. I guess they learned a lesson when they tried to make you a suspect. One straw is not enough."

"So it might be said that the second straw was the one that broke the case's back."

"I wouldn't say it. I don't pun. And I don't think Hockley did it."

"Why not?"

"You've heard of the Holy Trinity in murder cases, right?"

"Sure. Susannah is a big fan of murder mysteries, so I know about motive, means and opportunity."

"Hockley had the means and the opportunity, but so did everyone else in northern New Mexico. She was in the gallery alone for hours with no way to protect herself. Anyone could have walked in there and cut off her air."

"What about motive?"

"The theory is he was having an affair with Ximena. She threatened to tell his wife. So he killed her." He stared at me for a few seconds. "You buy that?"

"No."

"Why not?"

"Two reasons. First, Hockley doesn't strike me as someone who would have an affair with a student. But I don't know him well and could be wrong about that. I'm more certain of the second reason. I don't think Ximena would have been involved with a married man."

"You told me you hardly knew her."

"That's right. But I met her parents today, and I read a notebook full of poetry she wrote. I'm virtually certain she was not having an affair with Hockley."

He nodded. "You still have her notebook?"

I found it and gave it to him. He read the first few poems. Then he asked if I had any coffee.

I brewed the New Mexico Piñon Coffee he likes.

While Charles sipped coffee and read, I walked to the Golden Crown Panaderia on Mountain Road just east of Old Town and bought some cuernos de azucar.

I came back and brewed more coffee.

I fed Geronimo.

Charles finished the coffee, the cuernos and the notebook.

The furrows in his brow seemed even darker than his skin. I asked him what he was thinking about.

He held up the notebook. "I'm wondering if this could be introduced in court as evidence." He sighed and put the notebook on the table. "Maybe it won't get to court."

"Is there any evidence they were having an affair?"

"There's an allegation and a photograph of the two of them embracing. The embrace doesn't look intimate. It could just be a friendly greeting. The allegation is the problem."

"Who made it?"

"I'm going to tell you because I need your help. But you are not to tell anyone. Except Sharice."

"Why can I tell her? Do you also need her help?"

"No." He smiled. "I give you permission to tell her because I know you will, and I don't want you to feel guilty about it."

When I didn't say anything, he said, "People who sleep together share their secrets."

I nodded.

"The person who made the allegation is Jollo Bakkie."

"And the cops bought that? Don't they know she hates Hockley? She even gives bad grades to students who like him. The woman is a nut case."

"She has a written note from Ximena asking Jollo to help her break up with Hockley."

"Why would Ximena put something like that in writing?"

Charles just stared at me.

"Oh. Of course. Jollo doesn't know sign language, so Ximena would have to write to communicate with her. How do the police know the note is genuine?"

"The handwriting expert says it is. Needless to say, there are plenty of papers around with Ximena's writing on them. One of the challenges of being deaf—hard not to leave a paper trail."

"What does the note say?"

He showed me a photocopy of it. It read, "Hockley has been after me since I was a freshman. I fended him off for two years. But last semester, I gave in. It was great at first—exciting and new. Obviously something I'd never done before. But now he's making too many demands on me. I want out. But I don't know how to tell him. And I don't want to hurt him. Can you help me?"

"It's torn," I noted.

"You thinking part of the note might be missing?"

I nodded.

"Me too. But it's a complete story as-is. I don't think Hockley's attorney could prevent it being entered as evidence, and I don't think he would get far trying to speculate there was more to the note that would undermine what it clearly seems to say."

"So how can I help you?"

"I need information about the art department that only an insider can get."

"I'm not an insider. I'm just a first-semester adjunct teaching one course."

"You may be more of an insider than you think," he said. Then he gave me a big smile. "According to rumor, you sent their former department head to prison."

42

Visiting hours for Level I and Level II prisoners at the Central New Mexico Correctional Facility in Los Lunas are from 8:30 a.m. to 3:00 p.m. on Saturdays and Sundays.

Unless you know an FBI agent who knows the right people and sets up a visit on a Tuesday morning.

Los Lunas is thirty miles south of Albuquerque on Interstate 25. Unfortunately, that is not quite far enough to prevent it from becoming a bedroom community for Albuquerque.

If you're a language buff and thinking it should be *Las* Lunas because the Spanish word for moon is feminine, you are right. But the town is not named after moons. It's named after the Luna family that settled it.

The prison is on the east side of the freeway and is easily spotted because of its two parallel fences enclosing acres of bare sand on which not a single plant grows. Weed B Gon must be delivered there in tanker trucks.

Even though Charles had paved the way for my visit, it took half an hour to complete the required paperwork and be briefed by a corrections officer on the rule for visitors.

Frederick Blass was a Level I prisoner—lowest of the security levels—but I was still not allowed to be in a room with him. We faced each other through a polycarbonate window and talked via microphones.

I remembered Frederick as a leading man. Sort of a contemporary Errol Flynn. Tall and handsome with a high forehead, intelligent eyes, strong chin and sharp nose. He combed his wavy black hair casually back with no part. He had the voice and posture of an operatic baritone.

His penthouse on the top floor of Rio Grande Lofts looked more like a gallery than a residence, and he entertained there lavishly.

But the thing I remembered most about him was his sartorial flamboyance. The first time I ever saw him, he was wearing blue suede shoes. Likely the first man to do so since Elvis made them popular.

The man on the other side of the polycarbonate window wore black slippers. Shoelaces are on the contraband list. His shirt was faded blue cotton. "Blass" and "264983" were stenciled on it.

His hair was white and cropped short. The intelligent eyes were still there, but the glow of the raconteur was gone, replaced by a gaze that seemed to reflect wisdom.

"It's good to see you, Hubie."

"I thought you wouldn't want to see me."

"Why would you think that?"

"Because if it weren't for me—"

"I'm not here because of you. I'm here because of me. Or, more accurately, because of the man I used to be."

"You've changed?"

He nodded.

"This probably sounds weird," I said, "but even though your fancy clothes have been replaced with prison dungarees and your hair has gone white, you look good."

"That's nice to hear from someone on the other side of the glass. It's scary when someone in here says it."

"It must be horrible."

"The first few months were bad. I survived. Now I flourish."

"How so?"

"I teach. Not to a bunch of vapid youngsters like I did before. I teach hardened criminals to paint. They love it. The warden loves it. He says it's therapeutic. Maybe it is. What I see is guys who have always been losers, always done the wrong thing, finding out they can do something creative rather than destructive."

"What about your own art?"

"You saw my art. It was postmodernist crap. I knew what the collectors and critics liked, and I gave it to them. Calculating. But then that's who I was."

"And now?"

"I strive for authenticity." He smiled. "Like Sartre."

"Can I see your work?"

He held up a pencil sketch of Susannah dancing with a man out in the countryside. Only the jacket and the back of the man's head were visible. She was looking out from the picture.

"It's been almost five years since I saw her. Does she still look like this?"

I swallowed hard and nodded. He'd somehow managed to capture her impetuous and vulnerable side simultaneously. And the way he held the paper—gently, the way a Buddhist monk might hold a rice-paper lamp—told me he was still in love with her.

"If I mail this to you, will you give it to her for me?"

I nodded.

"And tell her I'm sorry?"

I nodded again.

"She always insisted you weren't her boyfriend, but I never completely believed her. When I tried to frame you, I rationalized it by saying I was eliminating the competition. I was a sick puppy. I hope you can forgive me."

"I did that the day you came here. I figured you had enough grief."

"Thanks. So why did you ask to see me?"

"I'm an adjunct in the art department this fall. I'm teaching a course called 'Anasazi Pottery Methods.'"

His eyes widened. "Did Melvin Armstrong or Junior Prather leave the department? Because there was never enough demand to justify the two of them, much less an adjunct."

"No, they're both still there. They greeted me on my first day to tell me they weren't talking to me."

"Is Milton Shorter the department head?"

"He's acting department head."

"Still acting after all these years? That's strange. So you wanted to visit me to get tips on how to teach a studio class?"

"Too late for that. I've already made every mistake possible. But the worst thing is that one of my students was murdered."

I told him about Ximena's death and the ongoing investigation. I told him about the informal and formal allegations leveled at Junior Prather, me and now Harte Hockley. I told him about Charles Webbe.

He told me about all the petty jealousies in the art department, most of which I had seen or at least heard about.

"Why did you start the tradition of serving tea?"

"Well, it wasn't so the straws could serve as clues. The departmental meetings were fractious. I thought if we spent the first few minutes doing something no one could argue about, it might reduce the bickering."

"Did it?"

He shook his head slowly. "When I introduced the idea, they bickered about whether the tea would be served to them according to academic rank or alphabetical order. They settled on academic rank in reverse so that the most senior full professor would be served last."

"I guess that explains why I was served first."

"And why Jack Wiezga is always served last," he added.

"He's retired," I noted. "Why does he still have a studio? Why does he attend departmental meetings? Why does he get to decide who teaches?"

"He's the glue that holds the department together. Like the alpha male in a pack of stray dogs. Even mongrels need order in their lives. They don't all like Wiezga, but someone has to be in charge."

"Shouldn't that be the department head?"

"Of course. But the department head is appointed by the dean based on administrative capability. The real power is informal and wielded by the lead dog."

"So Wiezga is the one who always knows which way the wind is blowing?"

He laughed. "I guess you've heard that a lot. It's sort of the departmental mantra. Let me give you the background. When I first became department head and found myself in a dispute with a faculty member over course assignments, travel funds or what-have-you, they would often defend their stance by saying they knew which way the wind was blowing. I was chatting with Wiezga near the end of that first semester and tried to make a few brownie points by telling him in a thankful tone that he was the only person in the department who never said he knew which way the wind was blowing. He smiled that heavy-jawed smile of his and said, 'I don't need to know which way the wind is blowing. I *am* the wind.'"

43

I divided my time that afternoon between watching my students put the final touches on the works they planned to submit for the student/faculty exhibit and thinking about what Blass had told me.

Sharice was working late, so I met Susannah at Dos Hermanas. Usually, she waits until Angie brings our margaritas before sharing any news, but that afternoon she started talking before I was seated.

"Ximena didn't die from asphyxiation."

"The Office of the Medical Investigator ruled she did."

"They're wrong. She was poisoned."

"And you know this how?"

"Call it a hunch for now. But it's based on sixteen years of experience."

"As a medical investigator?" I asked kiddingly.

"As a murder mystery reader. And hanging around with you has added a bit to my knowledge base."

"Don't remind me. So what kind of poison was it?"

"My guess would be cyanide. But we can figure that out after the experiment we're going to run tomorrow."

After she explained the experiment, I just stared at her dumbfounded.

"So tell me about your day," she said.

"I visited Freddie Blass at the Central New Mexico Correctional Facility in Los Lunas."

Now it was her turn to look dumbfounded.

After I recounted my conversation with Blass, she asked how he was.

"A changed man. Calmer. More reflective. Looks different too. His hair is white and he's too thin."

She shuddered.

"One thing hasn't changed."

"What's that?"

"He's still in love with you."

"Like I'm supposed to care? He's a murderer."

"He was convicted of manslaughter."

"Only because of a plea bargain. His killing of Gerstner was premeditated. The fact that he set up a possible frame of you proves that."

"That only proves the thought of killing Gerstner had crossed his mind. It doesn't prove he was actually going to do it. The actual murder was in the heat of an argument. His attorney said Gerstner attacked Blass."

"Attorneys are paid to lie."

I didn't reply.

"Why are you defending him?" she asked.

"I'm not defending him. He killed Gertsner. He went to prison. Now he's about to be released. He's done his time. And he's a changed man, Suze."

"They all say that to the parole board."

44

The experiment required Sharice to assist. It was seven the next morning. Susannah sat on my kitchen table at the back of Spirits in Clay. Sharice covered Susannah's body with alginate from her hips to her neck. The she wrapped gauze over the alginate.

I waited in my studio until Sharice beckoned me to join them.

I looked at Susannah. "You sure you want to do this?"

"Absolutely. How often does a girl get to have a free facial and solve a murder all at once?"

I inserted two straws. I slathered alginate on her head. I applied layers of gauze and plaster until they reached what I judged to be the same thickness that had been on Ximena.

We didn't bother doing Susannah below the waist. The experiment didn't require it, and having her sit on the table eliminated the need for an armature.

Sharice went to work.

I read *War and Peace*.

Actually, I read *The Journey Home* by Edward Abbey. It only seemed like *War and Peace* because my best friend was encased in plaster for hours.

When the hours finally came to an end, I stood up, faced Susannah's plaster head and pinched both straws closed.

There was a muted sound like someone clearing her throat in

the next room. Then a louder rumble followed by a slight rise in her shoulders. Then the head rotated a millimeter to one side. Then back the same amount.

A cracking sound was followed by her arms coming away from her side by an inch. Then another inch. They began to vibrate. More guttural noises. Louder at this point. A resounding crack was followed by a complete break in the plaster at her right elbow. Then it tore away at the shoulder as she reached up and swatted away my hands.

She gripped her jaw and began to move it left and right. A crack formed where her mouth should be. It arched down like a sad face. She worked her fingers loose and stuck them into the crack. Then she pulled off most of the face plaster. She removed the protective discs from her eyes and looked at me.

"Nothing to it."

"Welcome back."

"Thanks. That was the boringest time I ever spent. Is it too early for margaritas?"

"You're in luck. It's just past noon."

"Pull the rest of the plaster off my arms, then help me stand up."

I did. She walked unsteadily into my bathroom. Pieces of plaster came flying out onto the floor. Those were flowed by clumps of gauze. Then I heard the door close and the shower come on.

45

"Why did you run the shower so long?"

"A lot of plaster washed down the drain. I wanted to make sure it was long gone and wouldn't plug your sewer line."

"Thanks."

"On top of that, I kept finding pieces lodged in my hair." She bent her head down. "You see any plaster in there?"

"Your hair is so thick, there could be a plaster of Paris figurine in there without me seeing it." I paused then said, "I feel really stupid."

"You shouldn't. My hair really is that thick."

I shook my head. "What I feel stupid about is not realizing Ximena could have broken out of the plaster."

"Nobody realized it. Everyone just assumed she was a sitting duck. Er . . . standing duck? All the murderer had to do was just hold the straws shut for a few minutes while she suffocated."

"You didn't assume it."

"I did when you first told me about it."

"What made you change your mind?"

"Her poems. They showed grit, pride. Someone who wrote like that would struggle. I imagined her in that plaster, flexing every muscle in her body. Then I suddenly realized we had no proof that plaster would be strong enough to keep you from flexing. So we needed to run an experiment to find out. And now we know I was right about her being poisoned."

"Because it takes at least three minutes of air deprivation before you pass out?"

"Right. And it took me less than two minutes to swat your hands off the straws. But poison can act so quickly that you wouldn't have time to struggle against the plaster."

"But the OMI ruled that Ximena died of suffocation. Maybe Ximena wasn't strong enough to break the plaster. You're a lot stronger than most women."

"I'm stronger than a lot of men too. And I didn't have much adrenaline, because I knew you weren't going to suffocate me. But Ximena would have been in full panic. She would have been fighting for survival."

"But what about the OMI's finding?" I asked again.

"Easy. It has to be a poison that mimics suffocation."

"Since you guessed cyanide, I suppose it mimics suffocation."

"Right. It prevents red blood cells from processing oxygen. The victim suffocates even though she's got plenty of oxygen coming in. The effect on the red cells is almost instantaneous."

"But wouldn't the OMI have been able to detect cyanide when he did the autopsy?"

"You'd know the answer to that if you read murder mysteries. There was one by Agatha Christie called *Sparkling Cyanide*."

"Someone put cyanide in Champagne?"

"Exactly."

"That's awful."

"Well, of course it's awful. Murder is never pleasant."

"I meant spoiling Champagne. I hope it wasn't Gruet."

"Probably not. It was set in 1945. It starts when seven people go to dinner at a restaurant in London called Luxembourg."

"Or a restaurant in Luxembourg called London," I said, trying to sound like Groucho Marx.

"Do you want to hear this or not?"

Strangely, I did. And said so.

"A character named Rosemary dies at the restaurant while dining with her husband and some of their friends. Months later, her husband, George, gets an anonymous letter claiming Rosemary was poisoned. The husband contacts all the people who were there the night Rosemary died and invites them to join him at the same restaurant exactly one year after the evening of his wife's death. He hires an actress who looks like his wife and arranges for her to arrive a few minutes late and take the seat next to him."

"And he did that because?"

"That's obvious, Hubie. He expected the murderer to confess when he saw the ghost."

"Why didn't I think of that?"

"Doesn't matter, because the actress didn't show up. And George dies at the restaurant in the same manner as his wife—cyanide in his Champagne."

"Was this the beginning of the BYOB movement?"

"No. But it was the beginning of a long tradition of poison in murder mysteries."

"Always cyanide?"

"Of course not. There's hemlock, of course."

"Made famous by Socrates."

"Right. And Aconite."

"Another famous victim—the emperor Claudius."

"And then there's Mandrake."

"The magician?"

"No, the poison. The plant bears edible fruit. But the roots are poisonous. Extracts from it are used today to remove warts."

"Can we change the subject?"

"You don't want to know about strychnine and arsenic?"

"Not if I can help it. Remind me why we're talking about this."

"Because you asked why the OMI didn't find evidence of cyanide in Ximena. The answer is there are lots of poisons. So instead of running scores of tests, pathologists just test for things that the situation indicates might be possible. There was evidence of oxygen deprivation. She was encased in plaster with only straws to provide air. The obvious guess is someone pinched the straws closed."

"So now what?"

"You tell Whit to tell the OMI to test for cyanide."

"I know I sometimes make fun of you for reading murder mysteries, but I have to admit you may have solved this one."

"Not really. Before our little experiment, we thought someone pinched off Ximena's air supply. But we had no way of knowing who did it, since anyone could have gone in there and done it. Now we know she was poisoned. But we still have no way of knowing who did it."

"Maybe we do. If it really was cyanide, the police might be able to find out if anyone who knew Ximena had access to cyanide."

"I suspect most people who knew her had access to cyanide."

"Why?"

"She was an art student, Hubie. Cyanide is stored in the photography lab. It's used as the fixing agent in the wet-plate collodion process for large-format photographs. And another cyanide compound is stored in the metals lab. It's used in plating and finishing for metal jewelry and other sorts of metal artwork."

46

Because we moved the cocktail hour up to just past noon, I was at a loss when Susannah left. It was too late for lunch. I decided the salsa and chips would have to tide me over until dinner.

I returned to Spirits in Clay and relieved Glad. I took my position on the stool behind the counter hoping the crowd of Tuesday shoppers might be good for business.

That hope became a reality when the first person through the door bought the Zia bird jar Glad had taken subject to my approval. The buyer bargained me down from the forty-five hundred I had it marked at to an even four thousand.

Sometimes I go weeks without a sale. Now I had quadrupled my thousand dollars in just a few days. And I hadn't even paid the thousand yet.

I looked up at the sound of the bong to see Miss Gladys.

"Is that smile for me or for this treat for your tummy?"

I looked at the casserole dish. "You brought me lunch?"

"Just because I have a fiancé doesn't mean I can't look after you from time to time," she said. "But this isn't lunch. It's leftover dessert. But don't let the word *leftover* fool you. It's probably even better now that the flavors have melded."

I eyed the concoction warily. "What's the name of this dish?"

The names are often as bizarre as the dishes themselves.

Her eyes actually twinkled. "It's called the Next Best Thing to Robert Redford. When you taste it, you'll understand why. It has a frozen graham-cracker crust, a stick of margarine, an eight-ounce package of Kraft light cream cheese, a cup of sugar and two packages of Jell-O instant pudding, one vanilla and one chocolate. You stir everything with a little cream and dump in into the crust. Bake it at three fifty for fifteen minutes, then top it off with a twelve-ounce tub of Cool Whip."

The growling you just heard was my stomach.

"I think I'll save it for after an evening meal when I can appreciate it fully."

47

It was a brisk fall day with a light breeze and bright sun. Purple and orange deciduous trees dotted the Sandia Mountains, creating a patchwork with the green conifers. A dusting of snow along the ridge capped off the postcard vista.

Even though the walk from Old Town to the campus is uphill and the fresh fall air was 10 percent automobile exhaust, I was in a great mood when I entered the pottery studio.

Then I saw my students.

If the old saying about misery is true, they would have loved company.

"Why the long faces?"

"They rejected us," said Aleesha. "All of us."

"Who rejected you?"

"The gallery committee. Everybody in this class submitted a piece for the student/faculty show, and they rejected all of them. It's your fault."

I was stunned. Not by her allegation. I'd gotten used to that. But by the rejections. I know good pottery when I see it. Most of theirs were better than good. I couldn't believe not even one of their pieces had been accepted.

"It's not his fault," said Carly.

Aleesha looked at me. "Was our work good enough to make the show?"

"Absolutely."

She looked at Carly. "See what I mean? If the work is good enough, then it was rejected for some other reason. And the only other reason is because they're mad at him for something. Telling us not to pay the lab fee. Taking us on unauthorized field trips."

"Maybe it's because you filed an unjustified EEO complaint," said Marlon.

"What would you know about justification?" she shot back.

Carly jumped in, "He treats you just like everyone else, Aleesha. Better actually. Despite your constant complaining, he treated you the same way he treated the rest of us."

"That's because he's afraid of her," said Apache.

"No," said Raúl, "he has nothing to be afraid of. He's just an adjunct. It's not like they're going to fire him."

Bruce laughed and said, "He might want them to."

"It might be good if they fired him. He could file his own complaint," said Alfred, "and claim he was discriminated against because he's a straight white male."

"How you know he's straight?" asked Aleesha.

"I've seen him around town with his girlfriend. And, Aleesha"— he put the outsides of his wrists on the two sides of his waist— "guess what, honey. She's black."

Marlon laughed. "You dating a sister, Mr. Schuze?"

"No. She's an only child."

They all laughed at me.

"This class is like a sitcom," said Nathan, and they laughed some more.

When the laughter died down, Raúl said, "We should fight this."

"Fight what?" I asked.

"The rejection of our work."

"You can't fight it," said Aleesha. "The gallery committee picks which pieces get in, and that's it. It's not like the law"—she glared at Marlon—"where you can go the EEO office and right a wrong. There is no appeal."

"You're right," said Raúl. "We can't change the committee, but we can embarrass them."

"How?"

"By mounting our own show, a *Salon des Refusés.*"

"What's that?"

"It means exhibition of rejects."

Aleesha said, "That's us, all right—rejects."

"And we are in good company," said Raúl. "The first Salon des Refusés included Édouard Manet."

"Even I've heard of him," said Mia.

"Tell us about that," I said to Raúl.

"The Académie des Beaux-Arts in Paris started sponsoring art exhibits in 1667. They were the most prestigious art show in the Western world. An artist who got a work into the show was virtually guaranteed a successful career. The members of the academy were very picky about what got into the show."

"Like the gallery committee," said Aleesha.

"Worse," said Raúl. "At least our committee lets in contemporary and even edgy work. The academy accepted only art depicting traditional subjects painted realistically. But art cannot be frozen. By 1863, Impressionism was on the rise, and a central figure in the movement was Manet. The academy rejected his entry. He and the other rejects mounted their own exhibit in another wing of the building where the academy had their official show. A thousand visitors a day visited the Salon des Refusés, more than visited the official salon. Émile Zola reported that visitors pushed to get into the crowded Salon des Refusés to see Manet's *Déjeuner sur l'herbe.*"

Aleesha said, "It's one thing to have rejected works by Manet. But who's going to want to see rejected works by Aleesha Jones?"

"All the students," said Apache. "What could appeal to the natural rebelliousness of students more than attending a show of pieces rejected by the faculty?"

"He's right," said Mia.

"But where would we mount our show?" asked Carly.

"They won't let us use the gallery," said Aleesha.

"She's right," said Marlon. "But we could do it outside the building, set it up on the grass."

"It's November. It could be forty degrees out there. It might even snow."

"Have it in the hall," Raúl suggested.

"I don't think they'll let us do that," said Alfred.

Marlon said, "We're students here, right? We pay tuition. We have a right to be in the hall."

"But we don't have the right to put our pots in the display cases."

"Just hold them. We'll line up on both sides of the hall leading to the gallery. We'll hold our works in our hands for people to look at as they go to the gallery."

Bruce smiled and said, "Or we could write 'Homeless and Hungry—Please Help' on a piece of cardboard and hold that up."

"No," said Aleesha, "but we could each have a sign on our work saying 'This was rejected by the gallery.'"

Their nods told me they were going with Aleesha's plan. Which sent me to my lawyer's office.

48

Where I actually went was the country club. Layton Kent, my lawyer, maintains an office in the Albuquerque Plaza Office Tower, the tallest building in New Mexico. Although at only twenty-two stories it would be almost a walk-up in New York City.

Layton conducts most business from his table at the country club, which provides him with both visibility and food. The latter being important for a man who weighs a seventh of a ton.

Not counting his ego, which would likely kick him up to an even three hundred.

Most of his clients are also members of the country club, and many of them are also lawyers. They seek his assistance in hiding their wealth from the IRS. In perfectly legal ways, of course.

I have no wealth to hide. He represents me at the insistence of his wife, the lovely Mariela de Baca Enriquez Kent, who collects ancient pottery. She is my best customer, and I am his worst client.

Layton nodded his permission to the server, who finally looked at me.

"Something to drink, sir?"

"Water, please."

"Sparkling or still?"

Still what? I thought to myself. Still tasting faintly of the Rio

Grande? What I said out loud was "Sparkling, with a twist of lime please." One must try to fit in with the club set.

Layton's water also had bubbles. His twist was lemon. "I know one of your students was murdered. I know you were suspected of it."

I started to say something but he raised a palm to silence me. "I also know you have not come here to seek my assistance in extricating yourself from a murder charge as you have done in the past." He wrinkled his nose in disgust. "I know this because the district attorney told me you are no longer a suspect. So what bizarre predicament brings you here?"

I told him about my students' plan to stage a Salon des Refusés.

"Are their pieces worthy of display?"

"Good enough even for Mrs. Kent."

He raised his eyebrows. Oddly, no wrinkles appeared. Despite his bulk, he has no flab and no wrinkles. It is as if his skin is a size too small and serves as an all-over girdle. His complexion is as smooth and flawless as a cover girl's. His teeth are perfect. If he were a photo, you would suspect Photoshop.

My guess is he has both a dermatologist and a dentist full-time on retainer.

"What do you want me to do?" he asked.

"I think the faculty may try to prevent the students from staging their Salon des Refusés. We'll need to move quickly if they do."

"We?"

"You *are* a patron of the arts."

He raised his eyebrows again but did not dispute me.

49

Whit Fletcher gave me his cop stare. "One way you coulda known it was cyanide was you sprayed it up those straws."

"And the other way," I replied, "is what I just told you. Susannah figured it out."

"From reading murder mysteries," he said contemptuously.

"Exactly. And she must have been right, or you wouldn't be here."

I'd called him about Susannah's theory immediately after we ran the experiment. He said it was malarkey. But he showed up at the condo after I returned from the country club, skipped "hello" and went directly to "One way you coulda known it was cyanide was you sprayed it up those straws."

His professional pride was wounded. "So now what?" I asked.

"Footwork. We start checking on all the fruits and nuts in the art department to see if any of them bought some cyanide."

"Even if they didn't buy it, they all have access to it."

He raised his eyebrows.

"It's used in the photography labs and the jewelry-making studios."

"They let those kooks have cyanide?"

"It's in different compounds. Sodium cyanide and potassium cyanide. I'm no chemist, but I know either of those can kill you if you're not careful, and there may be some way to make it even more lethal by purifying it, concentrating it or whatever."

"I'll have the lab boys check into it." He looked around the condo. "So that really was her father I saw?"

"It was."

"And now that he's gone, you snuck back in."

"I didn't sneak in, Whit. I live here."

"'Cept when her father is here."

"Would be a bit awkward."

50

When Sharice got home, I pointed to the dish on the kitchen counter. "Dessert tonight is courtesy of Miss Gladys."

"After she and Glad get married, do you think she'll drop the *miss* part?"

I shook my head. "She was married to Mr. Claiborne for thirty years and was always called Miss Gladys."

"Even by him?"

"Probably. I think it's a Southern thing."

She peered warily at the dish. "What do we call this?"

"The Next Best Thing to Robert Redford."

She gave me an impetuous kiss. "You're even better than Robert Redford."

"And younger," I said.

Something I don't get to say as much now that I'm nearing the big five-o. Actually, I rarely think about my age, even less so now that Sharice and I are together.

She cooked a "meatloaf" made entirely from mushrooms and carrots.

I've never been a vegetarian, but I understand the appeal. Seeing a cute piglet gives me pangs of guilt for eating bacon. But I rationalize it. It's a bargain we have with livestock. We care for them and then eat them as our part of the bargain.

I'm not sure that would stand up to rational analysis. So I don't try to analyze it.

Speaking of bacon, I thought the mushroom-carrot loaf would have been better with a few crisp strips crumbled into it.

With regard to the Next Best Thing to Robert Redford, all it needed was some cold Gruet and the ability to forget all those chemicals.

I told her about my students and their plan for a Salon des Refusés.

"You think the faculty will let them do that?"

"The students have a right to be in the hall. All they're planning to do is hold the pots they made with a sign saying they were rejected."

"But the faculty might drum up some excuse, saying the students are blocking traffic or something. They might even call the campus police to have the students physically removed."

"That's why I talked to Layton Kent."

"It would probably take three of them to lift him."

"True. But it's not his heft we need. It's his ability to get an injunction at warp speed from Judge Aragon."

"When does the show open?"

"Tomorrow evening at six."

"Great. I get off work at five and we aren't doing the free clinic."

"You want to go to the student/faculty show?"

"No. I want to go to the Salon des Refusés."

51

We met in the pottery studio half an hour before the grand opening of the student/faculty show. Sort of a dress rehearsal combined with a pep talk.

Alfred had made a copy of the genuine Tularosa pot he'd hugged the first day of class. It wasn't as good as my copy, but I've been doing it for a quarter of a century.

Aleesha's pot was perfectly shaped. The face she decorated it with looked like one of the African masks in Picasso's *Les Demoiselles d'Avignon*. Appropriation, I guess.

Not surprisingly, Nathan's pot had a snake coiled around it matching the tattoo on his arm.

Bruce used the raku firing technique and got spectacular turquoise hues on his wide shallow bowl.

Raúl did an exact copy of a small Acoma thimble jug.

Apache knocked a hole in his piece to symbolize the harm done by colonization. I knew that because it was on the sign he was planning to hold.

Marlon's pot was twice as large as the biggest ancient piece ever discovered.

Mia never got the hang of it. Her point-and-click skills didn't transfer to 3-D. So she formed a clay rectangle and attached a picture of Ximena using a design program she had mastered in her interior-design courses.

Carly did a pair of pots with their handles intertwined. Unfit for any practical use but fascinating to see.

After looking at all their works, I made my pep talk. "The first day of this class, I showed you a copy I made of an ancient Tularosa pot."

"Apache complained about it," said Aleesha.

"I was wrong," he said, "but my heart was in the right place."

"Yes," I said, "you thought it was disrespectful. But now you know it was just the opposite. The people who made those pots have been wronged by history, their story told only by professional archaeologists. By liberating their work, I make it possible for them to tell their own story. Their story is in those pots." I looked at each of them in turn. "Your works also tell your story. You put some part yourself into them. Maybe a bit of your soul. But like the ancient potters, you want your work to be seen." Then I got a bit carried away. I'm not used to making speeches. "You are fearless. No rejection will stop you from showing your work. The gallery committee will not be your judge. The people will be your judge!"

"You sound like Coach Keys in the pregame meeting," said Marlon.

"I do?"

He nodded.

"Is that a good thing?"

"Hell yes," he said. "Let's march down the hall and kick some butt!"

"One thing first." I held out the box they had seen many times. "Cell phones in here. We don't want rings, buzzes and clangs interrupting our Salon des Refusés."

They all dutifully dropped their cell phones in the box.

"Aleesha, you can keep yours."

She stared at me wide-eyed.

I handed her a paper. "I want you to put this number in your phone so you can dial it with one touch. The person on the other end will recognize your number, because I gave it to him."

52

Manet would have been happy for us.

All the people on their way into the gallery stopped to look at the work by my students. Even better, many of them left the gallery after a brief walk-through and returned to the hallway to spend more time at the Salon des Refusés.

The euphoria lasted about ten minutes.

Junior Prather yelled at me. "You need to get your students out of here!"

"I thought you weren't talking to me."

"I'm not talking to you. I'm yelling at you."

"That's the first thing you've ever said to me that makes sense. But my students are not leaving. They have a right to be in the hallway."

"They're blocking traffic."

"You need to yell that. Otherwise, you're talking to me."

He raised his volume again. "Get them out of here right now!"

He was good at yelling. He stomped off.

The students enjoyed our exchange.

Jollo Bakkie showed up and asked us to leave. I told her we were staying put until the gallery closed. She said we were violating the fire code. I asked if she had a copy of it handy. She stomped off.

Helga Ólafsdóttir showed up late, explaining that her work had also been rejected.

"If I'd known this was planned," she said, "I would have joined in."

"Please do."

"I don't have my work with me. But I have a better idea."

She entered the gallery and clapped her hands together loudly. "Ladies and gentlemen. My name is Helga Ólafsdóttir. I'm a member of the art faculty. I wish to state publicly I am not affiliated in any way with this show. I was not on the selection committee. I have no pieces in the show. If you want to see genuine art, you are in the wrong place. Go out in the halls and enjoy the pieces done by the students in Mr. Schuze's pottery class."

Melvin Armstrong stomped out.

The campus police stomped in with Junior Prather pointing at me. I gave Aleesha the high sign. She punched her cell phone.

The cops looked scary but were actually nice.

The lead policeman's name tag said Burke. He asked if I was in charge of the students.

"They are in my class. I don't claim to be in charge of them."

"The faculty members hosting the gallery event say the presence of these students and their artworks are a distraction. I'd like you and them to clear the building."

"The hall is a public space. We have a right to be here."

"Professor Prather says the gallery committee reserved the entire building for tonight's opening event."

"Even the halls?"

"The entire building," Burke repeated.

"Even the bathrooms?"

"The entire building."

"What about my office? They can't reserve my office. It's reserved for me."

"It isn't your office," said Junior.

"There you go—talking to me again."

He clenched his teeth and spoke to Burke. "It isn't his office. It's used by all the adjuncts."

"That would be me," I said. "I'm the only adjunct."

I knew that because all the drawers Shorter hadn't assigned to me remained empty all semester long. Not only did I never see another person in the office, I never saw another object. Except for my grade book and red pencil, neither of which had been touched.

"Look," said Burke, "why cause trouble? You can set up in the student union. Or another classroom building. We'll escort you to the location of your choice."

"We aren't leaving."

He shook his head. "We'll have to move you."

Raúl shouted, "Everyone down on the ground."

The crowd that had been watching the exchange gasped as the students first sat then lay flat on the floor with their pots resting on their chests.

Officer Burke turned to his assistant. "Call for backup, Wes. Three more officers. And the wagon."

A wrinkled old guy in the crowd turned to his wife and said, "God, this takes me back to the good old days."

"The sixties were not the good old days, Harold. You only think so because you spent the whole decade stoned."

Layton Kent arrived sooner than the backup policemen, so I didn't get to experience being dragged away from a protest. He showed Burke the restraining order. Burke looked at Prather, "Looks like they get to stay. C'mon, Wes, let's get a doughnut."

Prather waited to grab me until Burke and Wes left the building. His eyes were bulging, the veins on his forehead like jungle vines and his cheeks purple. He's a skinny guy, but his long arms gave him leverage. The next thing I knew, Junior had me headed toward the door at a perilously low angle.

Marlon moved fast for a guy his size. He pried Junior's hands loose. Unfortunately, Junior was all that was holding me up. I broke my fall with my face. My vision blurred.

Something was hovering above me. I closed my eyes tightly. When I reopened them, I could see Junior's arms and legs flailing in the air. Marlon's right hand held Junior's belt buckle. His left hand held Junior's beard. Junior was slapping ineffectively at Marlon and trying to yell. It's hard to generate force when you're suspended in the air and even harder to yell when your mouth is pulled wide open by your beard.

The duo was headed to the door. Bruce was trailing behind, perhaps as backup if needed. After they exited, there was a shriek followed by a thud.

Everyone in the hall was staring at the door. Marlon reentered to see all eyes on him.

"I handed Mr. Prather to the campus police," he said calmly.

"More like tossed," said Bruce.

"Yeah," said Marlon, "and they missed him." He shrugged.

Sharice brought damp paper towels from the restroom and cleaned the blood off my face. Then she pulled my lips apart. "Thank God none of your teeth are broken."

Marlon pulled me up and held on to me while I steadied myself. "You okay, Mr. Schuze?"

I told him I was and turned to Sharice. "Let's go home."

She took my hand and turned me to the door just in time to see the camera flashes.

53

The smell of roasting coffee woke me up and the hot shower eased the soreness of having been manhandled by Junior Prather.

After brushing, flossing and gargling, I grabbed my razor, looked in the mirror and saw—to use an old chestnut of an expression—the goalie for a darts team. Running a blade over all those welts and scabs was not a good idea.

No problem. The scruffy look is in. And I was almost proud to be battle scarred.

It was then I realized I hadn't reflected on the success of the Salon des Refusés. Just as in the first one with Manet, our salon proved more popular with the public than the official gallery show. The publicity that would surely result from the confrontation with the campus cops and the assault on me would draw big crowds to Spirits in Clay for the sale benefitting the Ximena Sifuentes Memorial Scholarship Fund.

Sharice filled my now-notorious cup with fresh brew and handed me the morning paper. The headline read UNM PROFESSOR ARRESTED FOR ASSAULTING COLLEAGUE.

I told her I was hoping it would say "arrested for murder."

"You think he killed Ximena?"

"Of course. He was the one who chose her as the model. He was the one who put her in a defenseless situation. And although theoretically anyone could have walked in off the street and shut off her air or poisoned her, he's the only one we know for sure was in there. Furthermore, he demonstrated last night that he's willing to harm other people. Namely, *moi*."

"What about motive?"

"Remember the guy Charles told us about who assaulted a deaf person in the Library of Congress just because he was deaf? Maybe Junior hates deaf people."

"I know he's a nut case, but murdering Ximena seems like a stretch without a stronger motive."

"Maybe she rejected his advances."

"With his looks, if he killed all the women who rejected his advances, he'd have to be a serial killer."

I shrugged. As I'd told Susannah, it wasn't my job to discover a motive.

54

After the hubbub of the Salon des Refusés had calmed down and classes had returned to normal—or what passes for normal in the art world—it was time to sell the works the students had made. Sharice went with me to Spirits in Clay. She helped me wrap and box my own inventory, which we stored in my former residence at the back of the building.

The first thing Aleesha said after all the students showed up, was, "How are you going to decide who gets the choice spots to display the work."

"I'm not going to decide that. The artists are going to decide that."

The second thing she said was directed at Sharice. "You his girlfriend?"

Sharice smiled. "I am."

"I need to talk to you."

"No," said Sharice as the smile disappeared. "*I* need to talk to *you.*"

Sharice went out the front door and Aleesha followed.

"You gonna go after them?" asked Marlon.

"No way."

"Smart man."

"I'm going to the back. Let me know when the show is mounted."

I brewed some coffee and sat at my kitchen chair. I wondered what Sharice was saying to Aleesha.

I wondered if I wanted to know.

Since her decision not to undergo any further medical tests, she had demonstrated the sort of resolve that she must have exercised after the mastectomy. She was more sure of herself, more focused. I suspected Aleesha was on the receiving end of a stern lecture.

I picked up Abbey's *The Road Home* and eventually came to a passage that read:

> Gaunt and ganted, lean and bony deer, how will they ever get through the coming winter? A tough life. Always hard times for deer. The struggle for existence. All their energy goes into survival—and reproduction. The only point of it all—to go on. On and on and on. What else is there? Sometimes I'm appalled by the brutality, the horror of this planetary spawning and scheming and striving and dying. One no longer searches for any ulterior significance in all this; as in the finest music, the meaning is in the music itself, not in anything beyond it. All we have, it seems to me, is the beauty of art and nature and life, and the love which that beauty inspires.

It struck me that Sharice had that same philosophy. She was living in that dank apartment off San Mateo, recovering from chemotherapy and living like a nun because she was saving all her money for reconstructive surgery. Then—as I imagined it—she woke up one morning and said, "The meaning is in the music itself, not in anything beyond it."

Probably not those words. Maybe no words. Just a decision. She used her savings to buy the condo and change her wardrobe, which is really just a manifestation of a change in attitude. And now she had done it again. She was going to live life on her own terms instead of the dictates of medical fate.

Carly came back to tell me they had all their work on display.

"You like it?" she asked after leading me back to the store.

"Yes. Now I'll do my part."

I pulled the tented cards up from below the counter and began to write prices on them. As I do with my own merchandise, I wrote out the numbers instead of using the numerals. Under Carly's piece I wrote, "*Two thousand five hundred.*"

Luke looked at it and said, "Wow, Mom."

It was an unusual piece and well executed. It may not have been worth the price I set, but the sale was for a good cause, and the buyers wouldn't mind paying a bit more than retail.

After I'd priced all the pieces, Aleesha said, "How come you get to set the prices?"

"Because I own this place and I'm the lead dog in this pack of mongrels."

"Okay," she said, and laughed.

The crowd was large. Most were just curious because of the newspaper coverage. Some were buyers, including my best customers. Mariela Kent bought three pieces. Faye Po bought one. Donald and Dotty Edwards bought two. Elaine Chew from the Alumni Office bought one. Dr. Batres bought one. I bought the piece by Mia. It wasn't pottery per se, but I thought it would look good as part of a plaque that was planned in the art department. We made almost ten thousand dollars. Not bad for a small collection.

Only nine pieces when it should have been ten. Like her life, Ximena's pottery work was incomplete. I abandoned my plan to stay out of the investigation. I'd met her parents. I'd read her poetry. Things changed. So I changed.

55

The sale ended at four. The students left. Sharice helped me tidy up.

I thought about Abbey as we walked back to the condo. When he was a park ranger in a remote spot in the Canyonlands, a tourist from back east remarked, "The problem out here is there's not enough water."

Abbey smiled at him and said, "No, sir. There's exactly the right amount of water. The problem out here is that there are too many people."

And that's when I realized I might have a clue about Ximena's murder.

Not a real clue like a fingerprint or a smoking gun. What I had was a question that, if pursued, might lead somewhere.

The problem in the art program was not that there were too few students. It was that there were too many teachers. Freddie Blass had been surprised when I told him they hired me as an adjunct. There weren't enough students to fill up a normal teaching load for Armstrong and Prather.

So why offer ART 2330? Ximena and the other nine students could have been put in the existing courses taught by Armstrong and Prather with room left over. And it's not as though anyone needed Anasazi Pottery Methods to graduate. The course was new and had never before been offered.

So why was the course offered?

I thought of three possibilities.

First, maybe Shorter was so impressed by the noncredit course I taught in the spring that he wanted to bring me to the campus in the fall for a real course. After all, Olga brought me tamales.

Who was I kidding? Uncredentialed instructors of noncredit courses aren't offered real courses. It's like a guy in a slow pitch league being called up by the Dodgers.

Second, maybe Shorter thought Anasazi Pottery Methods needed to be included in the curriculum to demonstrate the department's commitment to multiculturalism. But hiring a white guy who's a pot thief to teach it doesn't fit with that scenario.

There was another explanation. It was the weirdest one. The first two were based on Shorter having a positive reason to offer the course—wanting to reward me or wanting to make the course selection reflect more diversity.

The third possibility was something negative. Maybe he wanted to punish me.

We were almost home when I told Sharice my theory.

She laughed. Actually, I think it may have been a guffaw, but I'm not certain how a guffaw sounds.

"Oh, come on." she said. "I know you had challenges with the class this semester, but you can't honestly call it punishment."

"Think about it. I had a deaf student. What are the odds of that? I had Apache, who thinks I'm insensitive to Indians. Shorter knows the majors. He advises them. Why would he put a student with Apache's outlook in my class? He must know about Aleesha's attitude and Nathan's immaturity. He probably knew Carly was going through a divorce. Even Raúl was a challenge, intimidating me with his intellect. And to top it off, I had Mia the temptress. He filled the class with kooks to get back at me."

"Get back at you for what?"

"I don't know."

She unlocked the door to the condo. "Does the word *paranoia* seem appropriate?"

"What about being charged with both an EEO and a sexual harassment violation?"

"Shorter didn't do that."

"He stuck me with the students who did. He may have put them up to it."

She just stared at me.

"I know. Paranoia. But what about the unauthorized field trip issue? Why would the safety guy even know about it if Shorter didn't report it?"

"Better question: How would Shorter know about it?"

That hissing sound you just heard was the air going out of my argument.

"One of my students would have told him." I sighed. "And I did have Bruce and Marlon, who were more or less normal. And the class had a great ending."

"Exactly."

"But don't you think it's a strange coincidence that I was kicked out of a session on deafness and had a deaf girl in my class?"

"It's also a coincidence that you had a deaf student and Susannah has a deaf brother."

She was right, of course. Coincidences don't prove anything.

But still.

56

Jack Wiezga's studio in the Fine Arts Building looked exactly as it did when I saw it five years earlier, except for the floor.

The old splatters of paint had reminded me of a Jackson Pollock painting. The current ones reminded me of a different Pollock. One with more red drops.

Wiezga spoke with his unlit pipe clinched between his teeth. "I wondered how long it would be before you showed up."

In fact, a couple of weeks had passed between my wondering if I should talk to him and my doing so. Among my other faults, I'm a procrastinator.

"Is Wiezga the word for 'wind' in some eastern European language?"

"It's a surname. Usually spelled W-y-z-g-a."

"So how did you get nicknamed 'The Wind'?"

"Ask Helga Ólafsdóttir. She's the one gave it to me. But you didn't come here to ask about my nickname."

Same old Wiezga. His tone as blunt as his forehead

I asked him if he knew why Milton Shorter scheduled ART 2330.

"The question you want to ask is how did the course get approved."

I frowned.

"A course can't be offered until it's approved. A faculty member proposes it to the departmental curriculum committee. If they approve it, it goes to the department head. If he approves, it goes to the curriculum committee of the College of Arts. If they approve, it goes to the dean of the College of Art. If he approves, it goes to the provost and the faculty senate. Only after they approve it can it be scheduled. That's the normal procedure."

"But not in this case?"

"No. ART 2330 was created by Shorter. He sent it directly to the dean. No one in the art department knew about it until it showed up in the fall schedule."

"Is that why Prather and Armstrong aren't talking to me?"

"Yes. They objected to the course because it reduced their already anemic class sizes."

"So why didn't they teach it?"

"It wasn't offered to them."

"I don't know much about academic politics, but isn't it unusual for a department head to create a course without faculty input?"

"I taught for forty years. Never heard of it happening."

He dug a tobacco pouch out of his pocket, filled his pipe and lit it. It smelled like fresh asphalt.

"Is Milton still just *acting* department head because of lack of faculty support?"

"Yes, but not because of failure to seek faculty input. Aside from this one incident, he never makes a move without getting everyone's opinion."

"Then what's the problem?"

"It's his field. Or, more accurately, fields. He seems like a dabbler. He started off as a studio artist."

"Was he good?"

"You've seen his work."

"I don't think so."

"You probably didn't recognize it as art. It's the silver coffee table in his office."

"Oops. That explains why he put a coaster under my tea when I put it on the table. I thought it was just a coffee table. I didn't know it was a work of art."

"Some of the faculty would question whether it's a work of art."

"The fossil designs are interesting," I said.

"They are. But he didn't design them. God did. Or nature. Take your pick. Shorter places the fossils on the metal surface and pours on some chemicals. Then he removes the fossils and you have a design. Not quite paint by the numbers. More like etch by the numbers."

"One could say the same thing about Prather's ill-fated attempt to cast from life," I said.

"Yes. The form would have been from the poor girl's body, not from Prather's artistic imagination."

"He has one?"

"No. His only interest in art seems to be money. He spends more time hawking his wares than teaching."

I had noticed he was always selling coffee cups. "Is there money to be made from casting from life?"

"Perhaps if the person you make a cast of is famous. Or if the cast itself is artistically posed. Which it wasn't. He just stood her there like a person waiting in line to buy a coffee cup."

"Why would he cast someone from life if there's no money in it?"

He shrugged. "He's still an associate professor. Maybe he thought doing something more creative than cups would get him promoted to full professor."

"Hockley told me Shorter is into art therapy. Is that why the faculty think he's a dabbler?"

He nodded. "Before that, he toyed with being an art historian. Studied Jonson."

"Who in New Mexico doesn't?"

He laughed.

Although Raymond Jonson is a revered figure in New Mexico, I rarely think about him. In the first place, I'm a traditionalist. He spent his career pushing modern art in a state rich with traditional art. I view him as partly responsible for the weird fusion art displayed in so many galleries here that blend Native American themes with odd materials and colors never seen among the native peoples.

In addition to rarely thinking about him, I also rarely talk about him. Mainly because I don't know how to pronounce his name. Some say Jones-son. Others say Yown-son. Still others say Yoon-son. I think he should have left the *h* in his name and been just plain Johnson.

Jonson taught at UNM for twenty years, retiring just after Edward Abbey graduated. Abbey's lifelong best friend was the painter John De Puy, who studied under Jonson. Abbey himself dabbled in painting. UNM was a small school back then and the curriculum less varied. Most students took the same general education courses. It wouldn't surprise me to discover that Abbey took an art course from Jonson.

57

So I was not paranoid.

Shorter hadn't offered the course to his regular faculty. For some reason I couldn't fathom, he gave it to me.

I went from Wiezga's studio to Shorter's office, where I intended to ask him why he chose me to offer ART 2330.

I got as far as the hall, where I saw Shorter through the window in his door. He was talking to a woman seated to the side of the desk. They were both in profile and didn't see me.

I returned to the condo and paced around the glass table until Benz bared his teeth at me and hissed.

Geronimo and I went out on the balcony and tried patience. He was good at it. I wasn't. At least Benz was able to relax with me and my mutt out of the way.

I wanted to call Susannah and tell her about the woman I'd seen in Shorter's office. But the condo doesn't have a landline, and I don't have a cell phone. So I sat on the balcony and thought.

It was good place to think. The urban clatter below emphasized the feeling of being isolated, alone in the crowd. In this case, above the crowd.

The December sky was clear, nothing between the sun and the balcony but clean cold air.

A light breeze drifted over me. I sneezed.

And realized Harte Hockley had not killed Ximena.

I left the balcony at half past four and walked to Spirits in Clay to pick up my mail. There was a letter from the penitentiary. I took it with me to Dos Hermanas.

When Susannah arrived, I told her I'd gone to Shorter's office to ask why he scheduled ART 2330 and why he chose me to teach it.

"What did he say?"

"I didn't ask him. There was a woman in his office."

"Why didn't you just wait till she left?"

"Because the woman in his office was Ms. Nose."

"And you were afraid she would kick you out of the Art Building?"

"I don't know what I was afraid of. Anyway, I didn't want to see her, so I quietly left the building."

Susannah tapped the screen of her cell phone. Her large brown eyes grew even larger. "Oh. My. God."

She turned the phone for me to see. Under a photograph of Ms. Nose was her name—Helen Shorter.

"She's his wife! How did you do that?"

"Deaf and Hard of Hearing Services is housed under the Accessibility Resource Center. Their website has picture of the signers. You cold?"

I was shivering. "No. Scared. I angered his wife. He assigned me a course with a deaf girl in it. Then . . ."

"Then what?"

"I don't know. But my weird theory that the course was punishment looks a lot less weird."

"Why does that scare you?"

"What if it's related somehow to Ximena's death?"

"How?"

"I don't know. Maybe he enlisted Prather to kill her and frame me?"

She just shook her head.

"Someone killed her, and it wasn't Harte Hockley."

"I know that. They only thought he did because of the straws. Now that they know she was poisoned, the straw theory is dead."

"No. The pinching-the-straws-to-cut-off-her-air theory is dead. The spraying-poison-up-the-straws theory is alive and well."

"Of course! Do you think they tested all those straws for cyanide?"

"I don't know. But what I do know is that someone tried to frame him just like they tried to frame me. And I think I know how they did it."

"You've learned from the master," she said, pointing her thumb at herself. "Or maybe the mistress, but that word's been corrupted. Give it your best shot."

"They got the straws with his prints on them the same way they got a straw with my print on it. They took them from the tea he drank at the departmental meeting."

"You weaseled out of the suspect list using that lame explanation about there being only one straw with your fingerprints on one end and Ximena's nasal gunk on the other. But in Hockley's case, they had two."

"That's because he had two glasses of tea."

"And someone saved the straws?"

"I don't think so. They were thrown in a trash can, which was eventually emptied into a Dumpster behind Hodgin Hall. I saw them while my class was searching for twigs but didn't realize they were those straws. Someone retrieved them and tried to frame Hockley."

She was shaking her head as I spoke. "How would they know which straws were his?"

"Because he doodled on both cups. So when they saw the cups with the doodles, they knew the straws were his."

"And how did they get Ximena's nasal gunk on them? Her body was with the OMI by that point."

"Remember the second incriminating piece of evidence was a note that seemed to imply she and Hockley were having an affair? I'm guessing that note did double duty. It not only provided a motive, it provided some of her nasal mucus, which was rubbed onto the straws."

"What? She blew her nose on the note?"

"She sneezed on it. She had allergies and sneezed a lot."

"Okay, all of that is theoretically possible. But it's also farfetched."

"Granted. So give me another theory about the straws that's near-fetched."

"I can't think of one. But there's a hole in your theory. The handwriting expert said the writing on the note was Ximena's. So unless the framer was able to copy Ximena's handwriting well enough to fool the police expert, then Hockley was having an affair with her and she was going to end it. That's enough motive to make Hockley a suspect. Turning over evidence related to a suspect is not a frame. It's just part of the investigatory process."

"The note was torn. Charles and I both think the torn-off part might change the meaning of the note."

"No way. I don't remember exactly what you told me the note said, but I do remember there was no doubt about what it meant."

I pictured the note. "It said something like 'Hockley's been after me since I was a freshman. I fended him off. But last semester, I gave in. It was great at first and exciting. It was something I'd never done. But now he's making too many demands. I want out. But I don't know how to tell him. I don't want to hurt him.'"

She just looked at me and sipped her margarita.

"I know it seems obvious," I said. "But it doesn't actually say they were having an affair."

"And when Mick Jagger sings about not getting any satisfaction, he never mentions the word *sex*, but that's what the song's about."

She was right, of course. I decided to share my farfetched theory with Fletcher. He would poke a hole in it. Which is what it needed. And what I needed in order to stop obsessing.

The letter from the penitentiary was on the table. It contained two things. A slip of paper saying it had been opened by an assistant warden and cleared for mailing. And Freddie's drawing of Susannah. I passed it to her.

She stared at it. "*Dance in the Country*."

"Huh?"

"A painting by Renoir. Except I'm in it." She looked up. "Where did you get this?"

I showed her the return address on the envelope.

"Freddie?"

I nodded.

Her eyes watered.

"Tell me about the Renoir," I said.

"It's one of my favorite paintings. I don't remember telling him that, but I must have. Why else would he choose that painting?"

"Maybe you and Freddie just happen to like the same painting. More likely it's because it's so romantic. He's still in love with you."

She looked back at the sketch. "It is romantic. They haven't finished their picnic. They're totally lost in dance, oblivious to all else. His hat has fallen off. Her fan is about to hit the ground. She's obviously looking forward to what will happen next."

"When I saw it, I almost choked up. He captured your innocence and enthusiasm."

"I'm hardly innocent, Hubie."

"Innocence isn't a matter of history, Suze, it's a state of mind."

She looked at the sketch again, transfixed. "This says more about him than me."

"How so?"

"I think artists' personalities show in their works. The person who painted this is less self-centered than the Frederick Blass I knew."

"You think the guy whose back we see is Freddie?"

She didn't answer that question. I don't think she even heard it. "If what you say is true and he still . . ."

After a minute, she dried her eyes, looked up and held the sketch toward me.

"It's yours," I said. "He asked me to give it to you."

58

After the first day in class, I'd starting looking forward to it being over. Now I was sad it was.

A lot can happen in one semester.

"We gonna have a final exam?" asked Aleesha.

"Is it normal to have a final in a studio class?"

"No, but you don't do normal."

"I'll take that as a compliment."

"I meant it as a compliment. I liked this class even though you don't like me."

"I do like you, Aleesha. And I like you even more when you don't have your cell phone."

The class laughed.

"I think we will have a final. But it won't be here. It will be at Dos Hermanas in Old Town."

"Isn't that a bar?" asked Bruce.

"It's a *tortilleria* that happens to sell alcohol. Attendance is optional. Want to know your final grade?"

"I don't want to know mine," said Mia.

"Why not? You made an A."

"I did?"

"Sure. Your clay piece was inventive, and the etching was good."

Raúl said, "If she made an A, the rest of us must have made A-pluses."

Everyone laughed including Mia.

"There is no A-plus grade. But you did all make A's." I thought for a moment before continuing. "I lost a student. You lost a class-mate. That will stay with us forever."

I brought them up-to-date by telling them that Detective Fletcher had reported to me that Ximena had been poisoned.

"I just hope they catch the guy who did it," said Aleesha.

"Or the woman who did it," said Raúl.

"Women don't do things like that," she said.

"On the contrary," said Raúl. "Poison is the preferred method of women murderers. Lucrezia Borgia, the little old ladies from *Arsenic and Old Lace*, the witch from *Snow White*."

"He or she will be caught," I said.

Aleesha said, "Don't bet on it. There were almost five hundred murders in Chicago last year, and the police only solved about a hundred of them."

Marlon said, "Is that why you came to UNM instead of going to school in your home town?"

"Somebody from LA don't need to be criticizing Chicago."

Bruce noted that the murder case solution rate in Albuquerque is 95 percent.

Someone else started to speak, but I cut them off. "Did any of you know Ximena was a poet?"

They shook their heads, except for Alfred, who said, "She wrote some for me."

"Do you want to share one of them?"

He shook his head.

I held up Ximena's black book of poems. "This notebook is full of her poems. I'm going to turn it over to the police. They want to see if there's anything in it that might help their investigation. After the murderer is caught and tried, they'll give it back to Ximena's parents."

"Can you read one of her poems to us?" asked Carly.

"That's why I brought the book. There's a poem about all of you. She titled it 'Friends.'"

I interlock my index fingers
and form the lip of my pot
using the v they create
I interlock them again

We are all friends
Silence does not bother them

"What's that index-finger thing?" Aleesha asked.
"Interlocking index fingers twice is the sign for friendship."
"You know how to sign?"
"No. I asked a friend of mine about it." I closed the book. "I've
enjoyed getting to know you. I'll be in my office for the next hour
in case any of you have paperwork that needs to be signed."

The first drop-in was Alfred, who said he wanted to apologize for
appearing uncooperative.
"I never found you uncooperative," I said.
He looked at his shoes. "You asked me why Ximena said I was
the only one she would allow to prep her for the body cast, and I
didn't tell you."
"That's not uncooperative, Alfred. Cooperation doesn't require
you to reveal personal things."
"And then in class today, you asked if I wanted to share one of
the poems Ximena wrote for me, and I didn't."
"Same answer. Those are both private things. You have a right
to keep it that way."
"I would have told you why she chose me if I thought it would
help the police."
"I know that."
He finally looked up from the floor. "She was a very special person."
"Yes. She was."
"We were sort of a couple."
He studied my face for a reaction. I don't think I showed one.
Maybe I did. After all, I couldn't see my face.
"You're probably surprised. Most people think I'm gay, but
I'm not."

I didn't think teaching pottery required me to know the sexual orientation of my students, so I didn't say anything.

"I'm not straight, either. I'm just not interested."

"You said you and Ximena were a couple."

"I said 'sort of.'"

"I enjoyed having you in class, Alfred."

We stood. We hugged. He left.

Bruce was waiting a discreet distance down the hall.

"Can I ask you for some personal advice man-to-man?"

I signed up to teach Anasazi Pottery Methods, I thought to myself, not to be a counselor. But I nodded.

"I'm thinking of asking Carly for a date. You think that's out of line?"

"Why would it be?"

"I'm twenty-three. She's thirty-two. She has a kid."

"You like Luke?"

"Sure. He's a great kid."

"You like spending time with him?"

"Yeah."

"Then what's the problem? She's a nice person. She's no longer married. And she's attractive. What else do you want?"

"What about the age thing?"

"I'm ten years older than Sharice."

"Yeah, but you're a man."

"It's 2016, Bruce, not 1950."

He smiled. "Got it. Thanks."

Mia was next. "Mind if I kiss you? I promise it's just to show how thankful I am for what you did."

"What did I do?"

"I guess it's what you didn't do."

"How about a hug instead? Sharice is the jealous type."

Aleesha said, "Sharice tell you about our little talk?"

"She did not."

"I don't believe you."

"Wouldn't be the first time."

She shook her head slowly. "Did you ask her about it?"

"No."

"Why not?"

"If she thinks I need to know something about it, she'll tell me."

"She said that?"

"No."

"So you saw the two of us out there talking by the gazebo, and you didn't ask her about it and she didn't tell you about it."

"Our version of don't ask, don't tell."

"I don't get it."

"I forget how young you are. It's a policy the military adopted when—"

"I know about that. What I don't get is you both ignoring it."

"We didn't ignore it. She obviously didn't think she needed to tell me about it."

"But don't you wonder what—"

"It's called love, Aleesha. And it's based on trust."

"Wow. Well, she loves you just as much, but you already know that."

I nodded.

"I never believed a mixed couple could make it work."

"You were wrong."

She smiled. "Yeah. I was."

Marlon crushed my hand and told me my class was his favorite.

"Will you take another pottery class?"

"Nope. This was my last class. Fact is, I'm dropping out of school."

"Why? You're a good student, Marlon. You should get your degree."

"I will. But I need to spend the next few months working out. No time for classes. I expect to be drafted in the spring."

"I thought the draft was abolished a long time ago."

"That's funny, Mr. Schuze. I'm hoping to be drafted in the NFL."

"NFL?"

"National Football League. You've heard of it, right?"

"Right. Denver Broncos. Dallas Cowboys. So you'll be an offensive lineman with one of those teams?"

"Any team would be okay with me, but I'm hoping for the Rams."

I didn't know that one. "I wish you the best, Marlon."

He gave me a one-arm hug and said goodbye.

Raúl and Apache arrived at the same time. Raúl said, "Weird class. But good." He extended his hand and I took it. Apache said, "What he said."

I realized I'd think about these students off and on for the rest of my life. I didn't want to teach again, but I was grateful for the experience.

Then I thought about Ximena. The dissonance between nine happy students saying goodbye and the one who never said anything.

59

Whit Fletcher peered into my office.

"They must still dislike you, giving you an office this small."

"This office is actually a clue."

"You been hanging around that Inchaustigui girl too much."

"You want to know why it's a clue?"

"I'm listening."

"I went to see Frederick Blass."

"Yeah. Webbe told me he got you in on an off day. Blass apologize for trying to frame you?"

"He did. He also told me the art department never hires adjuncts because they don't have enough enrollment to create basic loads for their regular faculty."

"So?"

"So that started me wondering why Milton Shorter hired me. And the only reason that makes sense is he hired me as a form of revenge."

He stared out from underneath those droopy eyes. "Revenge for what?"

"For upsetting his wife."

He did what I'd hoped. Punched a hole in my theory. One I could have driven my Bronco through.

"He ain't married."

"How do you know that?"

"Routine police work, Hubert. We always check out the family of victims, perps and even witnesses. Just in case there are any connections."

"But there's a woman named Helen Shorter who works as a deaf interpreter at the university. I saw her in his office."

"She's his sister."

"But she has a gigantic nose. His is small and delicate."

"You seen my wife. She's almost six feet tall. Her sister is a runt. People from the same family don't always look alike."

"She has a Nordic complexion. He looks Italian."

"What'd I just say?"

I gave up and asked him if the crime lab tested all the straws for cyanide.

"Of course. None of the ones given to us had cyanide on them."

"What about the two that were actually in her nose?"

"The paramedics and cops who were called after the Sifuentes girl keeled over didn't think about the straws. Probably didn't know there were any. Who the hell knows about covering someone with plaster and calling it art? We asked Prather about it the second time we talked to him. That was after the OMI ruled the death was by asphyxiation. He said he took the cast back to his studio. Said he must have thrown the straws away, since they weren't part of the art. He also said he planned to complete the project."

"Even though Ximena was dead?"

"Said her being dead made the project more meaningful. Said it would be a tribute."

"Baloney. Since when do murderers pay tribute to their victims?"

"You think he killed her?"

I recited the reasons I'd given Susannah. He was the one who chose her as the model. He was the one who put her in a defenseless situation. And although theoretically anyone could have walked in off the street and poisoned her, he was the only one we knew for sure was in there. And he demonstrated his willingness to harm someone when he attacked me.

Fletcher admitted Prather would be his prime suspect except for lack of a motive.

I told him my theory about Shorter assigning me the class as revenge. He laughed at me.

Instead of trying to convince him, I said, "Maybe it would help the investigation to clear up everything concerning the straws you were given as evidence."

"Hmm. Sort of clear the underbrush."

"Exactly."

"That why you asked me to come here?"

I told him it was. We improvised a quick good cop/bad cop script and walked down the hall.

Whit stood unseen to the side of her door, and I walked into Jollo Bakkie's office by myself.

"What are you doing here?" she demanded.

I didn't answer her question. I just started the script. "You went to the Dumpster behind Hodgin Hall and pulled two straws out of cups that had been doodled on. You recognized the doodles as being from Harte Hockley."

"Get out of my office."

Whit stepped inside and showed her his badge. "You want to continue this discussion at the police station?"

"You can't arrest me."

"You ever been strip searched?"

"You wouldn't do that."

"No, ma'am, I wouldn't. I'm too much of a gentleman. Bobcat would do that."

Jollo's eyes widened. "Bobcat?"

"That's the nickname the officers hung on the jail matron 'cause her butch haircut is dyed yellow and black. Lots of muscle for a woman. Lifts weights. Be good-looking if she lost about fifty pounds."

She glowered at us for thirty seconds. "I'm listening."

I said, "You knew Hockley's fingerprints were on those straws. You brought them back here and rubbed the other end of the straws on a note Ximena Sifuentes had sneezed on."

"Then you mailed them to us," said Fletcher. "You tried to frame Hockley for Ximena's murder."

"Why would I do that?"

My turn. "Because you want to teach painting and can't do that unless he's out of the picture."

"That's ridiculous."

His turn. "We know Hockley didn't do it. Ximena was not suffocated. She was poisoned. The straws you dug out of the Dumpster had no trace of poison on them. I can arrest you for interfering with a police investigation and falsifying evidence."

My turn. "Don't arrest her. Maybe she can help."

She looked at me. "How can I help?"

"On the day Ximena was killed, Shorter turned off the security camera in the gallery so that Ximena could cover her naked body with alginate and then gauze. He was supposed to turn it on again after the plaster was in place, but he forgot."

"So?"

"So there was a gap. Sometime after the plaster was applied and before the first guests arrived to view the removal of the plaster cast, someone entered the gallery and poisoned Ximena. We don't know who it was because the camera was off."

"What's that got to do with me?"

"Shorter says you're the reason he forgot."

She looked confused. "How did I make him forget?"

"You were in his office shortly after he turned off the camera. You tried to convince him that you should be teaching painting instead of Hockley. By the time you left, it was almost time for the removal of the cast."

Her anger and fear gave way to confusion. "Yes. That was so strange. Usually, he can't wait for me to leave. Like he's already made up his mind before I give him the reasons why I should be the painting instructor, and he just wants to get rid of me. But on that day, it all changed. For the first time, he allowed me to state my case completely. It was like he had all day and nothing better to do than listen to me. At one point, someone came into his office. I asked if he needed me to leave. He said hearing why I should be the painting instructor was more important than his other meetings, so she'd just have to wait. He listened so long that she just left. I guess she got tired of waiting."

"Then what?"

She sighed. "Then nothing. That was weeks ago, and Hockley is listed again next semester on all the painting sections. It doesn't make sense. Why did he listen so intently and show such interest if he wasn't going to change anything?"

I had an answer. Instead of giving it to her, I said, "There's one more thing you could do to be helpful."

"What's that?"

"Tell Lieutenant Fletcher about the note Ximena gave you concerning Hockley."

She continued looking at me. "I don't have to tell him about it. I gave it to him."

"No. You gave him part of it. The part he didn't get must have started something like 'Hockley really wanted me in his painting course.' Then the part you gave the police says, 'Hockley's been after me since I was a freshman. I fended him off. But last semester, I gave in.' You altered that note to make it sound like an affair. It wasn't about having an affair with Hockley. It was about being caught up by a demanding teacher who expected more commitment to painting than she was willing to give. She came to you for help, and you tried to sully her reputation."

"What does it matter? She's dead."

I resisted the temptation to slap her. "It matters to her parents."

Her shrug was cruel. "Okay. You're right."

She pulled a piece of paper out of her desk drawer and handed it to Fletcher.

"It's Prather's fault," she said. "He's the one who killed her. And it's obvious he tried to frame you by giving that straw to the police that he took out of your tea. That's what gave me the idea to get Hockley's straws. But Hockley's off the hook now because of the poison thing. So I didn't really do any harm." She looked at Fletcher. "I'm cooperating. There's no reason to arrest me."

"I'll think about it," he said.

60

I asked Whit why Bakkie would keep the torn-off part of the note.

His explanation was simple. "Criminals are stupid. That's why we catch them. She also lied about her meeting with Shorter. You told me he tried to shoo her out of his office. She says he listened patiently."

We were walking down the hallway. Empty classrooms and studios on each side because the semester was over.

I said, "Maybe Bakkie was telling the truth and it was Shorter who lied."

"Why would Shorter lie to you about his talk with Bakkie?"

I gave him the answer I had not given to Jollo. "He wanted her to stay so he'd have an alibi."

"An alibi for what?"

"I'm not sure. Try this. Shorter was afraid Prather might kill Ximena and he wanted an alibi to keep from being dragged into it."

"You'd make a lousy cop, Hubert. In the first place, if he wants an alibi, all he's got to do is go to a bar and make sure the barman and the customers see him there. It's a better alibi for two reasons. First, his office is less than a hundred feet from the gallery. He coulda slipped down there, poisoned her and been back behind his desk in less than five minutes. Sure, he can say he was with Bakkie all afternoon, but what about if he went to take a leak but didn't?

The bar gets him totally away. And on top of that, he don't have to put up with that wacky dame all afternoon."

He was right about my making a lousy cop. Which didn't bother me because it's about the last thing I'd want to be. I lack both the stature and the nerve.

We reached Prather's office.

I made my solo entry and got the same response from Junior that I got from Jollo.

"What are you doing here?"

"You took the straw from the cup of tea you served me at the departmental meeting and inserted it into one of Ximena's nostrils. Then you gave it to the police in an attempt to frame me for her murder."

It almost seemed he and Bakkie had coordinated their responses because he also said, "Get out of my office."

Whit stepped inside and showed his badge. "You want to continue this discussion at the police station?"

"You can't arrest me."

"You ever been strip searched?"

Junior was a lot less stoic in the face of that question than Bakkie had been. He swallowed audibly. His voice broke as he said, "I was just trying to help. I figured he must have killed her, so I was trying to point the police in the right direction."

"Why would I kill her?"

"You were having a lot of problems with your students."

Whit and I looked at each other and shook our heads.

Whit said, "I'm impounding the body cast." He nodded to me. I picked up one of the two halves of the cast. He picked up the other one. "Also, I'm going to prepare a statement. You're going to sign it. If you don't, you go to jail and get to meet Bulldog."

"Bulldog?"

"He's the guy does the strip searches."

"Two more things," I said. "Why did you decide to do the casting and why did you decide to use Ximena as the model?"

"Helen Shorter offered me a stipend to do a body cast of a deaf student for use as a display in the Deaf and Hard of Hearing Services lobby. I didn't know any deaf students, so she arranged for one. Also I thought doing something edgy might help me get promoted." He looked up at me. "I wish I hadn't attacked you."

I started to accept what I thought was his apology, but he kept talking. "Now I'll never be promoted," he said.

I guess he figured his lost promotion opportunity was my fault. Whit and I carried the two parts of the cast to my office. Even with them jammed into a corner, the door wouldn't close. My mind drifted back to the first day I was in the office, and Helga Ólafsdóttir caught me trying to pose like a Duane Hanson sculpture. What would she think if she saw the plaster mold?

I snapped back to the present and said to Whit, "Bobcat? Bulldog?"

"Funny what a simple nickname can do. Made 'em up of course. But they fit, don't they? Speaking of fit, let's check this out." He held up the note Bakkie had given the police weeks ago and the piece she had given him fifteen minutes ago. "Perfect fit."

As I suspected, the first part of the note made it clear that what Ximena wanted out of was not an affair with Hockley. What she wanted out of was his demanding painting course.

"You were right about the straws. Clearing that up gets rid of a distraction. But we're back at square one. I don't buy Prather as the killer and Bakkie's not a suspect. Hockley's off the hook."

"That's good. It exonerates Ximena from the alleged affair."

Not many people knew about the allegation, but that didn't matter. Even one would be too many. I felt happy for her. For her parents. For Alfred, her partner or friend or whatever. She was special to him. It would break his heart if he thought she had an affair with Hockley.

And that was when I thought about another note. The one Ximena wrote to Alfred about agreeing to be the model for the body cast.

I knew who killed Ximena. It was in that note. I didn't realize it at the time, of course. I didn't even know who it referred to then. It was an irrelevant detail. Or so I thought.

Maybe you remember that note. Maybe you paid more attention than I did. If so, you remember that it read, "I'm willing to be the model because I need the money. And because that stupid

Helen S. asked me to. Even though we don't get along, she seems to think I owe it to her. But I don't want Prather touching me. I don't want him wrapping gauze on me. I want you to do that. And I want you to make sure there's no monkey business."

Helen S.

Helen Shorter.

I told Whit about the note.

"So you think the Shorter woman conned Prather into putting the Sifuentes girl into plaster so that she could kill her by spraying poison up the straws?"

"Yes."

"What's the motive?"

"A clash of cultures."

"What the hell does that mean?"

"Helen Shorter is an activist for deafness being a culture and sign language being their native language. She thinks lip reading is a form of colonialism. The dominant culture—the people who can hear—are forcing the subjugated minority—deaf people—to adopt the culture of the hearing people. Like Europeans did when they conquered the Americas and forced all the native peoples to learn English."

He shook his head. "That sounds like some egghead theory, not a reason to kill anyone."

"Look at the Middle East. Sunnis and Shiites kill each other. Turks and Kurds kill each other."

"This is Albuquerque, Hubert. Murders here are motivated by jealousy or money."

"Most of the time. But this is a unique situation. Ximena learned to read lips so well that she got along fine in the hearing world. I had her in class and didn't even know she was deaf. She was an honor student. She was popular. But from Helen Shorter's point of view, Ximena was a turncoat. Her success in a world she could not hear undermined Helen Shorter's political thesis that deaf people are a repressed minority."

"Too deep for me. You got something more practical? Like someone heard her threaten to kill Ximena? Or she bought some cyanide? 'Cause otherwise, I got nowhere to start."

"How about you ask Milton Shorter about his sister?"

"What would I ask him?"

"Ask him why he scheduled me to teach a course. Ask him why he put Ximena in it. Ask him if he knew his sister arranged for Ximena to be the model."

61

We waited in the hall until a student left Shorter's office.

"Come in, Hubie. Sorry for the wait. The poor girl just got her academic suspension notice for next semester. I couldn't reinstate her. Only the dean has authority to do that. But I can listen."

"Art therapy, right?"

He smiled that soft smile of his. "Sometimes I don't have to pull out the brushes. Just listening is enough. Who's your friend?"

"This is Detective Whit Fletcher from the Albuquerque Police Department."

Milton shook Whit's hand then looked at me. "You in trouble again, Hubie?"

"Not that I know of."

Whit said, "Hubert and I just talked to Junior Prather."

Milton smiled and said, "So he's talking to you now?"

"Helps if the guy with you has a badge and a gun," I replied.

Whit rolled his eyes at me then looked at Milton. "Why did you ask Hubert to teach a class?"

"Actually, my sister suggested it. She said one of her student clients needed a pottery course."

"Ximena Sifuentes."

"Right."

"But why ask Hubert to teach it? You already got two pottery teachers."

"Helen is very protective of her student clients. She said Ximena would not be comfortable with Prather or Armstrong."

"So how do you explain her agreeing to be the model for Prather's body cast project?"

"That does seem odd, doesn't it? Maybe she needed the money."

"Did you know your sister selected Ximena as the model?"

"Heavens no. I didn't even know she and Prather knew each other."

"Seems like she would know your faculty."

He shook his head. "She works across campus. She comes here only when a deaf student needs her services. She, uh, doesn't interact much with the hearing community."

"She went to the trouble to get you to offer a new course so Ximena wouldn't have to take a pottery class from Prather? Then she arranges for Ximena to be Prather's model? That make sense to you?"

Milton bit his lower lip. "I'm a therapist, Lieutenant. What makes sense is not an objective fact."

"You told Hubert the reason you forgot to turn the security camera back on was because Jollo Bakkie was in your office."

"Yes, making her usual plea to teach a painting course."

"You told Hubie you tried to shoo her out. She says you listened patiently."

"Diplomacy. I tried to shoo her out gently. Evidently, too gently."

I asked Milton if he knew his sister had kicked me out of the new-faculty orientation session.

"I had no idea. Why did she kick you out?"

"The written version of her presentation claimed signing is the natural language of deaf people. During the ensuing discussion, I said signing is not a language any more than typing is a language. It's just another way of conveying a language."

"Ouch. No wonder she kicked you out. You belittled her most basic belief."

"I did not belittle anything. I said I appreciated the importance of signing and the skill it takes to master it. But the same can be said of Morse code. It's not a language."

"I agree with Helen on that point. I guess you and I will just have to agree to disagree."

"Fair enough. But why would she ask you to create a course with me as the teacher and put Ximena in that course if I had undermined her most basic belief about deaf people?"

He shrugged. "Therapy trains us not to make assumptions about motivations. Oftentimes they are unknown even to the person who has them. Perhaps she saw a nurturing side of you. After all, you weren't going to teach Ximena about deaf culture. You were going to teach pottery. Ximena needed a nurturing pottery teacher. From what I've heard from the students, Helen's judgment seems to have proved correct. They loved your class."

Whit and I walked to his car. I noted aloud that he was illegally parked.

"You think the campus cops are gonna ticket an APD car?"

"Guess not. Is Helen Shorter a suspect?"

"You think she should be?"

"Of course. Ximena didn't want to be the model, but Helen Shorter talked her into it. That left Ximena defenseless. And she put Ximena in my class even though she thinks I'm anti-deaf. If I got blamed for the murder, she kills two birds with one stone."

"You're forgetting one little detail, Hubert. It was Prather who tried to frame you, not the Shorter woman. Or do you think they were working together?"

"Maybe."

"And as far as putting Ximena in your class, I think what Milton said makes sense. You were the right teacher for her. It ain't important that you disagree with Helen Shorter about all that sign-language crap. What's important is you were a good teacher. You should feel good about what Milton said about the students liking your class."

"I guess you're right. But I still think you should check her out."

62

Nine days after Whit's visit to the campus, I lowered myself into one of Dos Hermanas's gaily decorated ladder-back chairs and told Susannah that Helen Shorter had just been arrested for the murder of Ximena Sifuentes.

She said, "I just heard the five o'clock news. They didn't mention it."

"That's because they don't know about it yet. Whit called right before I started over here."

"Why would he call you so fast? You offering a reward?"

"Funny. He called me because I was the one who cracked the case."

"'Cracked the case'? Since when do you talk like that?"

"Like Whit said, it comes from hanging around with you."

"The last time you said you solved the mystery, all you solved was one clue and even that depended on some hag of a fish."

"Hagfish."

"Whatever. What did he tell you?"

"First, she was uncooperative when he questioned her, and that made him suspicious."

"Being uncooperative is not a sign of guilt. And it may be hard to appear cooperative if you're a deaf mute."

"It's not like they're going to use that in court. It's just what made him probe a little deeper."

"What did he find?"

"Emails on her home computer. She called Ximena names and threatened her."

"She put a murder threat in an email?"

"No. Threats to 'out' her to the deaf community as a traitor. To turn the other deaf students against her. To withhold letters of recommendation from the Office of Hard of Hearing and Deaf Services, things like that."

"Doesn't sound like evidence of a murder."

"How about a spray bulb with cyanide traces on the inside and Ximena's nasal mucus on the outside."

"Wow. Even better than a straw. But why would she keep that?"

I told her that when I asked Whit why Jollo Bakkie kept the torn-off part of Ximena's note, he said, "Criminals are stupid. That's why we catch them." Then I said, "My hunch is she was afraid that no matter how she tried to get rid of it, someone would find it."

"She could have buried it out in the desert."

"And a police dog could have sniffed it out."

"Why would a police dog be out in the desert?"

"Maybe his handler collected cactuses. How would I know? The point is that if you've got something that could get you convicted of murder, you might think the best place to hide it is a place you control. So you bury it in your backyard."

"Because the guy who handles the police dogs can't go there to collect cactus."

"Exactly."

"Is that what she did with it—bury it in her backyard?"

"No."

"What did she do with it?" As I've told you before, Susannah loves murder mysteries.

"I can't tell you."

"You don't know?"

"I do know. But Whit told me not to tell anyone. The police want to keep all the details secret."

"Oh, come on. When he said don't tell anyone, he didn't mean me."

"How do you know that?"

"Did he mention me by name?"

"No."

"So, there you go. He knows we're friends and you tell me everything."

I couldn't argue with that. I leaned close to her and whispered, "Helen has one of those wide dog bowls with a sort of inner tube-shaped rim that stops it from sliding around. She glued the bulb under the rim. Clever, right? You pick up the bowl to look under it, and nothing's there."

"Very funny," she commented on my whispering. "But what if someone turns the bowl over?"

"All the food spills out. Who would do that?"

"The police, obviously. They found it."

"They did not. The dog found it."

"So it *was* sniffed out by a police dog."

"No. It was sniffed out by Helen Shorter's dog. He evidently didn't like the smell next to his food. So when the cops picked up the bowl and then sat it down again thinking there was nothing under it, he grabbed it in his jaw and turned it over. Smart dog with a weird name—Bram. I guess she liked Dracula."

"I'll bet he wasn't named after Bram Stoker. He was named after another dog named Bram who's deaf."

"There are deaf dogs?"

"Yeah. They used to put them down because they thought they couldn't be trained. And some people thought they were aggressive because they couldn't hear someone approaching, which is ridiculous because they can smell people. But there's a dog named Bram who learned to understand sign language. And he even makes a few signs."

"So why didn't he just sign to the police that there was something poisonous-smelling under his bowl?"

She ignored that. "Now that I think about Bram, I'm beginning to think maybe signing is a language."

"Why?"

"I've always bought your argument that signing is just a way to convey a spoken language like English or Spanish. But dogs can't speak. So signing doesn't depend on language."

"Dogs have always been taught how to respond to signs. You spin your finger and they roll over. You extend your hand and they shake it. But I don't think you can say dogs know languages just because they can respond to visual signals."

"Yeah, I guess. The horse called Clever Hans could add any two numbers his trainer gave him by tapping his hoof to the correct sum, but only if the trainer was in sight. Hans was reading the trainer's body language and realized when to stop tapping."

I pointed to my mouth, and she handed me a chip.

"Good doggie," I said.

She took one for herself and ate it. "So the police have the motive and the weapon. What about opportunity?"

"She was seen in the Art Building during the period when Ximena was in the body cast and the security camera was off."

"Too bad the security camera was off. That would have cinched it."

"I'd say finding the murder weapon in her houses cinches it."

"Maybe not. She can just say someone planted the squeeze bulb there to incriminate her."

"I don't think Whit would buy that."

"Forget about Whit. Think about a jury. Her lawyer will point out that there was an attempt to frame you. And then an attempt to frame Hockley. So why wouldn't a jury see this as just one more frame attempt?"

I had to admit that made sense. Which worried me for a moment. Then I realized it was pointless to worry. The police would still be gathering information. It would be weeks, maybe months, before they turned it over to the DA's Office. And who knows how long before it went to trial. If it did. Maybe there would be a plea bargain as there had been in Blass's case. As far as I was concerned, it was over. I didn't need to waste time worrying about what came next.

63

Sharice and I were in bed, her head on my chest. Benz was on my stomach, curled up under Sharice's chin. Geronimo was stretched across my legs at the foot of the bed.

One big happy family.

I was probably the happiest one. Benz and Geronimo had just returned from exile on the balcony.

Sharice said she was glad they caught Helen Shorter. "She must be deranged. Going to all that trouble. Getting her brother to schedule a course. Getting Prather to do a body cast. Spraying poison into it after it hardened. Why not just get a pistol and shoot the poor girl?"

I tried to shrug but couldn't. Too much weight on me. "Maybe she was afraid the gunshot would damage her hearing."

She laughed and bit at my ribs. Then she turned serious. "How about you? You had a roller-coaster semester."

"Nothing compared to what you have faced. With courage and aplomb."

"And your love and support."

I would have kissed her but I still couldn't move.

"My class got off to a rocky start, but by the end, I liked all nine of them. Wish it would have still been ten."

"The scholarship is a nice memorial."

"I wonder if she would have wanted it."

"Why wouldn't she?"

"Before Edward Abbey died, he made his friends agree that there would be no undertaker. No embalming. No coffin. The day he died, they put him in an old sleeping bag and transported him in the bed of a pickup out into the desert, where he was buried in an unmarked grave."

"He didn't need a marker. His books are his legacy. The scholarship is Ximena's legacy."

"A memorial maybe. But not a legacy. It's not something she did."

"It's something her fellow students did because of the person she was."

"True."

64

I drove to campus to retrieve the body cast from my office.

In case Whit asked for it as evidence, I wanted to be able to say truthfully, "I already destroyed it."

Getting rid of the cast would close the chapter. I hauled it out to the Bronco in two trips. I climbed in and started the engine.

Then I turned it off.

I couldn't leave in good conscience without saying goodbye to Milton Shorter. He had treated a lowly adjunct well, even become a sort of friend. Normally, I would have looked forward to chatting with him.

But his sister had just been arrested for murder. And he may have guessed from the visit I made to his office with Whit Fletcher that I had a hand in the case.

One shouldn't have to apologize for unmasking a killer. But still.

I felt less awkward when he smiled at me and rose to shake my hand. He motioned to his guest chair and I sat. He offered me a bottle of water. He handed me a coaster. I put it on the silver coffee table before putting the bottle down.

Might as well get it out, I thought. "Sorry about your sister."

He took in a deep breath then slowly exhaled. "Thanks, Hubie." He was silent for a few moments, looking down. "As a therapist, I should know how to handle guilt." He looked up and smiled. "I'm a better therapist than patient. I felt guilty about not turning the security camera back on. Now I feel guilty about not being a better brother to Helen."

I couldn't think of anything appropriate to say.

"My parents adopted her when I was fifteen. She was six. I thought it was cool that they were adopting a deaf child. It made them seem even more special as parents. And it seemed like a sort of adventure for me. We all learned to sign."

So that's why they didn't look alike. "Sounds like a good way to create a bond with a new family member."

"It was. But we never became really close because of the age difference. Three years after she arrived, I went away to college. I thought when she got a job here at UNM, we might find that brother-sister thing, but it didn't happen. My signing skills had declined. She was wrapped up in her clients. I was immersed in my job. We . . . I would say grew apart, but that's not it. We were never close to begin with. And now . . . I still can't believe she murdered Ximena."

"Maybe the police made a mistake."

He shook his head. "I wish I could believe that. But they found a squeeze bulb with cyanide on it under her dog bowl."

I hoped Milton didn't notice me shudder. Or feel the icy air that wafted across me.

The floodgates opened and everything I missed rushed in.

Susannah telling me that Ms. Nose—now known to me as Helen Shorter—had made snide remarks about the guest lecturer on Raymond Jonson, calling him a spoiled brat. Wiezga telling me Milton dabbled in art history specializing in Jonson. How would Helen know the lecturer was a spoiled brat if it weren't her brother?

And the coffee table was art because it had designs etched into it. A process using cyanide.

And Jollo saying he kept her in his office even though another woman was waiting to see him. Helen, no doubt. He wanted Jollo to see her there. She was probably the one who had placed Helen in the building while Ximena was in the body cast unseen by the security camera. And Helga telling me he was obsessive, yet he forgot to turn the camera back on.

And the final nail—more like a railroad spike—he could know where the squeeze bulb was found only if he had planted it there.

I looked up to see his countenance change from friend to menace. He had silently reasoned along with me.

"Guess I slipped up," he said.

Then his smile returned. He relaxed. After all, he had nothing to worry about.

Except me going to the police.

Which he didn't think was going to happen because he had pulled a pistol out of his desk drawer.

He laughed. "This is perfect. The story everyone will believe is the obvious. You attacked me because of the negative evaluation I gave you, and I had to shoot you in self-defense."

I was surprised I could talk, given how much I was shaking. "What negative evaluation?"

"The one I'm going to write after you're dead."

"No one will believe that. Fletcher heard you give me a positive evaluation."

"I'll figure something out. Can't have you setting Helen free."

"She's your sister!"

"She's a usurper. My parents left everything to her because they figured she needed it more than me. Me! Their natural child! Why should Helen get it all just because she's a deaf-mute?"

He aimed the pistol at me.

I dived off my chair just as it fired. I heard the bullet shatter the glass. I had to move before he came around the desk for a second shot at me.

I bolted up, but he had disappeared.

I froze. My first thought was he was hiding behind the desk. My second thought was more coherent. He's the one with the gun. Why would he hide?

Then I saw the blood splatters on the wall behind the desk. I tried to lean across the desk and look down. But the thing was too big. So I tiptoed around it and saw him crumpled on the floor, blood pooled around his head.

He had committed suicide. At the last moment, he had turned

the gun on himself. He couldn't face taking another life. He had realized what a terrible person he was and decided to end it all.

Wrong.

I turned to leave and saw Helen Shorter standing in the hall with a gun in her hand. I made a sign everyone knows. I raised my hands above my head in surrender.

She bent down and placed the gun on the floor. Then she made the only ASL sign I know. She interlocked her index fingers, creating a V. Then she separated them and did it again.

Friend.

65

Helen sat on the floor across the hall from her pistol.

I didn't know whether to call the campus police or the APD, so I let the phone decide. I lifted Milton's desk phone and punched in 911. After I told the dispatcher there had been a shooting in the art department office, I called Susannah.

She got there first. I told her what had happened. She crossed the hall and signed to Helen. Helen signed back. Susannah sat next to her. A conversation began.

The 911 call must have gone to the campus police, because Burke the campus cop arrived. I told him where Milton Shorter's body was. He looked at it then spoke into a microphone attached to his epaulette.

He went to the gun he'd spotted on the hall floor. He took a snapshot of it. He slid his right hand into a plastic glove. He picked up the gun, sniffed the muzzle then turned to me. "You teaching next semester?"

I told him I wasn't.

"Good."

His sidekick, Wes, arrived with an oddly shaped briefcase. He retrieved a plastic bag from it. Burke dropped the gun into the bag. He went back to Shorter's body and snapped some pictures.

He and Wes took more pictures and bagged all sorts of things, including my bottle of water and the coaster it sat on.

After I told him everything that happened from the time I arrived in Milton's office, he looked at the two women on the floor. "Which one is the deceased's sister?"

"The one with the prominent nose."

I felt bad describing her that way, but it was the most obvious difference between them.

"Who's the woman with her?"

"Susannah Inchaustigui. I-n-c—"

"I know how to spell Inchaustigui."

When I raised my eyebrows, he said, "We have lots of Basque students. What's she doing here?"

"She's a friend of mine. I asked her to come here after the shooting."

His eyes narrowed. "You invited a friend to a murder scene?"

"Ms. Shorter is a deaf-mute. Susannah knows sign language."

His only reply was "Hmm."

I introduce Burke and Susannah. They spoke for a moment. Burke briefly questioned Helen, with Susannah translating.

Helen admitted to shooting her brother. She claimed to have done so to save my life. I verified that. She refused to answer any other questions.

The field deputy medical investigator finally arrived with two guys and a gurney. The FDMI took a look at Milton Shorter and pronounced him dead.

A good guess, since a large portion of his head was missing and he hadn't taken a breath in over an hour.

The two guys with the FDMI put Milton in a body bag and lifted him onto the gurney.

Burke told Susannah and me to leave. He was going to secure the area.

Wes led Helen away.

Susannah judged me unfit to drive and took me to the condo, saying I could retrieve the Bronco later.

Milton's pistol aimed at me. His blood on the wall. His blown-open head on the floor. Helen standing there with a gun. The body being put in a bag. I wondered how I was ever going to get those images out of my consciousness.

66

The answer was a bit of romance, followed by a wedding.

Not my own, alas.

Sharice reminded me that Glad and Miss Gladys were getting married at noon on Saturday in the gazebo in the Old Town Plaza. So we walked downtown and spent the night in my residence at the back of Spirits in Clay.

Benz was a bit out of sorts; savannah cats don't handle change well. It was probably just my imagination, but Geronimo seemed to have a smirk on his snout.

I marinated a thick fillet of mahi-mahi in cumin and lime, then grilled it along with an ear of corn and some sliced red onions. I cut the fish into chunks and made fish tacos with corn kernels scraped from the cob, grilled red onion, diced avocados and a final spritz of lime juice.

We ate on the patio surrounded by the high adobe wall and the chamisa.

Then we left Benz and Geronimo on the patio (there being no terrace at Sprits in Clay) and drew the curtain so that they would not be embarrassed by our behavior.

We slept late the next morning. Knowing Sharice would not enjoy the coffee I brew, we walked across Central to the Central Grill and Coffee House, where Sharice had a latte and I had the house brew black. She had one of their house-baked scones. I had two.

We had just settled back in at Spirits in Clay when Tristan arrived. "I'm starting a new career as a wedding planner," he said, and handed us a large package. "See you soon."

The package contained two pairs of hiking boots, two pairs of cargo shorts, two floppy broad-brimmed canvas hats and two bright yellow T-shirts with GLAD AND GLADYS BECOME EVEN GLADDER printed horizontally and the date printed vertically in bright red so that the shirts mimicked the state flag. But the most surprising thing in the package was the instruction that we were to wear this getup to the ceremony.

"Do you suppose this is a joke?" I asked Sharice.

"Are you hoping it is?"

"Yes. You know I always wear long pants because I don't like the sun on my legs."

"And you have skinny legs."

"Well, that too. But I'm light brown to begin with and darken quickly in the sun."

"Great. If you get real dark, I'll take a snapshot of you and send it to Dad."

"Funny," I said, and donned the ridiculous outfit.

Sharice, on the other hand, looked terrific in shorts because of her long, sinewy legs. But the hat looked as weird on her as the shorts looked on me, as she agreed when she looked into the mirror.

One of the invited guests, Faye Po, had explained that the Chinese tradition is that gifts are always given by older people to younger people. Glad and Gladys had adopted that practice and specified that there be no presents. The clothes for the wedding were their presents to the guests.

We all gathered in front of Felipe de Neri shortly before noon and were joined by a mariachi band. Fortunately, they were dressed in the traditional *trajes de chorro*. Seeing someone in cargo shorts and a T-shirt playing a *guitarrón* would have verged on cosmic dissonance.

The mariachis played "Las Mañanitas" as they led us around one full circle of the plaza and then up to the gazebo. Glad and Gladys were followed by her son, Zachary, who was best man, and her daughter, Sarah, who was the bridesmaid. The other guests were Faye Po and her house boy, Diego; Martin Seepu; Tristan; John and Susan Hoffsis and John's father, Jim from the bookstore; Dr. Batres and the rest of the staff from his clinic; Susannah; the priest and several parishioners from Miss Gladys's home church, St. Mark's Episcopal Church in Nob Hill; and Whit Fletcher, whom Gladys adores.

Had we been Shriners wearing fezzes and riding scooters, we wouldn't have attracted more stares than we did in our cargo shorts and colorful tees. We encircled the gazebo, and a crowd of tourists encircled us.

A lady behind me whispered to her husband, "Do you think this is a Native American ceremony?"

"Who knows," he replied, "and what's the deal with the guy in the cut-off robe?"

The guy in question was Father Groas, who had shortened one of his old robes (using a kitchen knife, judging by the ragged hem around his waist) and was wearing cargo shorts and hiking boots. As he recited the opening prayer, I sent one heavenward myself, beseeching the Almighty not to allow anyone to take a picture of the priest.

Despite the costumes, the ceremony was traditional, with Glad and Gladys promising "to have and to hold from this day forward, for better or worse, for richer or poorer, in sickness and in health; to love, cherish, and to obey till death us do part."

After Father Groas announced them man and wife, the mariachi band played and sang "Contigo Aprendí":

Contigo aprendí a ver la luz del otro lado de la luna
Contigo aprendí que tu presencia no la cambio por ninguna
Aprendí que puede un beso ser mas dulce y más profundo,
Que puedo irme mañana mismo de este mundo,
Las cosas buenas ya contigo las viví
Contigo aprendí que yo nací el día que te conocí.

I sang along sotto voce in English for Sharice:

With you I've learned to see the light behind the moon
With you I've learned that I wouldn't change you for any-
    one else
I've learned that a kiss could be bigger and deeper
That I may leave this world tomorrow
Because I've already lived the best things with you
And with you I've learned that I was born the day I met
    you.

The band then switched back to "Las Mañanitas" and led us
to the reception in Moreno Hall at Felipe de Neri, where another
surprise awaited us. The dishes in the buffet line were Emma's
tuna, summer squash pie, King Ranch chicken, seven-layer Mexican dip, veggies and grits, dolmades casserole, Irish casserole and
spaghetti pie.

It seems the ladies of St Mark's all have Miss Gladys's casserole
recipes and had prepared them for the reception.

While I dithered, everyone else grabbed a plate and filled it
with mounds from each dish.

"Aren't you going to eat?" asked Sharice.

"I had two scones this morning," I reminded her.

She joined the line and eventually returned with a plate of veggies and grits for her and some seven-layer Mexican dip for me. If
you don't think of it as Mexican food, it actually tastes good. And
paired well with the cold Dos Equis on offer.

By the time the crowd began to thin out and the happy couple
left for their honeymoon, the casserole dishes were empty and the
beer was all gone.

Susannah, Tristan, Martin, Sharice and I cleaned up the hall,
then walked over to Dos Hermanas, where we were relaxed enough
to kick around what had happened at the university.

Susannah pointed at me and said, "Let me do the sleuthing
from now on."

"I wasn't sleuthing. I just went by Shorter's office to say
goodbye."

Tristan said, "Just in the nick of time, I'd say," and we all laughed.

I asked Susannah what Helen Shorter told her while they were seated on the floor.

"She figured out her brother had framed her. He asked her to meet him in his office on the day of the body cast event. When she arrived, there was another woman in his office. From the description Helen gave, it was Jollo Bakkie. Helen waited in his outer office for half an hour and then left. When she was arrested, the police told her they knew she was in the building on the day Ximena was murdered. She realized he had asked her to come merely so people would see her there. Then the police found the squeeze bulb with traces of cyanide on the inside and Ximena's nasal mucus on the outside. She knew her brother worked with cyanide. And had a key to her house. After she made bail, she went to confront him. She got there just as he was aiming his pistol at you. She shot him through the glass wall without even thinking about it."

"Since she was carrying a pistol," I said, "my guess is she was going there not merely to confront him but to shoot him."

Susannah shrugged. "She said she has a carry permit and always has her pistol with her."

"Why?"

"Because she can't yell for help."

We were silent for a few seconds.

"Lucky for me," I said.

"And for her," said Tristan.

"Why?"

"Because I think your guess was right. She went there to kill him. And she did. But because you were there, she walks. According to the law, what she did is justifiable homicide. She killed him to save your life."

Susannah said, "She also asked me to tell you something."

"What?"

"She signed that she was a friend because she didn't want you to think she was going to shoot you too. But that doesn't mean she's changed her mind about you. Your refusal to recognize signing as a genuine language is an act of oppressing a minority."

Tristan asked Sharice if she thought the refusal of most schools to recognize ebonics as a language was an act of suppressing the black minority.

She made a sound that might qualify as a scoff. "The people who pushed that claimed English is our slave language. In one sense, that's correct. My ancestors learned English only because they were taken as slaves to an English-speaking place. But other Africans were taken to Cuba, Brazil or Suriname and their descendants now speak Spanish, Portuguese or Dutch. Language didn't enslave us. People did that. We've risen out of slavery. So how is speaking English like ignorant white people supposed to help? To me, blacks in the diaspora have only two legitimate choices: Embrace the language of the place you happen to be born and speak it even better than everyone else. Or learn the African language of your distant ancestors. Anything else is just street politics."

"Or you could do both," said Martin.

"Yes," Sharice said, "that would be even better. It speaks well of your people that you have retained your language."

"Some of the young people don't understand that. They are immersed in popular culture with their phones."

"You should do what Uncle Hubert did with his class," said Tristan. "Take their phones away."

Angie showed up to take our order, and we all ordered margaritas.

"You don't drink spirits," I said to Sharice.

"I do to celebrate something special."

"Yes. That wedding was indeed special," I said.

"That's not what I'm referring to" she replied. "Stand up," she commanded.

I did. She stood up, wrapped those long arms around me and kissed me passionately.

Everyone in the place applauded.

"The special occasion is you being alive," Sharice said.

"It's like you got a reprieve," Tristan observed.

"And I should make the most of it," I said. I dropped down on one knee, Sharice's hand still in mine. "Marry me."

More applause from the crowd and shouts of "Say yes!"

Sharice teared up. "You know I love you, Hubie. And I want to be with you forever. But marriage is . . . I mean my father . . . uh . . ." She looked to our friends at the table. "I could use some help here."

Martin spoke. "There's a quote from Lao-Tzu that might help."

"You know Asian philosophy?" Sharice asked.

"I am Asian," he said with a smile. "My people came to this land across the ice bridge from Asia."

"He falls back on the land-bridge theory when it's convenient," I said, my knee beginning to hurt.

"What's the quote?" Sharice asked.

"He who speaks does not know. He who knows does not speak."

"Perfect," she said.

Acknowledgments

I am indebted to the beta readers of this book: Carl Durnberg, Beverley and Rufus Gentzen, Richard and Sally Matthews, Ofélia Nikolova, Stephanie Raffel, and Steve Wilson.

I am saddened to report that two among that group—Carl Durnberg and Rufus Gentzen—recently passed away. Both of them were brilliant and funny. Carl was responsible for a character in the book: Benz, Sharice's savannah cat. He raised them.

Peggy Hegeman did such a great job as editor of *The Pot Thief Who Studied Georgia O'Keeffe* that I requested her again, and Open Road obliged. She knows what I am trying to write even better than I do.

Thanks to Tim Hallinan and Anne Hillerman for reading the book and proving blurbs.

Special thanks to Lai-Kent Chew Orenduff for . . . well, everything really.

Mike Orenduff

About the Author

J. Michael Orenduff grew up in a house so close to the Rio Grande that he could Frisbee a tortilla into Mexico from his backyard. While studying for an MA at the University of New Mexico, he worked during the summer as a volunteer teacher at one of the nearby pueblos. After receiving a PhD from Tulane University, he became a professor. He went on to serve as president of New Mexico State University.

Orenduff took early retirement from higher education to write his award-winning Pot Thief murder mysteries, which combine archaeology and philosophy with humor and mystery. Among the author's many accolades are the Lefty Award for best humorous mystery, the Epic Award for best mystery or suspense ebook, and the New Mexico Book Award for best mystery or suspense fiction. His books have been described by the *Baltimore Sun* as "funny at a very high intellectual level" and "deliciously delightful," and by the *El Paso Times* as "the perfect fusion of murder, mayhem and margaritas."

THE POT THIEF MYSTERIES

FROM OPEN ROAD MEDIA

OPEN ROAD

INTEGRATED MEDIA

Find a full list of our authors and
titles at www.openroadmedia.com

FOLLOW US
@OpenRoadMedia